The Apprentices

THE
APPRENTICES

Maile Meloy

with illustrations by
IAN SCHOENHERR

G. P. PUTNAM'S SONS
An Imprint of Penguin Group (USA) Inc.

G. P. PUTNAM'S SONS
An imprint of Penguin Young Readers Group.
Published by The Penguin Group.
Penguin Group (USA) Inc., 375 Hudson Street, New York, NY 10014, U.S.A.
Penguin Group (Canada), 90 Eglinton Avenue East, Suite 700, Toronto, Ontario M4P 2Y3, Canada
(a division of Pearson Penguin Canada Inc.).
Penguin Books Ltd, 80 Strand, London WC2R 0RL, England.
Penguin Ireland, 25 St. Stephen's Green, Dublin 2, Ireland (a division of Penguin Books Ltd).
Penguin Group (Australia), 707 Collins Street, Melbourne, Victoria 3008, Australia
(a division of Pearson Australia Group Pty Ltd).
Penguin Books India Pvt Ltd, 11 Community Centre, Panchsheel Park, New Delhi—110 017, India.
Penguin Group (NZ), 67 Apollo Drive, Rosedale, Auckland 0632, New Zealand
(a division of Pearson New Zealand Ltd).
Penguin Books South Africa, Rosebank Office Park, 181 Jan Smuts Avenue,
Parktown North 2193, South Africa.
Penguin China, B7 Jiaming Center, 27 East Third Ring Road North,
Chaoyang District, Beijing 100020, China.
Penguin Books Ltd, Registered Offices: 80 Strand, London WC2R 0RL, England.

Published simultaneously in Canada. Printed in the United States of America.
Design by Ryan Thomann. Text set in Adobe Caslon.
The art was done in ink and acrylic paint on Strathmore Aquarius II paper.

Library of Congress Cataloging-in-Publication Data
Meloy, Maile. The apprentices / Maile Meloy ; [illustrated by Ian Schoenherr].
pages cm
Summary: "Two years after parting, Benjamin and Janie reunite via
magical communication to prevent a global catastrophe"—Provided by publisher.
[1. Alchemy—Fiction. 2. Magic—Fiction. 3. Adventure and adventurers—Fiction. 4. Voyages and
travels—Fiction. 5. Southeast Asia—History—1945—Fiction.] I. Schoenherr, Ian, illustrator. II. Title.
PZ7.M516354App 2013 [Fic]—dc23 2012048715
ISBN 978-0-399-16245-9
1 3 5 7 9 10 8 6 4 2

For Gwendolyn, Scarlett, and Sawyer

PART ONE

Separation

1. the action or state of being moved apart
2. the process of sorting and then extracting
   a specified substance for use or rejection

CHAPTER 1

Grayson Academy

The space between the stone library of Grayson Academy and the red brick science building created a ferocious wind tunnel, in any decent wind. Janie Scott ducked her head and leaned forward into the blast, on her way to dinner with her roommate's parents in the town of Grayson, across the street from the school. It was November of 1954, and a cold autumn in New Hampshire. Janie wore a warm wool peacoat, but the wind cut through her clothes. It made its way under and over the wraps of her scarf. It found the vulnerable gap between the peacoat's sleeve and her glove, where her wrist lay bare.

She had found the coat in her closet in London, when she was still at St. Beden's School, and it had a strange combination of smells: seawater, smoked meat, and something sweet that Janie couldn't identify. A girl from school named Sarah Pennington had said the coat belonged to her. But then she had taken one sniff, raised her eyebrows, and said that Janie could keep it.

Sarah Pennington also said that Janie and a boy named

Benjamin Burrows had borrowed a necklace from her, with a little gold heart pendant. Sarah said they had melted the necklace down, and were supposed to bring it back whole, as some kind of science experiment. Janie had no memory of borrowing anything from Sarah, but it seemed doubtful that she could bring a melted necklace back. Three weeks of her life had been erased from her mind, and she had lost so many important facts and experiences that she wouldn't have listed the coat or the necklace among the ones that mattered.

But Benjamin Burrows—that name had nagged at her. Sarah Pennington said he had sandy-colored hair, and was stubborn and defiant. Janie had concentrated, feeling the memory like something deep underwater, so deep it was lost in darkness. Before she went to sleep each night, she willed the memory to come up to the surface. After months of struggle, she thought she knew the shape of Benjamin and the sound of his voice. She couldn't remember exact conversations, but she had a sense of him. Fragments started to come back, things he had said. She began to remember a flight over water. A plunge into bitter cold. The fear that Benjamin was dead.

Then a parcel arrived at her parents' London flat, wrapped in brown paper: a diary in Janie's own handwriting, with a note from Benjamin saying that he thought it was safe for her to read it now. The diary entries explained what she had lost, and some of her memories came back flooding and whole. Some came in scraps and wisps that vanished when she tried to focus on them.

Now she was sixteen, and had recovered most of her memories—or thought she had. It was hard to know.

She had been on a journey by boat to Nova Zembla, an island off the northwestern coast of Russia, with Benjamin Burrows and his father. Benjamin's father wasn't an ordinary apothecary who sold medicine. He was trying to make the world safe from nuclear war. He had a book called the Pharmacopoeia with hundreds of years of secrets in it: alchemical secrets, elixirs made from plants, and ways of altering matter and transforming the human body.

Using the Pharmacopoeia, Janie and Benjamin and their friend Pip had become invisible—*actually* invisible—as they tried to rescue the apothecary from his enemies. They had become birds: Benjamin a skylark, Pip a swallow, and Janie an American robin. They had found the apothecary's colleagues: a beautiful Chinese chemist named Jin Lo and an exiled Hungarian count named Vilmos Hadik de Galántha. Together, they had stopped a Soviet nuclear test that would have killed or sickened the people who lived in Nova Zembla, and the reindeer and fish that kept them alive.

Janie's trusted Latin teacher, Mr. Danby, had turned out to be a Soviet spy. He had taken Janie prisoner in Nova Zembla, with the help of an East German agent they knew only as the Scar. Benjamin had become a bird again to try to rescue her. But it was dangerous, too soon for his body to repeat the transformation, and he couldn't keep his shape. She had watched him plunge sickeningly from the sky into the Barents Sea. A man in a kayak rescued them both from the freezing water and took them back to Benjamin's father.

In the meantime, not surprisingly, Janie had fallen in love with Benjamin.

But then something happened that she couldn't quite forgive: Benjamin and his father had erased her memory with a glass of drugged champagne. The apothecary said that Janie was only fourteen and had to stay with her parents, in school. So, fine: Benjamin and his father got to be mysterious, magical peacekeepers, while Janie had to memorize French verbs and eat institutional English food. Was this a fair arrangement?

No, it was not. Not according to Janie. She had received exactly three letters from Benjamin after the diary, all with blurred postmarks from locations that she couldn't make out. The letters didn't say anything about where he was or what he was doing.

In London, Janie's parents had been working as writers on a television program about Robin Hood. They had moved there from Los Angeles to escape investigation for being Communists, which they weren't—that was another thing that hadn't been fair. But now they were in Michigan, teaching at the university in Ann Arbor, without fear of U.S. marshals showing up at the door with a subpoena. The tide was turning against Senator McCarthy, who had never produced a single Soviet spy for all his insistence that he had a whole *list* of spies.

Her parents had been given the drugged champagne, too, and their memories of Janie's vanishing were gone, which was good. It would have worried them too much. They would have made her come to Ann Arbor with them, which she didn't want to do. Instead, they had settled for letting her board at Grayson Academy.

The original founders of Grayson had been Quakers, and the school prided itself on its progressive attitude toward women. It admitted a few girls every year, at a time when most girls' boarding schools were training young ladies to become suitable wives. Janie wanted to study chemistry. She'd become preoccupied with chemistry at St. Beden's, and had won a school prize there, and had gotten a scholarship to Grayson.

She couldn't imagine going back to Hollywood High now—the easy, sunshiny school she had once missed so much. Hollywood High was the place to be if you wanted an agent to spot your blond hair and your violet eyes and put you in movies. But Janie knew enough about show business not to want that, and besides, she didn't have blond hair or violet eyes. She had what Benjamin Burrows had called "American hair," by which he meant there was a lot of it—brown—and it was a little out of control. In the chemistry lab, she tugged it back in a ponytail so it wouldn't dangle in the hydrochloric acid or sizzle into smelly ash in the Bunsen burner.

Jin Lo, who was Janie's role model, wore her hair in a long, smooth braid down the back of her neck. Sometimes Janie tried to braid her own hair like that, but wayward wisps escaped around her face by lunchtime, and the braid was never as perfect and smooth as Jin Lo's.

The peacoat was Janie's best reminder of everything that

had happened. It had been cleaned, sadly, and no longer had its strange smell, but it convinced her that Benjamin and his father and their friends were real, that they had taken that long journey north together and returned, against terrible odds. It made her feel safe.

Her roommate at Grayson was a girl named Opal Magnusson, and on that windy night, Opal's parents had invited the girls for dinner at Bruno's, the Italian restaurant across the street from the Grayson campus. Janie leaned into the wind, peacoat clutched tight at the neck, and crossed the street into town. She pulled open the restaurant's glass door and was enveloped in the cozy smell of tomato and garlic. The sudden warmth made her cheeks tingle, and the soft light from sconces on the walls made her blink.

Bruno, the owner, called out *"Buona sera!"* and the white-coated waiters turned and beamed at Janie. She thought they must be tired of serving Grayson students by now—so many of the kids were spoiled and entitled—but the waiters were always kind.

"Janie!" Opal's father said, standing from his table. Mr.

Magnusson had thick, wild, white-blond hair, sparkling blue eyes, and a ready grin. He held out his big arms to welcome her.

His wife, Opal's mother, was tiny, with wide dark eyes. Her thick black hair was pulled back in a chignon at the nape of her neck. She gave Janie a demure smile and a nod. She had been a Malay princess, as Janie understood it, the young-est daughter of a powerful sultan. Mr. Magnusson had vast holdings in Southeast Asia, and had met the princess there and whisked her away. The war had been inconvenient for him, but after the Japanese were defeated, he had become richer than ever.

Opal gave Janie a wan smile, looking sick of her parents already.

Janie took the empty chair at their table, and a waiter tucked it under her. "Sorry I'm late," she said, unfolding her napkin. "I was in the chemistry lab."

"On a Sunday?" Mr. Magnusson asked.

"The teacher gave me a key."

"Such devotion to your studies," Mr. Magnusson said. "Opal could use some of that."

Janie cast around for some response. Mr. Magnusson was infuriating because he made his disappointment with Opal the subject of every conversation. "It's just something I'm playing around with," she said.

"But it shows you have real purpose and drive," Mr. Magnusson said. "Unlike *some* young people I could mention. Now let's order some food." He waved to the waiter.

Janie caught Opal's eye and mouthed, *"Sorry."*

Opal just gave a tiny shake of her head and rolled her bread into round pellets. Opal had long silken brown hair, green eyes, and honey-colored skin. She made Sarah Pennington, who'd been the prettiest girl at St. Beden's School, look ordinary: just another blonde. Opal was so beautiful it was hard to look at her, and she seemed to know it, so she hid behind heavy, clunky glasses she didn't need. It was as if she were in disguise, like Clark Kent.

"So," Mr. Magnusson said, after they had ordered. "The great experiment. Tell me everything."

"Well," Janie said, glancing again at Opal, "I'm trying to find an efficient way to desalinate large amounts of seawater. To take the salt out, and make it drinkable, without using a generator. So that the ocean could be a water source more easily."

Mr. Magnusson's blue eyes grew wide. "But this is magnificent," he said. "It could alleviate so much suffering."

"I hope so," Janie said, tearing off a piece of warm bread.

"Wars will be fought over water," Mr. Magnusson said. "It will be the great commodity. Cheap, large-scale desalination would change everything."

"I haven't done it yet," Janie said.

"But you're close?"

"I think so."

"Who gave you the idea?"

Janie nearly choked on her bread. "Sorry?" she asked.

"Well, it's not an idea that a schoolgirl has on her own. Am I right?"

Janie felt her cheeks getting hot. Why had she had to brag about the project? She couldn't say anything about Jin Lo or the Pharmacopoeia. "I just—figured it out by working on it," she said, which was sort of true. "It's been a slow process."

"But how did you become interested in chemistry?"

All Janie could think of was Jin Lo, who was not a normal chemist in the way that the apothecary was not a normal apothecary. "In London," she said. "I had a good teacher. I won a prize there, and that got me the scholarship here."

"Remarkable!" Mr. Magnusson said. "I'll be your first customer! I can use your desalination in the islands. I predict, Janie, that you will do great things."

Janie smiled, uncomfortable. "And so will Opal."

Mr. Magnusson waved the idea away. "Oh, Opal will inherit a lot of money," he said. "She might do good things with it. And she could marry a very rich man, if she stops making herself ugly."

"Daddy!" Opal said.

"Seriously, though, Janie," Mr. Magnusson said, leaning forward. "I would like to buy your experiment."

"It's not for sale," Janie said. "Anyway, it isn't finished."

"When it's finished, then," he said. "I insist."

There was a silence. Opal crossed her arms and slumped in her chair, her heavy glasses sliding down her nose. Her mother took up her wineglass and glanced at Janie like a frightened rabbit.

Food arrived, carried by a teenage busboy, and Mr. Magnusson made a big production of making sure there was room for everything on the table. Then he kept up a steady stream of anecdotes, so there was no room for other conversation.

Janie turned her attention to her plate of spaghetti. It was delicious, and she'd been hungrier than she knew. She concentrated on twirling the noodles on her fork and not splashing sauce onto her shirt.

But then her reprieve was over. Mr. Magnusson asked, "How soon do you think you'll be finished with your experiment?"

"I don't know," she said. She meant to stop there, but he looked at her encouragingly, waiting. "It all depends on the recrystallization process," she said, "and perfecting my seeding method."

Opal yawned in protest. "This is so *boring* I'm going to cry!"

"Your capacity to be bored is the stuff of legend," her father said.

"I'm tired, too, Magnus," his wife said quietly.

"Raffaello!" Mr. Magnusson called to the busboy. "May I have the check? I must get these ladies home to bed."

They were gathered by helpful hands into their coats. Mr. Magnusson held open a vast black fur cloak for his tiny wife, ready to swallow her up. As she backed into the fur, the princess shot Janie the frightened rabbit look again, and this time Janie thought it contained either a plea or a warning—or both.

Janie walked back with Opal to their room in Carleton Hall. The wind had died down and wasn't so cutting, especially now that Janie had a belly full of food. They were silent for a while, and Janie was trying to think what to say that wouldn't embarrass them both, but Opal burst out first.

"Why do you try to show me up with Daddy?" she asked.

Janie was startled. "I don't!"

"He's *my* father, you know."

"Of course he is."

"He's not *yours*."

"I have my own father."

"When you act all smart with him, it makes him think I'm stupid."

"I wasn't trying to act smart," Janie said, though she kicked herself for not shutting up. "I just answered his questions."

"He said that all I can do with my life is marry someone rich!"

He *had* said that. Janie couldn't deny it. She thought of her own father, who had always been so supportive and encouraging—when he wasn't teasing her and joking. Her parents had talked to her as if she were an adult, and played games with her as an equal, for as long as she could remember. She couldn't imagine what it was like to have none of that confidence behind you. She said, "I think your dad was just making a joke."

"No," Opal said, shaking her head. "He meant it."

"He said you'd do good things with the money," Janie said. "It takes skill to be a good philanthropist."

"It's not like being a *scientist.*"

"So be a scientist, then," Janie said, losing patience. "Show him he's wrong."

"I'm failing math!"

"Then let's go over some problems. I'll help you."

"Don't you *dare* patronize me, Janie Scott!" Opal said.

"I wasn't!"

Opal marched ahead, the heels of her expensive boots striking the pavement, and Janie followed helplessly.

Their room in Carleton Hall was barely big enough for two narrow beds pushed against opposite walls, two desks, two dressers, and a single closet, but still Janie and Opal managed to get ready for bed without speaking. They stepped around each other with cold constraint. Janie wanted to bring up tomorrow's math test, but she didn't dare.

In bed, she lay looking at the ceiling, listening to Opal toss back and forth on her pillow, just a few feet away. She tried to think of something to say to apologize, but could only imagine Opal shooting it down. Then Opal's restless rolling stopped, and her breathing became steady.

If she could sleep, then Janie could, too.

CHAPTER 2

The Test

In the morning, Opal seemed to have forgiven Janie. She wasn't exactly friendly as they dressed for the day, but she didn't seem furious, either. Janie was grateful. She grabbed a sweet roll from the dining hall and unlocked the chemistry classroom to check on her experiment, so she wouldn't have to sit with Opal at breakfast. She was hoping to see salt crystals on the thread.

Her experiment was really an exercise in imitation. In London, she had gone with her parents to the National Gallery, where they had watched a young man set up an easel in front of a Rembrandt portrait. He was making a copy of the portrait, and Janie's father had said it was a way of learning to paint, to re-create the brushstrokes of a great master. Janie felt that she was doing something like that with her experiment.

On the boat to Nova Zembla, Jin Lo had shown her a glass vial of clear liquid. It was for emergencies, in case they became stranded without fresh water. When Jin Lo dipped a thread into the liquid and then dropped the same thread into a beaker of seawater, salt crystals began to form. It was like watching dissolution in reverse, as all the salt was drawn out of the water. Less than a minute later, there was a hard salt crystal attached to the thread, like rock candy. Jin Lo had removed the crystal, set it aside, and handed the beaker to Janie.

"Drink," she'd said.

"It's safe?" Janie had asked.

"No, I poison you," Jin Lo had said.

Janie drank. The water was cold, silvery clear, and almost sweet, as if it had come from a mountain stream. At dinner that night, their friend Vili, the Hungarian count, had taken out a pocketknife and happily scraped some of the crystallized sea salt onto his food.

In London, with her memories erased, Janie had found the vial of desalinizing liquid in the pocket of her peacoat. At first, she hadn't remembered what it was. But she had set the vial aside. As she recovered her memories, she realized how important it could be. People all over the world needed clean water, and the oceans were endless. The instructions for removing the salt must be in the Pharmacopoeia, the apothecary's ancient book, but Benjamin and his father had the Pharmacopoeia with them, wherever they were.

So Janie's experiment was to see if she could re-create the liquid *without* the Pharmacopoeia, by careful analysis of the vial's contents. She thought she had figured out the components, but she hadn't been able to repeat the crystallizing effect.

When she arrived in the chemistry classroom with her books and her half-eaten sweet roll on Monday morning, there were still no crystals, and the water was as salty as ever.

Discouraged, she ran to trigonometry before the first bell, sliding into her seat as Mr. Evensong passed out the test.

Opal sat two seats over, and Janie wished they'd gone over some problems before they went to sleep. Opal was staring straight ahead, through her heavy glasses, nervously chewing her bottom lip. Janie wished Opal wasn't so afraid. She got tangled up in her own fear and couldn't see the problems clearly. Janie liked math: It was like a puzzle. The prospect of finding a definite, provable answer was reassuring, when other parts of her life had been muddled and confusing.

"You may begin," Mr. Evensong said.

Janie turned the test over and considered the diagram and the first problem:

1. Calculate the length of the side x, given that $\tan \theta = 0.4$

Her pencil started scratching on the page, and she worked the problem in a kind of trance.

When she finished the test, she looked around, coming out of a world made of circles and angles and lines. Her classmates were still hunched over their test papers. The tip of Opal's tongue stuck out of her mouth in concentration.

By the clock over Mr. Evensong's head, Janie had fifteen minutes of class time to go. Mr. Evensong was bent over his desk, grading homework. He was a slight, balding man in a frayed sweater who had endless patience for his students—especially the ones who struggled.

Janie went over her test to make sure she had written the answers correctly and shown all of her work, but that only took a few minutes. Then she reached under her desk and brought out the small red notebook in which she kept notes on her chemistry experiment. She hadn't had time to record her observations from the morning, and she started writing her guesses about what had gone wrong. Too high a concentration? Not high enough? Temperature too high? Not high enough? Was the thread the wrong texture? She twirled the pencil between her fingers and wondered what else the trouble could be.

When Mr. Evensong announced that the time was up, Janie tucked the red notebook away and turned in her test paper with everyone else. The bell rang, and she gathered her things. In the hall, she waited to see if Opal was coming—they usually walked to history class together—but Opal didn't follow her out. She must be talking to Mr. Evensong about the test. Finally Janie couldn't wait any longer without being late, so she walked on alone.

Grayson was laid out like a college campus, with classrooms in separate buildings, and Janie stepped out onto the stone steps of the math and science building. She felt a tug on the end of her scarf and turned to see Tadpole Porter, his hands jammed in his pockets, whistling and looking innocently up at the sky. Tadpole's name was really Thaddeus, but only teachers called him that. He was a round boy with glasses and thick, unruly brown hair, and he was the smartest boy in her history class. She wondered if having a lot of ideas stimulated hair growth—all that blood flow near the scalp.

"That's funny," she said. "I thought I felt someone pull on my scarf. I must have imagined it." She started walking again.

"You know what happens when you start imagining things," Tadpole said, falling into step beside her. "They cart you off to the loony bin."

"I don't know what you're talking about," she said. "Imagining what?"

"Your scarf being pulled," he said.

"What scarf? Now *you're* imagining things."

Tadpole laughed. "Where's your roommate?" he asked. "You always have protection on this walk."

Janie looked at him sideways—did Tadpole have a crush on Opal? "She stayed behind in math," she said. "To talk to Mr. Evensong."

"Good," he said. "I wouldn't dare pull your scarf when she was there. I mean, not that I did, or ever *would* pull your scarf. But I really wouldn't if Opal was around. She's scary."

"She's not," Janie said. "Just kind of short-tempered." Then she regretted saying something so honest about her roommate.

"That's what I mean!" Tadpole said. "She'd turn on you in a *second*."

They were already inside the building, and they joined the press into the classroom. Tadpole's desk was in front of Janie's.

Mrs. McClellan, the history teacher, wore a long, straight purple skirt and a black sweater. Her streaked gray hair made her look wise and a little witchy. When the bell had rung again and everyone had settled down, Mrs. McClellan said,

"Today we're going to talk about Indochina." She pulled a map of Asia down like a window shade over the chalkboard.

All of Janie's American history and social studies classes before Grayson had begun with the Pilgrims and the Declaration of Independence, and ended with the Civil War. Then the next year they started over again with the Pilgrims. It was as if history had stopped on the night John Wilkes Booth shot Abraham Lincoln. But Mrs. McClellan was different. She liked to remind her students that history was happening right *now*, today. At the top of her chalkboard was a quotation from the philosopher Edmund Burke: *Those who don't know history are destined to repeat it.* Tadpole had raised his hand on the first day of class to point out that George Santayana had said almost the same thing, and Mrs. McClellan had replied that Edmund Burke said it first, and that maybe those who don't know their great quotations are destined to repeat them. Tadpole was her best student, but they had been sparring ever since.

"The war in Korea ended before any of you could be drafted to fight in it," Mrs. McClellan said. "But Asia is still in tumult. There's a good chance that the United States will be drawn in, now that the French have been defeated in Indochina. You're sixteen now. Eighteen will come before you know it, and you'll be eligible for the draft. So it will serve you to know something about the region."

"They won't want *me*," Tadpole said.

There was general confirming laughter in the classroom. It was true that with his roundness and his glasses he didn't seem very military. Janie wished Tadpole wouldn't bring mockery on himself—but maybe it let him control the laughter. Her father was always joking, too, and she wondered what he had been like as a boy.

"I wouldn't be so sure, Thaddeus," Mrs. McClellan said. "Intelligence is much more important in this nuclear age, and the military will need brains. You might be just the kind of draftee they're looking for."

"Except that I'll be in college," Tadpole said.

"Of course you will," Mrs. McClellan said. "Because life always goes exactly as we plan it." She turned to the map. "Now, these countries are Vietnam, Cambodia, and Laos."

Even as smart as he was, Tadpole couldn't really imagine war, Janie thought. None of her classmates could imagine anything truly bad happening to them. All they remembered of the Second World War was the end: flag-waving and parades and the end of butter rationing. Their fathers had been too old for Korea. That was true for Janie, too, but she knew how the apothecary had suffered when his wife was killed in the London Blitz, and how Jin Lo's family had been murdered during the Japanese invasion of China, and how Count Vili's parents had been killed in Hungary. Janie herself had been present at the detonation of a hydrogen bomb. All of that sometimes made her feel out of place at Grayson. But she reminded herself that she was here to learn. She wrote *Vietnam, Cambodia, Laos* in her history notebook.

"The French took control of the territories that are now Vietnam and Cambodia," Mrs. McClellan was saying, "when they defeated China in the Sino-French war in 1885."

Janie wrote that down: *Sino-French war ended 1885.*

The lecture went on and class was almost over when a girl with curly red hair came to the door and gave Mrs. McClellan a slip of paper. The teacher looked up, and her eyes landed on Janie. "Miss Scott," she said. "You're wanted in the headmaster's office."

Janie had no experience with being summoned. Flustered, she gathered her books. The other students stared at her, and Tadpole gave her a questioning look. She wondered if something had happened to her parents, then tried to block out the thought. She left quickly, following the red-haired girl down the hall. "Do you know what this is about?" Janie asked her.

"Nope," the girl said. "But Mr. Evensong is there."

"Mr. Evensong the math teacher?"

The girl shot her a look. "No, the *other* Mr. Evensong."

Janie had been in the headmaster's office only once before, with her parents, for a brief meeting when she'd arrived at the school. Afterward, her father had joked about the unoriginal casting of Mr. Willingham, the headmaster. He looked exactly like you'd expect a headmaster to look. He was tall but not too tall, slightly portly, with a round belly. He was balding, wore tweedy three-piece suits, and smoked a pipe. Janie guessed the school had chosen him for these attributes—for his very unoriginality. It must be reassuring for parents to leave their children with a headmaster who was so perfectly headmasterish.

Also in the office, as the girl had said, was Mr. Evensong, the math teacher, in his mustard-colored cardigan with the hole in the elbow. He sat stooped in a curved wooden chair in front of Mr. Willingham's desk, and he turned to look at Janie as she walked in. There was something in his face she couldn't identify.

"Ah, Miss Scott," Mr. Willingham said, rising.

"Hello," Janie said.

"Mr. Evensong has brought me some disturbing news."

"Oh?" Janie looked to the teacher, who was still sitting. Could she have failed the math test? But that wasn't possible—she could do those problems in her sleep.

"Please sit," the headmaster said.

Janie reluctantly took the other chair. She slid back an inch on the smooth, polished wood, but stayed near the edge, her books on her lap. Her stomach felt tight with nameless fear.

"I know you've read Grayson Academy's Honor Code," Mr. Willingham said, "because I have your signed agreement here." He lifted a piece of paper from a slim folder on his desk marked *JANE SCOTT.* She had a *file*, her own file; there it was.

"Yes," Janie said. "I've read it."

"So you know that the consequence of cheating is expulsion."

"Yes. But I still don't understand."

Mr. Evensong must have been holding his breath in the chair next to her, because he let it go with a little explosion of exasperation. "*I* don't understand!" he said. "You're my best student, Miss Scott. I feel utterly betrayed!"

Janie looked at him in surprise. "By what?"

"By your cheating on the trigonometry test!"

Janie stared at him. Then at Mr. Willingham. Then at Mr. Evensong again. "But I didn't cheat!"

Mr. Evensong, still full of righteous anger, said, "Ten minutes before the end of the exam time, you took notes from beneath your desk and used them to fill in the answers on the test."

Janie nearly laughed with relief. "Oh, *that!*" she said. "That was my chemistry notebook. I mean, the one I keep about my experiment." She looked at the two men, expecting their faces to relax into understanding, but they didn't. "I had gone to check on the experiment before class," she went on. "I finished the test early, and there were still ten minutes left, so I got out my notebook to write down some hypotheses about my results."

Mr. Evensong still looked angry, and Mr. Willingham looked disappointed. "You got every single answer correct," he said.

"I'm good at math."

"You *are!*" Mr. Evensong burst out. "So I can only imagine it's a kind of perverse . . . *perfectionism* that would drive you to cheat. But the information I received stated quite clearly that you took the answers from your notebook."

The tightness turned to an ache in Janie's stomach. "The information you received—from who?"

"From *whom*," Mr. Willingham said. He seemed to regret the necessity of correcting her lapse in grammar as much as he regretted the necessity of correcting her lapse in conscience.

"From *whom?*" Janie asked.

"A reliable source," Mr. Willingham said.

"It was Opal, wasn't it?" Janie asked, and a flicker in the math teacher's eyes confirmed it. It all began to make sense. Opal's fury at her the night before, then the apparent truce this morning. Opal's staying after class to speak to Mr. Evensong. Tadpole Porter had been right: Opal could turn on you, fast. "We had a fight last night," she said. "Opal was angry at me. But I *swear* I didn't cheat on that test."

"We must take the allegation seriously," Mr. Willingham said. "The Honor Code is very clear."

"But you have no proof!" Janie said. "It's her word against mine! And Mr. Evensong, you *know* I know how to do all those problems. I have no motive to cheat, and she does have a motive to get me in trouble—she's mad at me! That's all this is!"

Mr. Evensong looked briefly uncertain, but Mr. Willingham cut in. "I'm sorry, Miss Scott," he said.

"Let me show you the notebook," Janie said, fumbling through her things. "I can show you what I was writing. It's all notes on my experiment. I'm desalinating seawater. That means taking the salt out." She thrust the red notebook at the headmaster, who looked away.

Janie took the rejected notebook back into her lap, stunned.

A thought occurred to her. "How much money has Mr. Magnusson given to Grayson Academy?" she asked.

"We would never disclose such a thing," Mr. Willingham said. "And it has no bearing here."

"I think it does," Janie said. "Opal's a terrible student. You know that. Even *she* knows that. But she's valuable, isn't she? Has her father promised you a building?"

Mr. Willingham actually blushed, scarlet blooming on his portly cheeks.

"He has!" Janie said.

"Her father is irrelevant."

"He is *not*! Opal and I were fighting because her dad thinks I'm smarter than she is. She's failing math, and I'm good at it, and now you want to expel me because she's mad, when I didn't cheat!"

Mr. Willingham's face was now the color of a ripe plum. "We don't *want* to expel you, Miss Scott," he said. "We *are* expelling you."

"Did Opal threaten you?"

"This matter is closed. I've written a letter to your parents."

Janie stared at him. "You wrote to them before you even talked to me?"

"Yes. The case was cut and dried."

She was silent with disbelief.

"I'm sure you'll find a place in another fine school," he said.

"Oh, sure. Schools love cheaters."

"As an expelled student, you are no longer permitted in the dormitories," he said. "You may stay in the infirmary until your parents collect you."

"The *infirmary*?" she said. It wasn't enough to kick her out, they had to put her in the grim sick beds, with the terrifying nurses?

"You'll be perfectly safe there," he said.

Janie's mind raced. She needed to stay near the school, to be near her experiment, but *not* in the infirmary, under Willingham's control. She had to buy time. "I have an aunt in Concord," she said quickly, the words coming out before she had thought them through. "I can go there until my parents come."

"Oh, splendid," Mr. Willingham said. He seemed relieved to be rid of her. "You may telephone her from my secretary's desk. But please reverse the charges, if you don't mind. Concord is a toll call."

Janie almost laughed. They wouldn't even pay for a phone call to Concord? But it didn't matter, because her aunt didn't exist. "Right," she said. "I'll reverse the charges."

"You may go," Willingham said.

She looked at Mr. Evensong to see what he thought about all of this, but he was looking down at his hands.

Janie left the headmaster's office, dazed, and closed the heavy door behind her. Mr. Willingham's secretary was rummaging in a file cabinet against the wall. Janie wondered where she would actually go.

Her eye fell on a wire tray on the secretary's desk, where she saw her parents' names and address in Ann Arbor typed on a stamped white envelope.

The secretary still had her back turned, and Janie picked up the envelope and tucked it between her books. Hugging the books close, she slipped out of the room.

CHAPTER 3

Exile

Janie went back to Carleton Hall in a daze. The building was weirdly silent as she walked up to the second floor, and she stood in her room looking around. Most of the things in it were Opal's. Janie had come straight from London, with only her clothes and a few books. The Persian rug on the floor was Opal's. There was also a framed photograph of Opal doing a split in a handstand on the back of a trotting horse. When Janie asked about it, Opal had only shrugged. "It's something I used to do," she said. Janie didn't understand how someone who had the confidence to do *that* panicked when faced with a trigonometry problem.

Janie took out her duffel bag and unzipped it on the bed. Where would she go? She sat down on the bed with Mr. Willingham's letter and opened the envelope.

November 8, 1954

Dear Mr. and Mrs. Scott,
I regret to inform you that your daughter,

Jane, has been found cheating on a
mathematics examination here at Grayson
Academy. Our Honor Code, which Jane signed
on arrival, is very clear on the subject of
academic dishonesty. A single infraction
requires immediate expulsion.

It saddens me to dismiss a promising
student, but we must be rigorous in our
adherence to our school's principles. Please
make arrangements to collect Jane as soon
as possible.

Sincerely,

M. Linus Willingham

HEADMASTER, GRAYSON ACADEMY

The letter enraged Janie all over again. The accusation
was a lie, and Mr. Willingham had no proof. She understood his greed and desire to keep Opal's father's donations
coming in. But she didn't understand Mr. Evensong turning
her in without talking to her first. He *knew* what kind of
student she was.

She gathered her shampoo, hairbrush, toothbrush, and
toothpaste, and put them in the duffel. Then she sat down
in despair. If she left now, and dismantled all her glassware
and her titrating apparatus, she wouldn't have any answers,
after spending the entire fall designing the experiment. The
thought of all that wasted time made her feel sick. And she

was so close! To go to Ann Arbor now, to her parents, would be like leaving in the last ten minutes of a movie, before she found out what happened. But it was much more important than a movie. She couldn't move the equipment; it was too ungainly and fragile, and some of it belonged to the school. She didn't want to tell her parents to come get her. She just wanted to finish her project. And maybe she could still clear her name.

Janie heard the door to the room open—Opal back—and she spun around. But it wasn't Opal. It was Mrs. Jericho, the Carleton Hall housekeeper, with her plump face and white apron. "I thought I heard someone up here," Mrs. Jericho said. "You're not meant to be here between classes, you know."

"I have to leave school . . . for a while," Janie said, because she couldn't imagine leaving for good.

Mrs. Jericho's forehead wrinkled with concern. "Is everything all right?"

Her kindness surprised Janie, and she felt tears burning behind her eyes. She willed them back. "Yes," she said. "It's all fine."

Janie walked away from the dormitory, duffel bag slung over one shoulder, knapsack over the other. She crossed Kingsley Street, at the edge of campus, and wandered through the town of Grayson, trying to think.

Her parents would understand. They knew all about being falsely accused. She thought she understood a little better now how they had felt when the U.S. marshals started following them around. She remembered her father pounding the table in helpless rage. His fury had startled her when she was fourteen and knew nothing about the world. It didn't surprise her now.

So her parents would help her fight Mr. Willingham. They would go to the board of trustees. Or they would help her find a better school, with a less corrupt and infuriating headmaster. At the very least, they would take her back to Ann Arbor. It was almost Christmas break, and she could curl up on her parents' couch by the glowing fireplace, reading novels. Her dad would crack jokes to make her laugh, and her mom would be witty and compassionate. There would be many variations on the name Willingham—Mr. Willing-Sham, Mr. Wimpy-Ham—and many impersonations of him with his belly and his waistcoat and his pipe. Janie could eat cereal in pajamas and socks, instead of having to dress in a chilly dormitory and shiver through the frosty morning to the dining hall.

But she didn't want to go home. She couldn't let Willingham win like that. She had to finish her experiment, its maze-like apparatus so precariously assembled in the chemistry lab, and to do that she needed to stay quiet and unnoticed for just a little bit longer. Her parents wouldn't understand. They would show up ready to fight, or they would sweep her away in indignation, and that would be the end of it.

But where to stay? She hoped she might see a sign in a window on one of the streets in Grayson—some sweet old lady advertising a tiny, cheap room for rent. She had a little money, but it wouldn't last long. The hotel where most parents stayed was expensive. There was a cheaper hotel at the edge of town, but the clerk would call the police if a sixteen-year-old girl tried to check in by herself.

She saw no signs in any windows, and was walking back

past Bruno's restaurant when she saw the teenage busboy, Raffaello, hosing off rubber kitchen mats in the alley. He was one of the few people in town she knew by name. He kinked his hose to shut it off. "Hi," he said. "It's Janie, right?"

She nodded.

"Don't you have school?" he asked. He had dark eyes and glossy black curls. He didn't have Bruno's Italian accent, but he didn't talk like the kids at Grayson, either. She guessed he went to East High.

"Not today," she said. "Don't you?"

"They let me leave early so I can come here and work for my dad," he said. "I only miss gym and study hall."

She eased the duffel bag strap off her tired shoulder and put the bag on the ground. The lunch service at Bruno's was over. Where had the time gone? She had been wandering in a daze. "Do you make money, working for your dad?" she asked.

"Of course," Raffaello said. "You think I clean these things for fun?"

"I wish I had a job."

"We need a dishwasher."

"Really?"

"Yeah, but I'm joking. You wouldn't like it."

"Why not?"

"The pots are greasy. The water is hot. You burn your fingers until they get so tough and calloused you don't feel them anymore. You smell like dishwater at the end of the night. It's no job for girls."

She bridled at that. "*I* could do it. I'm good at doing dishes."

He laughed. "Yeah, at home, washing three or four plates, right? Not for a hundred people. But you don't need a job. You go to Grayson."

"So?"

"So you must be rich. And smart."

"I'm not rich. And I don't go to Grayson anymore."

"What happened?"

"I'm not sure."

"Your parents stop paying?"

"No. And I had a scholarship."

"So you're extra smart."

"Just extra poor."

"You could go to East High with the rest of us poor kids."

She smiled. "I was really looking for a room to rent, first," she said. "But I'm not sure how much it will cost. Do you think I could get the dishwashing job?"

Raffaello tilted his head in thought. "No," he said. "Maybe."

Maybe was good enough. "Will you let me try?"

CHAPTER 4

Dishwashing

J anie helped Raffaello haul the rubber kitchen mats inside. She hadn't eaten lunch, so she ate a bowl of spaghetti with him. It was the same spaghetti she'd eaten in the dining room, but it tasted different in the kitchen. Raffaello introduced her to the cooks and showed her around the kitchen. When his father showed up for the evening shift, Raffaello spoke to him in rapid Italian. Bruno looked skeptically at Janie and disappeared into the front of the restaurant.

"What's the answer?" Janie whispered.

"He's deciding," Raffaello whispered back.

"How can I improve my chances?"

"You can't."

Then his father came back into the kitchen and shrugged. "We try," he said.

"Thank you!" Janie said, but Bruno just shook his head.

Raffaello showed her how to aim the spray nozzle at the best angle into the deep sink so it didn't splash water everywhere, and how to load the big new industrial dishwashing machine—Janie had never seen a dishwashing machine before—and slide the steel door closed. Then she started scrubbing pots. Dinner started, and more greasy plates came in with the busboys, and Janie scraped leftovers into a giant trash can and started the whole process over again.

By the end of the evening, every muscle in her body was sore, her fingers were pruned and red, and she never wanted to see Italian food again. But then someone put a bowl of tomato soup on the counter in front of her and it looked delicious. So she sat on a stool and ate, leaning on her elbows. She was too tired to care about manners.

Her mouth was full and her eyes were nearly closed when a woman came in through the back door. She was tall and buxom, in a long coat, and she had snow in her pinned-up hair. Janie had just had time to register that it was snowing, and she still had nowhere to sleep, when the woman demanded, *"Dov'è la ragazza?"*

The kitchen went silent. Even Bruno, that imposing figure, looked afraid. Janie froze and tried to swallow.

The woman zeroed in on Janie, slinging her coat over her powerful forearm, and put her hands on her hips. "You have a name?" She had a stronger Italian accent than Bruno's.

Janie managed to say, "Janie Scott."

"This is my aunt Giovanna," Raffaello said. "She lives with us."

Giovanna ignored him. "Where your parents?" she asked Janie.

"Michigan."

"Mitchigan?"

"It's a state. West of here."

"Mitchigan," the woman said skeptically. "You Grayson?"

"Not anymore."

"Why no?"

"They kicked me out."

"Why?"

"They said I cheated."

"You cheat?"

"Never."

Giovanna made a doubtful face. "Everybody cheat sometime."

"I didn't. It was a math test. I'm really good at math."

"Oh, yes?" Giovanna said. She hung her coat on a hook, strode out of the kitchen into the restaurant, and returned with a stack of white slips, a long roll of adding machine paper, and the tray of money from the till. "This is tonight," she said. "Always it comes out wrong."

Janie felt the weight of the woman's eyes on her. Everyone else was watching, too. She pushed her soup bowl away, wiped her hands on a napkin, and pulled the stack of slips closer. Then she studied the numbers on the roll of paper. She looked up. "Do you have a pencil?"

Giovanna snapped her fingers. One of the waiters ran to her with a pencil, and she handed it over.

Janie, her fingers stinging from the hot plates, began to go through the slips, balancing out the night's take against the register. Everyone else went back to work. A few times Janie had to stop and puzzle out a mistake. Eventually she got to the end, but the amount still didn't balance with what was in the till. She rubbed her eyes, went back again, and found the error.

When she was finished, Janie pushed the totals to Giovanna, who looked them over. Then she told Janie what percentage of the evening's tips went to each of the employees—every waiter and busboy—and asked her to divvy them up.

"You didn't include the dishwasher," Raffaello said.

"We don't have dishwasher," Giovanna said.

"We do now," Raffaello insisted.

"It's okay," Janie said. "It was my first night."

"Doesn't matter," Raffaello said.

Giovanna frowned. "Hmph," she said.

"And she needs to stay with us tonight," Raffaello said.

"Absolutely no!"

Janie was too weary even to be disappointed. It was too cold to sleep outside in the snow, but she went blank when she thought about other possibilities. Could she go knock on the door of the infirmary? She thought she could sleep right here on this stool, she was so tired.

"She doesn't have anywhere else to go," Raffaello said.

"This is my fault?" Giovanna asked.

"She did a good job tonight. Two good jobs."

"I am no hotel!"

"Per favore, Zia Giovanna."

The woman folded her arms over her formidable chest. Then she threw her hands up in the air. "Okay!" she said. "Fine!"

Janie, blushing furiously, nodded her thanks and set about dividing the tips. She wound up with an astonishing nine dollars in cash and checked her math, but it was correct. The money felt hot in her pocket as they left the restaurant, Bruno locking up after them.

Raffaello lived with his father and his aunt in the apartment over the restaurant, and Janie followed them upstairs. She wanted to ask what had happened to Raffaello's mother, but she was too tired. The living room was worn and cozy even in the dark, with gauzy flowered curtains over the windows.

Giovanna threw some sheets and a blanket over the couch to make a bed. Janie said good night and thanked them all, brushed her teeth in the small bathroom, and fell into an exhausted sleep.

CHAPTER 5

A Reprieve

When Janie woke, it took some time for her to recognize the room: the couch she'd slept on, the floral curtains with early morning light coming through. She couldn't remember her dreams, but they nagged at her as if they were important. She closed her eyes and tried to fall asleep again, but it was hopeless.

The apartment was quiet, the others still asleep. Janie reflexively wondered if she was late for class, then remembered that she didn't have class anymore. But she still had her key to the chemistry classroom. She got up and dressed silently, folded her blanket and sheets on the couch, and let herself out of the apartment.

She crossed Kingsley Street where it divided the town from the Grayson campus. The sun still wasn't up, and the sky was a dark gray blue. Squirrels darted up the trees. A few of the boys from crew were running back from morning rowing practice on the river, flushed in their jerseys, with halos of steam rising up around their heads. They grinned at Janie with the euphoria of being healthy and sweaty and awake so early, and she tried to smile in return. The science building was unlocked and the hallway was empty. She let herself into the dark chemistry classroom with her key.

The lab seemed cold and forbidding now that she wasn't supposed to be there. She didn't want to turn on a light and draw attention. Familiar objects cast spooky shadows in the dimness, and the usual chemical smells seemed sinister. She wished Pip and Benjamin were here. Everything had been easier when her friends were with her. She hadn't been afraid to sneak into a school chemistry lab, or into a military bunker. She hadn't even been afraid to stow away on a boat to Nova Zembla. But Pip was in London, and Benjamin was *somewhere,* trying to slow down the world's ability to destroy itself. It was hard to fault him for that, but the result was that Janie was alone, and she was afraid.

She made her way along the lab tables to the back of the room where her experiment was set up. Mr. Kase, the chemistry teacher, was from Kentucky, and he'd joked that her apparatus looked like a distillery, and she must be making homemade corn whiskey. She supposed it did look like that. There were glass bottles and pipes and tubes, all arrayed in a three-dimensional maze, and there was a medium-sized water tank, like an aquarium. She was relieved to see that the apparatus hadn't been moved. Maybe everyone would just forget it was there until she had the information she needed. They would never notice the small adjustments she made each morning, and they wouldn't know how to move it or what to do with the pieces. It seemed like a long shot, but it was all she had.

She checked the saline levels in the tank, and they were lower than her last reading. The test thread was suspended from a ruler across the top of the tank. She pulled the thread out and it had a few salt crystals attached to it, sparkling like rough diamonds—more crystals than she'd ever had before. She felt a glow of excitement, and weighed the crystals on a small scale. She was so absorbed that she didn't notice the door opening at the other end of the room, or hear the footsteps behind her.

"Miss Scott," a voice said.

The warm glow winked out, like a snuffed candle. She turned and saw the portly headmaster, frowning in his three-piece suit. "Mr. Willingham."

"I thought I had made myself clear," he said. "You were to leave campus at once."

"I *did* leave," she said. "But I had to check on my experiment."

"How did you get in?"

She decided to make a stab at lying. "The room was open?"

"I'll take that key," Mr. Willingham said, holding out his hand.

Janie took the key out of her pocket and handed it over, careful not to touch his palm.

"*Thank* you," he said, with exaggerated formality.

"I'm so close to finishing," she said. "The saline levels are lower than ever. I just wanted a little more time."

Mr. Willingham's eyebrows rose. "Clearly this experiment is important to you, Miss Scott. And I support the spirit of inquiry, of course. But you are no longer a student here. How much time do you need?"

"I was thinking before that I needed a month," Janie said, the words tumbling out. "But this morning, I think—well, I don't know for sure, and I don't want to jinx it, but I might only need a week."

"I see."

"If I could just come in the morning before class," she said. "That's what I've been doing all term. I wouldn't disturb anything, or anyone."

Mr. Willingham frowned. "How would you get here from Concord?"

Concord! She'd forgotten about Concord. "My aunt can give me a ride," she said. "It's on her way to work."

"Work? Where?"

"At . . . the hospital," she said. Her father liked to quote Mark Twain: *If you tell the truth, you don't have to remember anything.* So much for that.

"She's a nurse?" Mr. Willingham asked.

"A doctor." Janie instantly cursed herself. Why a *doctor*? The headmaster was going to be curious about the lady doctor at the hospital.

The thready eyebrows shot up again. "Oh? What is her area of practice?"

"Um, she works with kids." That seemed plausible.

"A pediatrician."

"Yes. I can't believe I forgot that word!"

Mr. Willingham sighed, as if this pointless conversation had gone on long enough. "It's highly irregular to have students on our campus who are not enrolled," he said. "I'll give you until the end of the week."

Janie couldn't believe her luck. It was only Tuesday. "Really?"

"I can arrange to have the classroom door open by seven thirty each morning. Will that do?"

"Yes! Thank you!"

"Are you finished for today?"

"Almost."

"See that you're out by the time our *actual* students arrive." Mr. Willingham turned on his heel and left the room.

Janie hurried to write down the weight of the salt that had crystallized, and to adjust the solution and hang a new thread. One last week of research time! She was giddy with hope. It might just be enough.

CHAPTER 6

Success

Raffaello invited Janie to go to East High with him, and at first she said no. She couldn't enroll without her parents' help. And why would she go to school when she didn't have to? But then she imagined the empty day stretching out ahead of her while she sat on the flowered couch and stared at the wall or made conversation with Giovanna, and she changed her mind. She was used to going to class every day. And she was curious about the big public school.

"Won't the teachers question me?" she asked.

"Not for long," Raffaello said. "You'll see."

The school was a loud, busy, crowded place, compared to Grayson. Raffaello led Janie to a tiny, silver-haired English teacher in a blue dress, and said, "Mrs. Lloyd, this is Janie Scott. She's a new student but she's not on the roll sheets yet."

"When are they sending new roll sheets?" Mrs. Lloyd asked.

"The office doesn't know yet," Raffaello said. "Soon."

The teacher sighed. "See if you can find her a desk."

"Thank you, ma'am."

Janie sat with Raffaello and his friends, who did nothing but talk to each other. In the next class, Raffaello gave the same explanation about the roll sheets to a young math teacher in a suit, and added, "You can ask Mrs. Lloyd."

The teacher nodded and pointed to an empty desk, and Janie had infiltrated East High—it was as easy as that.

Raffaello was popular, with his quick smile and his easy manner, and there were girls among his friends as well as boys. Their rough, relentless teasing of each other reminded Janie of her almost-forgotten days at Hollywood High, but not of Grayson or St. Beden's. She felt as if the kids were speaking a language she'd once known but had forgotten. When it was time for Raffaello to go to work, she slipped out of the school with him, relieved.

At the restaurant, Giovanna wanted Janie's help with the wholesale food accounts. Janie combed through them as well as she could, until the dishes started to pile up and she put on an apron. At the end of the night, she closed out the till and divided the tips. Her share was eleven dollars this time. Then she climbed upstairs and fell into bed on the couch, more exhausted than she had ever been in her life.

Wednesday morning, she woke early and ran up to Grayson, afraid that the chemistry classroom wouldn't be unlocked. She only had three days left. But Mr. Willingham was true to his word, and the knob turned. The salt crystals on the thread were twice the size of the ones the day before, and the saline levels in the water even lower—she was getting closer! She did her measurements, adjusted the solution, treated a new thread and lowered it into the salt water, then slipped out before the first students came in.

Back at the apartment, she ate scrambled eggs on toast with Raffaello, then went to East High again. She would go crazy sitting alone all day, electrified by the knowledge that at this rate, she might have full crystallization by Friday. If she could make fresh water, it wouldn't matter where she was enrolled in high school or what she was going to tell her parents. She needed to write them her weekly letter soon so they wouldn't worry, but she couldn't bring herself to pretend that everything was normal and fine. She wished she could contact Jin Lo and tell her that she'd re-created the solution without the Pharmacopoeia's help.

Fingers were snapping in front of her face, and one of Raffaello's friends was grinning at her, a blond boy with a crew cut. "You here?" he asked.

"You were in some kind of trance," a girl with pin curls said.

"Maybe it's dangerous to wake her up," another boy said. "Same as sleepwalking."

"Sorry," Janie said. "I guess I drifted off."

"She's got a lot on her mind," Raffaello said. He reached out and tousled her hair.

Janie looked sharply at Raffaello to see what that hair tousling meant, but he had already turned away from her and moved on to another conversation. He had seemed to make the gesture without much thought, as one might pat a friendly dog on the head. So maybe that was all it was. She had become the family pet: the sleepy girl who did the dishes and kept the accounts and tagged along during the day.

Thursday morning, Janie hurried up to the science building again. Her tiredness disappeared when she saw that the crystals were larger than ever, the test water less salty. She was going to make her deadline. The water was drinkable at this point. There was still the hint of salt, but it was almost undetectable.

She wrote down her measurements and made what she was sure would be the final adjustment to the solution. Then she ran back across Kingsley Street for breakfast at the apartment.

It was hard to keep her voice down, with Bruno and Giovanna still asleep. What she really wanted to do was dance around the living room and shout "I'VE DONE IT!" Instead, she resorted to kicking her legs in the air and grinning like an idiot, and Raffaello watched her with a baffled smile. He slid an egg on toast onto her plate.

"I wish I could tell Jin—my old chemistry teacher," Janie said.

"Why can't you? You've got your tip money. Send a telegram."

Janie reminded herself to be careful, in her excitement, not to tell Raffaello things she wasn't supposed to tell. "I'm not sure where she is," she said. "I think she got a new job somewhere."

"You could write to your old school, and ask them to forward a letter."

"Sure." She was distracted for a moment by the tangled lie: Jin Lo had never been at her school. Then she broke into a happy smile. "Raffaello, I did it!"

He grinned back. "I knew you would."

"I wasn't sure." She took a bite of toast.

"Yes, you were. Finish your breakfast, or we'll be late."

She sat happily munching the crunchy toast and the soft, salty egg, thinking about how delicious salt was in small quantities, and how important the ability to remove it was. The vast oceans of the world could be drinkable.

She sailed through the day at East High, chatting with Raffaello's friends at lunch, joking about who was going to try out for the school play, a production of *A Midsummer Night's Dream*.

"I'd want to be the guy with the donkey head," Raffaello said.

"They aren't going to cover those curls with a donkey head," a girl said. "They'd make you one of the lovers, Demetrius or Lysander."

Raffaello made a face. "What kind of dumb names are those?"

"This from a boy named *Raffaello*?" the girl asked.

"I can't be in a play anyway," he said. "Some of us have responsibilities, you know."

He sounded like he was bragging, and the girl laughed at him, but Janie heard a tinge of regret in his voice.

That night in the restaurant when the dishes were done, Giovanna closed out the till, and Raffaello stacked breadbaskets. One of the cooks made Janie a bowl of linguine pesto. She ventured, "They're doing a play at school."

"*Sixty, sixty-five, seventy,*" Giovanna said, under her breath.

Janie took a bite of creamy green pasta and waited for Giovanna to finish counting, then said, "I think Raffaello would be great in it."

"Raffaello can't be in a play. He has a job."

"It's only for a few months."

Raffaello watched their conversation from across the kitchen, pretending not to listen. The rest of the kitchen staff was cautiously interested in anyone taking on Giovanna for any reason.

"It will make him a better waiter than being a busboy will," Janie said.

"Oh?" Giovanna said, accepting the challenge. "Why?"

"Because you have to memorize lines, and speak clearly, and perform. Those are all things waiters have to do well."

"He can practice being a waiter by being a *waiter*," Giovanna said. "In fact, Raffaello, you should start. No more busboy."

This was going the wrong way. "But if he gets one of the romantic leads, people will see him and talk about him," Janie said quickly. "Girls will want their parents to bring them to the restaurant where he works."

"And if he's only the boy who holds the spear?"

"Then he'll get the lead in the next play. And people will come here to see him."

Giovanna shook her head, looking down at her neat piles of cash. "We have many customers now."

"You wouldn't be happy with more?"

"We have better ways to make the advertisement."

"You can do those, too. Put an ad in the play's program. All I'm saying is that Raffaello is underused here, clearing dishes. You should get him onstage where more people can see how charming he is."

Giovanna gazed across the kitchen at her nephew, sizing him up as an undeveloped asset. "You want to be in this play?" she asked him.

He nodded nervously, which made his curls bounce around his temples.

"Speak up, child!" she commanded. "They don't hear you in the back of the theater like this!"

In the morning, Janie splashed water on her face and dashed up to Grayson, hoping that Mr. Willingham had remembered, one last time, to leave the chemistry door unlocked for her. The knob turned in her hand. She sent the headmaster a silent *thank you* across the campus, expecting the largest crystal yet on the thread in the tank at the back of the room. Then she stopped, staring.

There was no crystal.

There was no tank.

There was no apparatus.

Her salt, her beakers, her condensation-collecting tubes, the roll of thread, the carefully capped bottles—the whole thing was gone.

Janie closed her eyes for a few seconds, thinking she was hallucinating with tiredness, and opened them again. Nothing had changed. The back counter was still empty. She walked slowly toward it, feeling her feet touch the hard floor, so she knew she wasn't dreaming. The room was quiet and she could hear her own pulse in her ears.

She was awake, and this was real.

The countertop was black stone, and there was a shiny, clean rectangle where the tank had stood. She touched the stone. There wasn't a lot of dust, but there was enough to show that something had been there. There were a few white spots where salt water had dripped and dried. There was another circle of faint dust where her titrating apparatus had stood. But everything else was gone.

CHAPTER 7

The Headmaster

Janie marched into the headmaster's office, past the secretary, who looked up and started to say something. Janie ignored her and threw open Mr. Willingham's heavy wooden door.

"Where's my equipment?" she demanded.

Mr. Willingham, smoking his pipe, looked up at her mildly. "I beg your pardon?"

"It's not there! Everything's gone! That whole heavy tank!"

"What tank?"

"*My* tank, for my experiment! You saw it, in the chemistry classroom!"

"This tank was your personal property?"

Janie exhaled in exasperation. "No," she said. "But it's not about the tank. It's about my experiment. It's gone!"

"So you're saying there's been a theft of school chemistry

equipment?" Mr. Willingham asked. "That's a very serious matter."

She tried to calm herself down. "You know exactly what I'm talking about, and I want to know where it is."

Mr. Willingham set his pipe down carefully, put his elbows on the desk, and interlaced his plump white hands. He rested his nose on his knuckles as if he were thinking. Then he raised his head again. "Here is what I know," he said. "I know that you are no longer a student of this institution. A door was left unlocked at your request, and now you tell me that the school's valuable chemistry equipment has gone missing."

"It's not valuable in it*self*," Janie said. "It's a glass tank and some beakers and tubes. What's valuable is what I'd *done* with it."

"I see. Well, I think you'll find in our bylaws that all work done under the guidance of Grayson Academy belongs to the institution."

"So you took it?"

"No," he said. "I'm merely pointing out the fallacy of your claim to ownership."

"But I wasn't acting under anyone's guidance! It was my own experiment, done on my own time!"

"On the school's equipment and using its resources."

"The beakers and the tank?" Janie said. "That's ridiculous! I bought the other things—the thread and a carton of salt."

"So let us be clear," he said. "You are here to report the theft of some thread and a carton of salt?"

Janie wanted to scream with frustration. "Why would you *want* it?" she asked, stamping her foot. "I don't understand!"

And then suddenly she did understand. A cold flush of adrenaline spread through her body. "Wait," she said. She could barely breathe. "Mr. Magnusson. He said he'd be the first customer. He said he could use it in the islands."

"Did he?" Mr. Willingham asked mildly.

"You gave my experiment to him!"

"Why don't you just begin again?"

"I *can't*. It's taken months to get to this point. You told him I was close, and then he took it away. Or you took it and gave it to him."

"I do not broker the dabblings of children."

"It wasn't a *dabbling*." Her voice was low and unfamiliar, and frightened her. "It was valuable property and you knew it."

"I am the headmaster of a large and busy school, Miss Scott," he said. "Try as I might, I cannot keep abreast of the individual projects of each student in our care."

"But you knew about *mine*."

"I knew that you would like me to leave the chemistry door unlocked for one week, ending today. I know nothing more. You're lucky I'm not holding you liable for the loss of the equipment. In fact, I might call the police." He reached for the telephone on his desk.

Janie's mind was still tumbling over the events of the week. "Did you kick me out in the first place so he could take it?" she asked. "Mr. Magnusson never lets an opportunity go by, does he? He even gave me the week to perfect it."

The headmaster held the telephone receiver to his ear. "You're beginning to seem paranoid to me, Miss Scott.

Perhaps it's not the police I should call. Perhaps we should arrange a psychiatric evaluation." He started to dial.

Janie backed toward the door. If she wasn't careful, she was going to end up in a padded cell. Carted off to the loony bin. Who had said that? Tadpole Porter. But he wasn't part of the conspiracy. Or was he? She had to get out of here. She started to say something about her aunt in Concord, anything to make Mr. Willingham think that an adult was looking out for her, when she bumped into someone behind her and whirled around.

But it wasn't an orderly carrying a straitjacket. It was just the headmaster's fluffy-haired secretary, looking concerned. "Is everything all right?" she asked.

Janie darted around her and out the door, through the reception area, and into the hall. She made her way outside the building and stood on the steps, gulping air. She felt as if she hadn't really breathed the whole time she was in the office. The air outside was cold and clear, untainted by Mr. Willingham's noxious pipe smoke and his lies.

She wanted to crumple right there on the steps. But she had to move forward. Raffaello and his family had been kind to her, but they couldn't help her with this. She needed to find the only people who could help her fight back.

CHAPTER 8

Code-breaking

Raffaello was waiting for Janie on the sidewalk outside Bruno's restaurant. "We're late for school," he said. "Where have you been? It's the auditions today!"

"Sorry," she said. "I'm not feeling well. I don't think I can go."

Raffaello hesitated, puzzled. "You could be Hermia. Or Helena."

"I can't audition," Janie said. "They'd find out I'm not really enrolled at the school."

Raffaello's face fell.

"Go on," she said. "Go try out for the play."

He kicked the sidewalk and said nothing.

"I fought Giovanna for you!" she said. "Don't waste it!"

Raffaello looked up. "You really think I might get a part?"

Janie was losing patience. "I don't know!" she said. "But you won't get one if you don't *go*."

He yawned self-consciously, in that way boys did when they felt embarrassed and uncertain, and finally shouldered his knapsack and set off.

Alone in the living room upstairs, Janie got out Benjamin's

letters, the only hard evidence she had that he existed. She looked at the familiar handwriting, trying to see something she hadn't seen before. She had studied the postmarks a hundred times, and they all seemed deliberately blurred in the same way. She rubbed the paper with her thumb and guessed that Benjamin had treated the paper with something that resisted the postmark's ink, so it wouldn't take.

She took out the first letter again and unfolded it. It had arrived in London about two months after Benjamin first sent her diary back. The letter said:

Dear J.,
 How's all? Really beastly industrial nastiness, here. Can't help insulting natives, apparently. But so far no one's trying to run us out of town. So that's something. Miss you a lot. Tell your parents Figment says hello. My dad sends his regards.
                                             Bx

Parts of the letter were clear. The *x* was a kiss, which had made her knees go weak the first time she read it. "Figment" was her father's joking name for Benjamin; it came from "figment of your imagination." Her parents had invented a whole aristocratic English family called the Figments, fourteenth cousins to the Queen. Benjamin was supposed to be the son and heir. They thought the whole thing was hilarious. At the time, Janie had thought it was annoying. Now their dumb joke made her smile. But then she remembered that she needed to tell them that she'd been kicked out of Grayson—or tell them *something*, and soon. So she tried to think of a place where there might be industrial nastiness and easily offended locals. It seemed like that could describe most places in the world.

She'd received the next note about three months later:

> Dear J.;
> Might eventually return to England. Regardless, this lasts until Xmas. Even my batty old uncle recommends going. Home, I mean. I hope you'll stay in London. If you have to go, leave forwarding address. Missing you.
>
> Bx

That message had puzzled her at first, because she didn't think Benjamin had an uncle. But then she remembered the day they had followed a well-dressed man to the Connaught Hotel, trying to discover who he was. Benjamin had told the desk clerk that the man with the blackthorn walking stick was his uncle. So maybe the "batty old uncle" was Vili, the Hungarian count. But the only part of the letter that made sense was the instruction to leave a forwarding address, which Janie had done.

The third letter had arrived just before she left London, in September. It said:

Dear J.,

Experience says patience is required. I'm to undertake some asinine new trial on 2 November. Even with His Excellency's brilliance, really I don't expect success. Missing you—have I said that? Hope it won't be long now.

Bx

November 2 had passed, so the "trial" must be over. "His Excellency" would be Count Vili. But the rest of it was just confusing. Janie laid the three letters out next to one another. There was something odd about all of them. Benjamin was offhand and direct, and his way of talking was one of the first memories she'd recovered. The letters were strange and formal and sometimes stilted, as if he were writing a telegram and could only afford a certain number of words. She read each one again, and decided that it was only the *first* part of each letter that sounded strange. The last sentences sounded more like Benjamin, and convinced her that he was really the one writing them.

So maybe the false sound was deliberate. Benjamin didn't do things accidentally. Had he been trying to tell her something, with his strange stiltedness? He had once wanted to become a spy, not an apothecary. So maybe there was a code. Janie got out a piece of paper and wrote out the awkward words at the beginning of the first letter:

How's all? Really beastly industrial nasti-
ness, here. Can't help insulting natives,
apparently.

It wasn't Benjamin's voice. And it didn't contain information that did her any good. So what was it? It had to be a
message that he was hiding from other people—people who
wouldn't know that the words didn't sound like him or mean
anything to her. He was describing an industrial city of some
kind . . .

She let her eyes go out of focus over the piece of paper,
and then suddenly she saw it. She picked up her pencil again,
her hand shaking with excitement, and took the first letter of
each word:

HaRbinhChina

She tumbled off the couch and ran to the apartment's
small bookcase, hoping to find an atlas. There was a section for Raffaello's old schoolbooks, alongside Bruno's cook-
books and Giovanna's Italian romance novels, and he had a
slim paperback *Atlas of the World*. She pulled it off the shelf,
trying to keep her fingers steady as she thumbed through
the index.

There it was:

Harbin, China 22, B-12

She looked back at her transcription. There was no *h* at the end of Harbin. What did the *h* stand for? She looked at the sentences she'd written out. Really beastly industrial nastiness, *here*. Here, where he was. Harbin, *here*, China. That was the message. She could barely breathe. She flipped to page 22 and found the city. Harbin was in the far northeast part of the country, near the Russian border. They could easily have been there.

She picked up the next letter and read the first two sentences. "Might eventually return to England. Regardless, this lasts until Xmas. Even my batty old uncle recommends going." She fought to keep her pencil steady as she wrote out the first letters of each word:

MertERtluXembourg

She grabbed the atlas again and found the entry in the index:

Mertert, Luxembourg **10, E-5**

She was right! Count Vili was Hungarian, but he'd been living in the tiny country of Luxembourg, in the middle of Europe, before they met him. And he had money, and presumably a big house there. Benjamin and his father must have gone to stay with Count Vili!

Then the most recent message. "Experience says patience is required. I'm to undertake some asinine new trial on 2

November. Even with His Excellency's brilliance, really I don't expect success." She wrote out the first letters, her hand flying across the page. It read:

EspirltusantozNEwhebrldes

She looked it up in the atlas index. There was an Espírito Santo in Brazil, but that wasn't right, so she tried just looking up "New Hebrides."

New Hebrides 25, C-7

She flipped to the map on page 25 and saw the tiny islands, northeast of Australia, between New Guinea and Fiji. Espíritu Santo was one of them.

Janie had two conflicting feelings, with attendant questions, both equally strong. The first was: Why hadn't she figured out the code before? And the second: How had he expected her to figure it out? It wasn't a difficult code, once she was looking for it, but she hadn't been looking. Obviously, Benjamin had made it not too difficult so that she could find it without being given the key.

But she had to be looking. *That* was the key. And she hadn't looked, hadn't even thought to look, until now. Benjamin had given her a way to find out where he was *if she needed him*. And now she did need him. But the last letter had been sent months before. It had gone all the way to England before reaching her. There was no telling where he was now.

CHAPTER 9

An Invitation

The mailroom at Grayson was smallish, lined with racks of wooden pigeonholes, each with a student's name printed below. It was an annex of the cafeteria, and it always smelled like chicken soup, no matter what was for lunch.

Janie slipped in under the hum and buzz of lunchtime, and went to her pigeonhole: SCOTT, J. There was nothing inside the pigeonhole except a letter addressed to Miles Scouter, whose box was next to hers. Janie stuck the envelope in the SCOUTER box and went to the attendant's desk.

"Hi," she said. "I wonder if there's any mail for me?"

The woman looked up from sorting envelopes. She had dyed black hair, tortoiseshell glasses on a chain, and a sour expression. She had worked at Grayson for as long as anyone knew. Mrs. Andrews? Mrs. Anthony? "All the mail is in the pigeonholes," she said.

Janie looked at the pile still unsorted on the desk. "I just—"

she began. "It's just that I have to leave Grayson for a while, and I wanted to pick up anything that's here before I go."

The woman peered at her. "What's your name?"

"Janie Scott. Or Jane."

"Jane Scott," the woman said. "Right. I'm supposed to forward your mail to someplace—Minnesota?" She picked up a small bundle of envelopes and tilted her head back to look through her glasses at the note on top. "No. Michigan."

"Yes!" Janie said, reaching. "Michigan. That's me. I can just take them."

The woman pulled them away. "I have my instructions."

"But they might get lost in the mail."

"The United States Postal Service is very reliable."

"But I'm *here*."

The woman peered over her glasses. "Do you have any identification?"

"Of course not! I'm sixteen!" Janie's patience with all things Grayson was wearing thin. "I don't need identification when I take the mail from my pigeonhole."

"That's different," the woman said.

"Why?"

"Because then it's in the pigeonhole."

Janie closed her eyes for a moment. "Could you just—could you put it in the pigeonhole, like normal, just this one last time, and then I'll take it? The usual way?"

"Why are you leaving in the middle of term?"

"Because—" Janie began. "Because I've been expelled."

The woman pursed her lips. "I think I should call Mr. Willingham."

Mrs. Adelaide. Janie was 90 percent sure that was her name. "*Please,* Mrs. Adelaide," she said.

The woman looked up as if Janie had spoken a magical incantation, a secret password.

"My parents are coming to pick me up," Janie said. "And I'm trying to leave Grayson. I just want to make sure I have everything before I go. So that I can stay on top of all my responsibilities. You understand, Mrs. Adelaide."

The woman hesitated, looking at Janie's little stack of mail in her hand. Then she held it out. "Just this once," she said. "This is highly irregular."

"I really appreciate it," Janie said, taking hold of the stack. It didn't budge. Mrs. Adelaide wasn't letting go.

"*Thank* you, Mrs. Adelaide," Janie said, saying the magic words again. She tugged harder, and finally the letters were hers. She took a step backward to catch herself.

"Don't thank me," Mrs. Adelaide said, sighing. "Just go."

Janie stood outside the mailroom, on the edge of the cafeteria, amid the din of cheerful voices and clanking silverware. She shuffled through the stack, her hands trembling. An advertisement from the local department store. An announcement of a school poetry contest. A printed postcard from the Grayson Academy Social Committee, inviting her to the "Winter Wonderland" dance.

And there it was.

The Grayson Academy Social Committee
Invites you to the
WINTER WONDERLAND DANCE
Saturday 7pm
ember 1954

A letter addressed in Benjamin's handwriting. She felt as if she was awash in warm sunlight. "Thank you, Mrs. Adelaide!" she sang out.

The woman gave her a suspicious look.

Janie tucked the other letters into her peacoat pocket and studied Benjamin's envelope as she walked outside. It had a blurred postmark, as usual. She rubbed the envelope to see if it felt slick or waterproof, but it seemed like ordinary paper. She ran straight into someone standing in her path, scrambled back, and got ready to run.

"Easy there," Tadpole Porter said.

"Oh, it's you," she said. She stuffed the envelope in her pocket.

"You jumped about three feet in the air," he said.

"You surprised me," she said, trying to figure out how to get past him. He made a sizable figure in his wool coat.

"Who's your letter from?"

"What?"

"You were about to open a letter."

"Oh," she said. "A friend. In England."

Tadpole brightened. "Is she cute?"

Janie almost corrected him—then said, "Yes. Very cute."

"Blonde?"

"Kind of sandy-colored hair."

Tadpole's glasses had fogged in the cold and he took them off. His eyes looked naked in his plump face, without protection. "I hear English girls don't mind if you're endomorphic," he said hopefully, wiping his glasses. "Maybe because they had rationing for so long. So being well-fed just means you have resources, you know?" He put the glasses back on.

"Maybe," Janie said.

"So, did you really get kicked out?"

"I did."

"I heard that, but I couldn't believe it."

"They said I cheated on the trig test."

Tadpole burst out laughing. "You?" he said. "You'd have to cheat to get an answer *wrong*."

Janie's heart warmed toward him, for believing in her. "Thanks, Tadpole," she said. "I mean it. Thank you."

Tadpole blushed and seemed tongue-tied, and then recovered. "Hey, are you going to the dance? The, you know, Winter Wonderland thing?"

The question almost made her laugh. "No."

"Oh," he said. "I was just wondering."

"Okay." She started to make her way around him. She needed to read Benjamin's letter.

"No, wait!" he said, holding up both arms to block her. "Maybe you want to go. I mean, I'm on the dance committee. So I'm sort of supposed to make sure people want . . . you know, to go."

When Janie was still a Grayson student, she might have become self-conscious and unsure about whether anyone— even awkward, brainy Tadpole—was inviting her to the dance. But in the last week her evasiveness had gotten such a workout that she didn't have any of it left for the Winter Wonderland. "Are you inviting me to the dance?" she asked.

He blushed again. "Yeah," he said. "I mean, yes. I am."

"I've been kicked out," she said. "I'm not even supposed to be on campus. I can't go."

"Oh," he said. "Okay."

"But thanks for inviting me. I'd go if I could."

"Really?"

"Don't tell anyone you saw me, okay?"

"Oh!" he said. "No. Of course. I won't." Blushing so furiously had made his glasses fog again, and he took them off. Janie took advantage of his nearsightedness to dart around him and escape.

CHAPTER 10

Contact

J anie tore open Benjamin's envelope as soon as she got off campus. Something small and square slipped out of the letter, and she caught it before it fell.

The object was a flat glassine envelope that fit in her palm, and it was sealed with a double fold. She could see through the shiny, almost transparent paper to a coarse gray powder inside. She put the powder carefully in her pocket and read the letter, paying special attention to the first letter of each word.

Dear J.,

I'm sending you something we've just developed. Remember the homesickness remedy my father once gave you? Take a few grains like that. Make sure you're alone. Then sit quietly and close your eyes and think about . . . well, me. If you can stand it. Give it a try.

Bx

The letter wasn't stilted, but she tried the code anyway. *Isyswjd. Rthrmfogy. Tafglt.* Unless it was someplace in Iceland without many vowels, there was no code revealing where Benjamin was. She tried the last sentences, but there she found *Msya. Tsqacyeatawm. Iycsi. Giat.*

Nothing.

So maybe the instructions were all that the message was meant to convey. The apothecary, Benjamin's father, had given her a homesickness remedy when she first arrived in London. It was a combination of two powders, aspen and honeysuckle, dissolved in water. She'd met Benjamin on her first day using it, so it had been hard to determine what, exactly, had conquered her homesickness: aspen and honeysuckle, or a new friend.

She needed privacy to try the powder, but there was no privacy. Raffaello was at Bruno's when she got there, and she carefully tucked both envelopes away in her pocket.

"I auditioned!" Raffaello said.

He looked so proud that she had to laugh. "Congratulations," she said. "Was it scary?"

"Not as scary as facing Aunt Giovanna. Is that what made you sick? Do you feel better?"

She'd forgotten she'd said that she didn't feel well. The morning seemed so long ago. "Much better, thanks."

"Good, because my dad needs us to do some prep in the kitchen. Have you ever chopped garlic?"

She shook her head.

"I'll show you how," he said. "They'll put up the cast list over the weekend."

He told her all about the audition as they peeled and chopped. So it wasn't until late, when her fingers were pruned and the dishwater had soaked out all the garlic smell, and she had closed out the till and taken her tips, and the others had gone to bed in the apartment over the restaurant, that she was finally alone. Her hands felt clumsy from exhaustion or nervousness as she drew a glass of water. She tapped in a few grains of the coarse powder, letting it dissolve. Then she drank it down. Benjamin had said to think about *him*. Sitting cross-legged on the couch, she closed her eyes.

She thought about the first time she had seen him, a stubborn, sandy-haired boy arguing with the lunchroom matron at St. Beden's during a bomb drill. Janie had crouched obediently under the lunchroom table, like all the other students, and from there she had seen Benjamin telling the matron that hiding under tables wasn't going to protect them from an atomic bomb.

Then she thought about standing with him on the deck of an icebreaker at sea, heading north under a brilliant scattering of stars. He had reached out and touched her hair. She had known there was danger ahead, and still there was nowhere else in the world she had wanted to be.

Then something else happened. In that imagined space behind her eyelids, the inky sea faded away, and she saw lush green trees. She was no longer on the sea at night. It was day, but the sunlight filtered through dense foliage. She was crouched against a muddy slope in some kind of tropical jungle. The roots of a huge fallen tree, still hung with clods of dirt, provided shelter. She could smell the damp earth.

A blast of gunfire went off surprisingly close, and Janie flinched. Then she realized that the gunfire was steady and continuous, just over the rise.

She wanted to turn her head to look, but the imagining wasn't the kind she could control. It was like a vivid, uncontrollable dream, and it made her a little dizzy. Now there were two hands in front of her, not her own hands, rubbing some kind of liquid between them. The sharp smell of alcohol reached her nose.

A man's voice spoke nearby, and Janie's field of vision swung to take in the speaker. She gasped and nearly opened her eyes. Crouched next to her was the apothecary—Benjamin's father, Mr. Burrows. He wore a dark cotton shirt and a sweat-soaked blue bandana around his neck. "The firing's dying down," he said. "It won't be long."

Janie listened to the gunfire. Soon she only heard a distant, random shot every few seconds.

"Let's go," the apothecary said.

Janie seemed to be clambering up behind him, around the roots of the tree. Then her vision began to swim and break up. It was as if the illusion couldn't stand movement. The effect could only work when Benjamin kept still.

For it *was* Benjamin, she was sure of it. It was his hands she had seen, in place of her own. She had been seeing *through his eyes.* She sat very still on the couch, trying to bring the vision back. It was like trying to recover the fragments of a lost dream. But there was only darkness. She opened her eyes and saw Bruno and Giovanna's dim living room. When she turned her head, her vision spun, and she thought she might throw up, so she kept still. The curtains and books that had once seemed cozy and welcoming now seemed only dull and disappointing, after Benjamin's lush, dangerous world.

Benjamin's world! She closed her eyes to try to go back, but saw nothing. Where was he? Why was he in the jungle? Were they going into battle? How had he made the gray powder? Had he taken some? He must have.

And another question: Could Benjamin see through her eyes also, or did the effect only go one way? Did he know when she was doing it? She thought he must not, or he would have spoken to her. But maybe she could have spoken to him!

"Benjamin!" she called softly, in the empty living room.

Nothing. She had to try again.

She stood and moved carefully to the kitchen. The room didn't spin so much now. She filled her glass with water, tapped in a few more grains of powder, and drank it down. Her stomach seized, cramping, and she had to sit down on the kitchen floor to keep from falling over. She tried to be quiet, not to wake the others. She closed her eyes to find Benjamin again, but saw nothing, and felt only the disorienting dizziness and the pain in her stomach.

So maybe she wasn't supposed to take the stuff again so soon. The avian elixir, which had turned them into birds, worked like that: Benjamin had fallen from the sky after taking it too quickly a second time.

She waited for the nausea to pass, and tried to breathe, and thought about what jungle Benjamin might be in. She wished he had thought to write his location or some message on his shirtsleeves, just in case she looked in unexpectedly. "HI, JANIE, I'M IN _____." Or he could have used his old code in the letter, in some meaningless first sentence, to tell her where he was.

She remembered the arguments they'd had in London over how to use the Pharmacopoeia, and how to anticipate the hazards of whatever they were planning. She could imagine Benjamin retorting that he hadn't included a coded nonsense sentence because he wanted to be very *clear* about what she was supposed to *do*. And it was dangerous to keep using the same code, as someone might *break* it. And he didn't know exactly how the powder would *work* over such a great distance.

She smiled, imagining his indignant voice and his explanations. Benjamin was clearer to her now that she had seen his world through his eyes. She could try to reach him later, when it seemed safe to try again. She would look harder for signs of where he might be.

Then she remembered the gunfire, and Benjamin running out of their shelter. She hoped he and his father were safe, wherever they were.

PART TWO

Opposition

1. resistance or dissent, expressed in action or argument
2. (*the opposition*) a group of adversaries or competitors or political rivals
3. a contrast or antithesis (in Chinese philosophy and medicine, contrary forces are interdependent and connected in the natural world)

CHAPTER 11

Field Medics

Benjamin Burrows and his father were huddled in a makeshift foxhole, beneath the exposed roots of a fallen tree, waiting for the shooting to stop. Benjamin kept his arms protectively over his head and tried not to think about the grenade that could come flying into their shelter at any moment. He reminded himself that he had wanted a life of adventure. He had not wanted to run an apothecary shop in London. To keep his mind off the bullets flying through the air, he made a mental list of all the things that he had not wanted to make his living selling:

Aspirin
Hot-water bottles
Epsom salts
Milk of magnesia
Cod-liver oil
Cotton gauze

That last item brought him back to reality, and he reached for his satchel to be sure he still had plenty of gauze bandages.

They were going to need them when the fighting stopped. A grenade exploded not far away, and Benjamin rolled into the wall of earth beneath the upended tree roots. A spray of dirt and small rocks hit his back. He looked up at his father. "You all right?" he asked.

"Yes, yes, fine."

His father seemed to have shrunk in their weeks in the jungle. Benjamin was skinnier, too. They were living on rice, mostly, and green shoots his father found, and occasional bowls of stewed pork from the grateful families of men they had saved. But the villagers could barely feed themselves, let alone share with two hungry foreigners.

One night, Benjamin had woken with an itching head, his scalp crawling with something. He had leaped up shouting, clawing at his hair, and brought away dried blood and writhing ants beneath his fingernails. He woke his father, whose calm diagnosis had been that a leech had found its way onto Benjamin's head as he slept, injecting an anticoagulant to prevent blood clotting. When it had drunk its fill and dropped off, it left Benjamin's scalp bleeding freely. The ants had been attracted by the blood. "This whole jungle's out to get me!" Benjamin had cried. But his father had said that was a fallacy. The ants and the leech weren't out to get him. They didn't even recognize him as a particular individual. They were only doing what ants and leeches do: seeking nourishment.

"We need to get out of here," Benjamin said now, beneath the fallen tree.

"Not yet," his father said. "They're still firing."

"I mean out of this whole country. This place. We're not cut out for this kind of war."

"The people here need us," his father said. "We have an obligation to help them."

Benjamin sighed and settled back into the damp earth. They had come to Vietnam because his father had been looking for a particular plant with unusual medicinal qualities. But the Vietminh, who had fought the Japanese with the support of the United States, and defeated the French in a bid for independence, were now supported by Communist China. One day while Benjamin and his father were out collecting, Vietminh soldiers overran the rural village where they had been staying. The local people put up a fight and were slaughtered or captured. When Benjamin and his father returned, they treated the survivors. As soon as they were finished, a messenger begged them to come to the next village, where the same thing had taken place.

Now Benjamin's father wouldn't leave, and they were stuck in a place that seemed hotter, more humid, and more murderous every day. The Pharmacopoeia, the priceless leather-bound book stuffed with medical and magical secrets that their ancestors had passed down so carefully, was wrapped in oilcloth in his father's backpack. The oilcloth was a feeble barrier against mildew, paper-eating insects, bullets, and grenades. It was no way to protect a seven-hundred-year legacy.

The sound of gunfire was becoming less frequent. Benjamin was hungry. "This war isn't going to end," he said.

"So we should let these men die?"

"No! But we should—I don't know. Go back to thinking about the bigger picture." *And eating real food,* he thought. Benjamin was sixteen and would have been hungry a lot even if they were back in England, but here there was a gnawing emptiness in his stomach that wouldn't go away. The rice balls he carried, wrapped in a waxy leaf in his pocket, didn't help.

"We aren't very good at the bigger picture, you may have noticed," his father said. "Medicine is the great aim, the true aim. Paracelsus said it four hundred years ago. I only lost sight of it for a time."

Benjamin wanted to point out that Paracelsus didn't know about atomic weapons, but he didn't want to torture his father. After the war, in which Benjamin's mother had been killed, his father had become alarmed by the world-destroying possibilities of the atomic bomb, and started working on an antidote. In Nova Zembla, they had succeeded, containing a blooming mushroom cloud and shrinking it back to nothing, while the Quintessence scrubbed the radiation from the air. But they had been lucky there: They knew the test was coming, and they could get close to the bomb at the right moment. The great hope was that they could improve their methods, and neutralize a bomb *after* it had been dropped in combat. But now they couldn't even keep ahead of the escalating nuclear tests.

They had been late for two tests by the British in western Australia, and unable to get close to an American hydrogen bomb in the Bikini Atoll in March. An unlucky Japanese fishing boat *had* gotten close, though. The boat, the *Lucky Dragon*

No. 5, was forty miles away from the atoll when the wind shifted, covering the fishermen with ash. They had stopped to bring in their fishing gear before fleeing the strange powdery mist. By the time they got to shore, the fishermen had burns and blisters on their skin. Their irradiated tuna went to market, to be sold and eaten. Benjamin's father had followed the *Lucky Dragon*'s story with a tormented interest.

Then, in early September, the Soviets tested an atomic bomb in the Ural Mountains, in Russia. Benjamin's father hadn't even known that one was coming, and he cursed himself for his blindness. Three weeks later, the Japanese radioman of the *Lucky Dragon* died at the age of forty. He said, "I pray that I am the last victim of an atomic or hydrogen bomb."

After the Soviet test and the radioman's death, something happened to Benjamin's father. He became obsessed with their failure. He developed a tic, a muscle near his left eye that twitched so violently sometimes that Benjamin could see it. He had never been convinced by "deterrence," the idea that the great powers would keep each other from using nuclear weapons just by possessing them. But he *had* been convinced that a few idealistic scientists—and a teenage boy—could stop the great powers from having them. *That* was the fallacy, as far as Benjamin was concerned. They were so few, and so isolated. They had no resources beyond their own strange and secret abilities. How could they follow the intelligence traffic of so many different countries, and cover so much ground, *and* stay hidden? Of course they had failed! Staying here and giving up wasn't the answer.

Benjamin looked at his hands, which were dirty, and he wiped them down with alcohol from his bag. There would be casualties to deal with soon, and he would need clean hands. He thought of Janie, and wondered if she'd gotten his letter yet, with the little glassine envelope.

"The firing's dying down," his father said. "It won't be long."

Benjamin listened. There was a distant pop or two of gunfire, and the sound of men moaning, some of them surely dying. The Vietminh had retreated. They would return, of course. They had endless reinforcements and infusions of weapons from the Chinese. But for now they were gone.

"Let's go," his father said.

They crept out of their shelter and moved among the bodies. Benjamin had become good at triage, at knowing which men needed attention immediately, which could wait a little longer, and which were beyond help. He had learned useful first aid. He knelt beside a boy no older than he was, who was bleeding from an arterial leg wound, and he tied the boy's handkerchief around his thigh to stop the pumping flow of blood. Then he cut open the cotton pant leg to expose the wound and reached in with a pair of tweezers to remove the bullet, wincing at the pain he was causing. The boy screamed. They needed a fast-acting anesthetic—Benjamin had to remind his father about that.

Tossing aside the bullet, he daubed a pasty blue salve onto the wound. It was his father's latest concoction. Under the salve, the ragged edges of the wound re-knit themselves: Each torn piece of muscle and skin and artery wall sought the place it had been attached before. His father had mixed in something that made it sterilizing, so it devoured any bacteria that tried to colonize the wound. He had used it on Benjamin's scalp on the night of the ants.

Benjamin experimentally loosened the handkerchief on the boy's thigh, and the bleeding didn't start up again. The skin still had color in it, so he wasn't *out* of blood—which happened sometimes. Benjamin realized he'd been holding his breath, and let it go. The boy's face, distorted by pain, relaxed slightly. Benjamin wrapped the leg in the clean cotton gauze from his satchel and fashioned a crutch out of a fallen tree limb. He cut a notch in one end of a branch with his knife and set a short crossbar at the top, to go under the boy's arm, then wrapped twine from a roll in his pocket around the crossbar to secure it.

Benjamin knew some of the local dialect, thanks to a rare mushroom his father had found in China. Small, brown, and nonpoisonous, it stimulated the part of the brain that acquires language. Chewing a small dried piece of the mushroom dramatically increased the speed at which they had learned the villagers' language. It gave them a heightened linguistic focus.

Benjamin asked if his patient could walk. The boy nodded, standing with the aid of the crutch, and Benjamin moved on to the next casualty. A man his father's age had taken a bullet to the temple. His family would bury him before the animals found him, if he had family.

Benjamin followed the sound of a moan to a lean man in his twenties, shot in the chest. Air was coming through his wound with a sucking sound. Benjamin cleaned the blood away as well as he could, and applied some of the blue paste to the edges. Then he placed a square of thin, transparent plastic over the hole. He taped the square at the top and the two sides, leaving the bottom edge free, to create a valve. When the man breathed in, he sucked the plastic into the hole, sealing it so that air couldn't come in that way.

Benjamin was leaning over the next casualty, another teenager, who seemed to have taken a lot of shrapnel on the right side of the body, when he heard a metallic click near his left ear.

He turned to see the man holding the gun. It was a Vietminh officer, who told him to put his hands on his head. Benjamin obeyed. He could hear his father saying irritably in English, "You *must* let me finish treating this man," and then repeating the sentence in the local dialect, using the familiar, arrogant form of *you* that the soldiers had used. But the Vietminh clearly didn't feel there was anything they *must* do, at least not under orders from this Englishman.

The man with the gun gave Benjamin a shove in the back. With a regretful glance, Benjamin left the kid with the shrapnel bleeding on the ground.

CHAPTER 12

Homecoming

Jin Lo wandered the streets of her city. It was early morning, on a hazy gray day. An old man with white hair swept the sidewalk in front of a teashop. Had he lived here when she was a child, when the invading army came? Or had he been a soldier, away at war, seeing different horrors?

A striped cat stepped out of an alleyway and looked directly at Jin Lo. Its yellow eyes held hers until she was almost upon it. Then it darted away, into the shadows.

She'd had a cat of her own once, when she was eight, a black cat with a white spot on his nose and an unfortunate tendency to drool when happy. He left wet spots on her sleeve when he purred in her arms. But he was a very good hunter, and brought home mice, which he left outside the front door as offerings. When the soldiers came, he vanished. She sometimes had fantasies that he had been out hunting all this time, that he had grown huge, and could break the necks of the soldiers with one swift bite, and leave them at the door.

Or perhaps her cat had stayed away out of shame, because he had been able to do nothing to protect his family.

Or perhaps a stray bullet or a cruel and gratuitous swipe of a bayonet had ended him. But that she could hardly believe. Her cat had been too quick and nimble, too savvy and wary to linger near the soldiers.

When the soldiers came, Jin Lo's father ordered her into a wooden trunk near the door to hide. She didn't understand what was happening. But she had hidden in that trunk before, playing "eluding the cat" with her friends, when the object was to hide while someone searched. So she climbed in, sank down, and let her father close the lid over her head.

Then he opened the trunk again and tried to make her small brother get in, but her brother had screamed, and would have given both children away. Her mother took him into her arms. The lid closed, and that was the last time Jin Lo saw them alive. She carried the picture with her: her wailing brother, her mother shushing him, and her father looking afraid as she had never seen him afraid before.

She had stayed in the trunk, silent. Many times she had wanted to climb out, to protect her brother from anyone who might try to hurt him, but then she remembered the look of fear on her father's face.

After a while it was quiet. She crept out of the trunk in the dark, making no sound. She had always been good at "eluding the cat": silent and clever. She stepped outside and saw dark, still forms on the ground. She didn't want to look, wouldn't look. That couldn't be her father, who had always made her feel so safe. That couldn't be her mother, the most beautiful woman on the block. But her eye fell on a small hand sticking out from beneath the body of their next-door neighbor, old Mrs. Hsu. It looked as if Mrs. Hsu had been trying to shield the little boy.

Jin Lo had taken the small hand and tugged, imagining her brother gasping for air when she pulled him free. He would be afraid, but he would be happy to see his sister. His lip would tremble, and she would whisper reassurances and quiet him.

She pushed at Mrs. Hsu's body and wrenched her brother free. But the boy didn't tremble into tears, and he didn't reach for his sister with his fat, soft arms. A single bullet had gone through both of them. *The Japanese are efficient,* her father would have said.

Jin Lo let go of her brother's tiny hand and ran as fast as she could for the Safety Zone. Her father had told her to go to the Red Cross Hospital if she was ever alone.

She ran past more dark shapes and knew them to be the bodies of her neighbors and friends. Somewhere she heard crying, but still Jin Lo ran. Her mouth was open in a silent scream, sucking in the cold wind, which already had the taste of death in it. She would not be so foolish as to make a noise.

She reached the hospital, joined the nurses, and helped them all through the night. It was easy to tend a terrible wound if you had no heart. It didn't make your stomach turn, or your eyes melt into tears. The nurses whispered that the American missionary, the Reverend Magee, had been out filming with a camera. He was making a record so the world would know. In the morning she reported her story to Magee himself, and she didn't cry.

Sometimes, when she told the story later, it was she who had crawled out from under the body of Mrs. Hsu, unhurt, as she had hoped her brother would do. It was not so much that she was ashamed of hiding in the trunk. She knew that she had only been an eight-year-old girl, and she would have died at her family's side if she had tried to protect them. It would have been a kind of loyalty, but a futile kind. The reason she changed the story was that it made it a *story*, one she had control over, even as the heart of it stayed true. Her family had been killed, and she had survived. It was intolerable. But less so if she could change it, alter it, and move the details around.

Now that she had returned to her city, her feet took her to the street where she had grown up. She had not seen the place since she ran away to the Red Cross Hospital. Her feet moved more slowly. Many of the houses looked lived in, cared for, with small gardens in front, though there were no flowers now that it was winter.

A man was painting the front door of a house meticulously, as if the smooth brushstrokes were the most important thing in the world. A woman, visible in a backyard, hung white sheets on a line. Jin Lo's feet carried her on, against her will.

Then she stopped in front of a small, unpainted house. Its brown, dead garden grew only weeds. A window was cracked, and the gate hung off its hinge. She pushed the gate open, and it creaked. The front door gave when she pushed. There was no furniture inside the house. It had all been carried away. The wooden trunk she had hidden in was gone. A layer of dust covered the floor, and she left footprints in it. She looked at the tiny room she had shared with her baby brother, and at her parents' room, and at the kitchen where they had eaten their meals. She heard her father saying something sardonic, her mother saying something gentle, her brother squealing with delight. And then her legs seemed to collapse beneath her, and she sat cross-legged in the dust on the kitchen floor.

"I'm here," she said to the empty air. "I'm back. Please talk to me."

CHAPTER 13

First Do No Harm

The first thing Benjamin saw when they took the blindfold off was the oilcloth that had protected the Pharmacopoeia, thrown in a heap on the ground. One of the soldiers held the heavy book and flipped through the fragile, valuable pages with impatience, unable to read the Greek or Latin. Benjamin was about to say something, but then he saw a woman whose stomach had been cut open. She was alive, kneeling and begging for help in a low, persistent voice that had been lost among all the other voices in the settlement. It was the only thing he could hear, now that he could see her. His hands were bound behind his back.

His father, beside him, was speaking insistently to the Vietminh officers in the local dialect, then switching to French, which had been the language of authority in the country: "You must untie my hands. Let me help her. *Laissez moi l'aider.*"

"It is a punishment," one of the soldiers said.

"For what?"

"Eating rice that was meant for seed."

"And for this you cut her open?" his father asked.

"It is fitting. Too many people need food."

"She'll die."

"We all will die, without food."

"Please let me help her."

"We need you inside."

The men pushed them both across the dusty courtyard and into a wooden building. Benjamin wondered if the woman had been shown to them on purpose, as a warning of what might happen to them. But then he wondered if such brutality was so ordinary that their captors had simply taken off their blindfolds as soon as they reached the settlement, forgetting that there was anything disturbing there to see. He feared it was the second possibility—the soldiers had been thoughtless. That seemed worse than any threat. And they had the Pharmacopoeia. Would they destroy it? Keep it? All paper was valuable in the villages, as toilet paper, but he decided not to think about that.

It was dark inside the small building, and Benjamin's eyes took some time to adjust. There was a smell of bodies and also a smoky smell. The soldiers were respectfully silent, shuffling their feet nervously. In the middle of the room was a cot, and on the cot lay a man. He seemed to stare at Benjamin and his father without seeing, and he shook with chills. His high forehead shone with sweat.

"How long has he been in a fever?" Benjamin's father asked.

"Three days," said their guard.

"Does he hallucinate?"

The guard looked uncomfortable. "Perhaps."

"How is his vision?"

"Not good."

"He's your leader?"

"Our general."

"If I cure him, you let me tend to the woman."

There was a pause. "If you do not cure him, we kill you."

Benjamin's father switched to French again. *"Il a le neuro-paludisme. Il mourra sans traitement."*

Neuropaludisme was cerebral malaria. Benjamin looked at the sick general, who should be in a bucket of ice right now. His brains were being cooked by the fever as they talked.

"Alors traitez-le!" the soldier said: So treat him.

"Et puis la femme," Benjamin's father insisted.

The man waved a hand in impatience, as if they were bargaining for the life of a fly, not a woman. *"Oui,"* he said. *"D'accord."*

"Déliez nous."

Their hands were untied as he asked, and Benjamin's father knelt beside the general and reached for his bony wrist to take his pulse.

It occurred to Benjamin that his father might *pretend* to try to rescue the general, but instead let him die. It was the best thing he could do, to remove this man who had killed and enslaved innocent people.

But his father wasn't capable of killing a man while seeming to save him. His job was to heal, and he was stubborn in his principles. Murdering a man, even a dangerous and destructive man, would be impossible for him. And he had made his deal for the woman's life.

So they set about saving a villain. His father carefully laid out the contents of his knapsack, and asked for clean, boiled water. The men brought a tin cup, and he measured drops from a bottle into it. *"Barbaric,"* he muttered, almost to himself—he was still thinking of the woman, Benjamin knew. "The barbarity of it, Benjamin."

He helped the glassy-eyed general drink from the cup, then let his head down carefully on the pillow. He dampened a cloth and laid it over the man's sweating forehead. Then he took the man's listless hand and studied the fingernails. "You told me three days," he said to the soldiers in their dialect. "He's been sick much longer."

The men looked at each other. "Yes," one said. "The fever comes and goes."

"You have ice?"

"No."

Benjamin's father pressed on the general's abdomen, feeling for the edges of the liver, for the spleen. He seemed very much like a doctor, and Benjamin knew the men thought he was one. If they knew he was really a London apothecary, what would they say? "Let him sleep," he finally said. "I want to see the woman now."

The soldiers looked unsure, but he had such confidence and authority that no one dared to stop him as he moved toward the door. Benjamin followed, trying to look half as steady as his father did.

At the last moment, one of their captors stepped in their way. "You must stay until the general is well."

"My son will stay," his father said. "And I will return."

All eyes in the dim room turned to Benjamin, who hesitated, then went back to the bedside of the feverish man. He kneeled where his father had been. The men seemed to weigh the question of whether to allow a teenage replacement at the bedside of their leader, but then let his father pass.

The light outside was dazzling. The door closed and it was dim again. The remaining men looked at Benjamin, as if expecting him to do something medical, so he picked up the sick man's wrist. The pulse was thready and racing, and the skin felt like tissue paper over sticks for bones. His father was right; the man had been sick a long time. His mind would never be the same. He set the hand gently back on the cot, wondering what terrible things it had done.

He heard his father's voice issuing orders outside, and then he heard a woman's wail. There was silence in the hut. The wail turned to soft sobbing. How many stitches would the gaping hole in her belly require? The blue paste was effective in healing wounds quickly, but he had never seen it applied to anything so drastic.

The sounds from outside became indecipherable, and Benjamin fell into a kind of stupor as he waited. He was roused from it by his father calling, *"Benjamin!"*

He scrambled up and pushed past the startled men. As a group they were afraid. No one wanted to be the one to seize him. He got outside and blinked in the sunlight. The woman had been taken into the shade. His father, hands bloody to the elbow, was scattering something in the dust of the clearing.

"The book!" his father said.

The Pharmacopoeia lay discarded on the ground. Benjamin ran to wrap it up in the oilcloth, and tucked it under his arm, but by then the soldiers had surrounded them. Their faces were grim and their guns raised. One stepped forward. "You will stay until the general recovers. *Vous resterez.*"

Benjamin's father ignored the French command. "We must go. Evil spirits are coming to punish you for your deeds. You think no one sees. But the spirits see."

Benjamin saw something out of the corner of his

eye: a phantom shape, like a shadow, in human form. He stepped back with a cold jolt of fear. Then he saw another. The figures surrounded the clearing, swaying, reaching out with ghostly gray arms. His father turned and walked away from the soldiers, straight toward the ghosts.

"*Arrêtez!*" one of the soldiers said. "*N'allez pas!* Stop!"

But his father kept walking. After a paralyzed moment, Benjamin followed, carrying the book. He waited for a shot to ring out, but none did. They passed the old woman, her stomach bandaged and her body unnaturally still. They were walking right toward the phantoms. Benjamin heard a mournful, moaning sound. Was it a sound his father had created, or was someone howling in fear? The ghost figures reached out, mouths wide.

His father said, "Walk right through them."

Benjamin had to close his eyes, afraid he would feel the cold phantom fingers on his throat. He smelled something sharp and metallic, and then they were out of the clearing. They walked a hundred yards from the village. When they were out of sight in a bamboo grove, his father led him off the trail, smoothing and arranging the greenery behind them to cover their path. They hid under the wide, sheltering leaves of a *Hopea odorata* tree. After a few minutes, the soldiers mastered their fear and came running down the path in pursuit.

Hidden beneath the *odorata* leaves, Benjamin held the Pharmacopoeia on his lap. "Did you save the woman?" he whispered.

His father frowned. "She might live."

"And the ghosts? I thought you didn't like to encourage superstition. Evil spirits and all that."

The muscle in his father's eye jumped. He said, "I don't. But sometimes you work with what you have."

CHAPTER 14

YES or NO

Benjamin and his father spent the next two nights in one of the ruined villages, in an unburned hut. It was safer there than in the inhabited villages because it wasn't likely to be attacked.

Benjamin made soup over a tiny chemical fire that gave off no smoke and wouldn't give away their position. He had taken over the business of cooking. His father, who could work such wonders, ought to be a better chef, but he saw cooking as a task of refueling, delivering calories to the body.

There were mats in the hut to sleep on, and Benjamin stretched out on one. The moment he put his head on the rolled-up jacket that was his pillow, he had a vivid memory of Janie holding back her hair over a little pot, in her parents' London kitchen, boiling leaves that the gardener in the Physic Garden had given them. The smell of the steam compelled a person to tell the truth, and made Benjamin and Janie tell each other things they didn't want to say.

He sat up on the mat, in the abandoned hut. Janie had the glassine envelope. He was sure of it. He looked at his watch.

It was ten o'clock at night on a Sunday, which meant it was late morning for her. A good time to try.

The idea behind the powder, which he wasn't sure he had perfected, was that a thing split in half is still connected to its other half. It was meant to establish a means of communication over great distance. He had been thinking about the story of Zeus splitting human beings in half, out of fear that they would become too powerful. In the story, the halved people felt incomplete, and always yearned for their missing counterparts. Benjamin believed that the divided particles in his powder would behave the same way, and provide a link between the users. He dug in his knapsack, tapped a few grains into his canteen, and drank it down. Now he needed to concentrate. He closed his eyes and deliberately called up memories:

Janie ringing Sergei Shiskin's doorbell, making up a story about the science team needing the Russian boy's help. The brave, solemn look on her face as she took off her grandmother's gold earrings to melt them down for the invisibility solution. Janie on the deck of the icebreaker, cap pulled over her ears, hair blowing wildly. The way he had known that he could kiss her then—that she would let him and it would be all right.

And then he was in a place he had never seen, a small room with flowered curtains and a low bookshelf. He was sitting on a sagging couch. There was a thin paperback atlas open on his lap, and a hand—not his hand, but a girl's hand—turning the pages. *Janie.* It worked! She was looking at a map of Australia, and there were the New Hebrides. Did she know he had been there, from his letters? He wondered if he could move her hand. Could he *point*, if he concentrated hard enough?

He thought about her right index finger and willed it toward the speck of island on the map. But instead she turned the page. Now she was looking at South America. That didn't do him any good, but still he concentrated on her hands, trying to move them. He tried to stretch out the fingers on her right hand, but nothing happened. He made a fist with his own hand, and thought her fingers curled slightly, but maybe she was doing that anyway.

She turned the page again. He saw the South China Sea, and felt his heart start to race. She was very, very warm. He decided that her dominant right hand might be too strongly connected to her own logical left brain, so he concentrated all his attention on her resting *left* hand. Her fingers unfolded.

He thought harder and moved his own left hand as he wanted her to move hers. He focused hard on his index finger—on *her* index finger, the one they were pointing together. It came down on the long curving shape of Vietnam, and Benjamin nearly collapsed with the effort. He was sweating. He held the finger there on her map, both with his body and with his mind. As long as he didn't have to move it again, he thought he could keep it in place.

But then the atlas was thrown aside on the couch, and both of Janie's hands were moving outside his control. They caught up a small red notebook and a pen from the coffee table and flipped to a blank page. The right hand wrote in a hurried scrawl:

Benjamin! Are you in Vietnam? Point to answer:

YES   NO

With renewed effort and excitement, he shifted her left index finger toward YES.

Then he heard Janie's voice, as if from inside his own head. It was the strangest effect. "Can you hear me?" she asked.

He lifted her index finger a fraction of an inch and let it fall back on YES.

"Oh!" the voice in his head cried in amazement. "But I can't hear you, right?"

"I don't think so," he said aloud, but she went on talking:

"Because you're looking in *here* this time," she said, "and I can't see where you are. So it goes one direction at a time. Right? I have so many things to tell you. To ask you. I took the powder twice and the second time it made me really sick and didn't work. So I think we have to wait a day between doses. Does that sound right?" She rested her left hand lightly on the notebook.

He lifted her finger and let it fall back on YES. It was getting easier to move it, now that she was willing.

"Okay," she said. "This stuff wore off quickly before, so I'll try to be fast. I saw you and your father in the jungle, in a war. Are you in a war?"

His finger—and therefore hers—moved toward NO. But then he slid it back to YES. People were shooting each other and dying. If that wasn't a war, he didn't know what was.

"Will you please be careful?" she asked.

He left her finger on YES, but without any real conviction. He could be as careful as he wanted, but survival out here was mostly dumb luck.

"I feel you fading already," Janie's voice said. "Listen, I recreated Jin Lo's desalinization process for seawater, but someone stole it from me. His name is Magnus Magnusson, and he got me kicked out of school. He's a terrible—"

A door opened in the room where Janie was, and she abruptly stopped talking. A boy about their age walked in, maybe sixteen or seventeen. Dark curls spilled over his forehead, and his eyes lit up when he saw Janie. A bright smile flashed across his face, and Benjamin could see that the boy was smitten. "I got the part," he said shyly.

"Which one?" Janie asked.

"Demetrius."

"I knew it!" Janie cried, and she leaped off the couch, dragging Benjamin with her. His vision distorted with the sudden motion. She threw her arms round the boy's tall, lean frame. They were Benjamin's arms, too, and she was hugging the boy a bit carelessly, he thought. He wanted to draw back, but couldn't. She let go and caught the boy by the shoulders.

"I'm so proud of you," she said.

The boy was grinning at her like a fool. The connection was starting to fade. The living room had grown lighter and less defined, like an overexposed photograph. "Were you talking to someone when I came in?" the boy asked.

"No! Who? Can you wait a second?"

She let go of the boy and ran into a small bathroom. The blurring caused by her quick movement made Benjamin dizzy. She turned on the water in the sink and looked in the mirror over it. The image danced and then held still, and Benjamin drew in his breath sharply. It was the first time he'd seen Janie's face in two years. She was flushed with pleasure from congratulating the boy. There were high pink spots on her cheeks, and her hair fell in loose waves.

"Benjamin, you still there?" she whispered. "Listen, quickly. I want to explain. I'm living with this family because I got kicked out of school. They have an Italian restaurant in town, in Grayson. That's the son."

Benjamin tried to focus, through his nausea, to keep the picture clear. Her face had lost some of its childish softness. She had cheekbones. She pushed her hair impatiently behind her ears, and the look in her eyes was determined but also afraid. Benjamin wished she would explain everything, but she was disappearing fast, and her voice sounded like it was coming over a great distance.

"We have to talk again," she said. "Should we try at midnight tomorrow night? I'll be finished with work then."

That was morning for him. He nodded, even though she couldn't see him. But she seemed to nod slightly, too. Then the image faded, and she was gone.

Benjamin opened his eyes. He was sitting in the dark, abandoned hut, with the smell of charred thatch in the air, and his father breathing evenly on the mat on the other side of the room. Benjamin turned to look at his father, and the room whirled. His stomach heaved. He hadn't felt this bad since he drank too much rice wine at a village wedding.

Carefully, moving slowly to protect his spinning head, he lay back down on his mat. He knew that time had passed, of course. He had seen so many things that kids weren't sup-posed to see that sometimes he felt like he was a hundred years old. But in his mind, Janie was still fourteen, laughing at Count Vili's stories on the deck of the icebreaker and licking herring grease off her fingers. Or pleading with Benjamin to stay, as the train couplings corroded between them.

She had spent two years without him, two years growing up and having her own life. He *knew* that, in his mind. But he hadn't really understood it until he saw her. She could never have been a spy, broadcasting every thought the way she did. Everything she felt had always played visibly over her face. She was so happy for that kid Demetrius, or whatever his name was. Benjamin had been saving lives in the jungle, and this guy was going to be in a *school play*. And Janie was proud of him, and had hugged him. For a part in a *play*!

Benjamin rolled over on the mat. His head was clearing

now. *I'm so proud of you,* Janie had said to the grinning boy. And she had hugged him. There'd been something strange and unexpected in the hug, but Benjamin wasn't sure what it was. Then he realized with a shock: Janie had real breasts now, and they must have pressed against the boy as she threw her arms round him. That Benjamin had been forced to experience the hug in his own body seemed particularly unfair and revolting. He pulled a mosquito net over his head and tried counting to a hundred—then a thousand—to get to sleep.

CHAPTER 15

The Mickey Finn

Janie was elbow-deep in dishwater, scrubbing at a particularly stubborn bit of brown, baked-on cheese from a lasagna tray, still high from having made contact with Benjamin, when Raffaello came into the kitchen with a stack of plates.

"Your rich friend's here," he said.

Janie looked up, her face hot from the steam. "Who?"

"That pretty girl you used to have dinner with. With the ugly glasses."

"Opal?"

"With her parents."

Janie's heart seemed to trip through three or four extra beats. The Magnussons were bound to come in sometime, of course, for a Sunday night dinner, but she'd gotten caught up in thoughts of Benjamin and burnt cheese and the East High school play, and she wasn't prepared.

"That guy's a jackass," Raffaello said, pulling a bottle of wine from a rack. "Always pretending to be everyone's friend, but really ordering us around."

Janie barely heard him. Her thoughts were racing ahead of her. She might not get this chance again. "Did he order wine?" she asked.

"A glass. His wife's not having any."

"I'll pour it."

Raffaello grinned at her. "You gonna poison him because he's a jackass?"

Janie kept her voice light. "That's not a good reason?"

"Funny," he said. "Anyway, we have to pour the wine at the table."

Janie took off her rubber gloves. "Let me just make sure he has a clean glass. He's always complaining about things not being *spotless*." She found a clean linen towel and wiped the edges of a wineglass with her back turned. The pastry chef was teasing Raffaello in Italian, saying something about the great, famous actor—she could understand that much, by now—and Raffaello parried back with something she didn't follow. She slipped the glassine envelope from her pocket and tapped a few grains of powder into the bottom of the glass.

"What's taking so long?" Raffaello asked.

"There was a water spot," she said, palming the envelope. "Now it's perfect." She handed him the glass, glancing to see if the grains were visible. They were, but only if you were looking for them. Otherwise no one would notice. At least she hoped no one would notice. And the grains would dissolve as soon as the wine was poured.

Raffaello rolled his eyes. "He doesn't deserve such perfection," he said.

"Go pour," she said. "Keep the glass upright, though. He hates it when waiters swing them by the stems."

Raffaello made a skeptical face.

"He does!" she said. "He thinks it looks careless."

"I'll show him *careless*," Raffaello said, but he carried the glass upright into the restaurant, grabbing the bottle of wine by the neck as he left.

Janie felt a little faint. What if Mr. Magnusson noticed? He'd just think they were bits of breadcrumb, and toss them out. He wouldn't know what it was. He didn't even know she was here. She was still safe. It was all going to be fine.

But what if he drank the powder, and it turned out that *he* could see into *her* world? The thought gave her a moment of panic.

But Mr. Magnusson wouldn't know how to do it, of course. She'd had to deliberately concentrate on Benjamin, to see his world. And Benjamin had only seen *hers* because he'd known how to do it even better than she did. Mr. Magnusson knew nothing. She wouldn't let him know she was watching. She wouldn't tip him off by trying to push his hands around. She would wait until tomorrow morning, when he would be in his office. It should be safe to try it by then, and she might learn something there.

"Where are my plates?" a waiter asked, seeing the empty rack. *"Dai, dai, dai, ragazza! Madonna!"*

Janie shook away her thoughts and hurried the clean plates to the rack. Then she pulled on rubber gloves and plunged her arms back into the dirty water. She had just run another load through the machine when Giovanna came in.

"Your pretty friend is here," Giovanna said.

"So I hear," Janie said.

"You wan' go say hello?"

"No, that's okay."

Giovanna frowned and put a hand on her hip. "You embarrassed, working here?"

"Of course not!"

"You not friends anymore?"

"Not really."

"Ah," Giovanna said, nodding sagely. "It is over a boy?"

"No!"

"This is a thing that happens."

"It isn't like that."

Giovanna shrugged. "Okay. You don' have to tell me."

"There isn't anything to tell."

"Just talk to her. I tell you, this is the best thing, to *face* this trouble with your friend. I know."

"Really," Janie said, "I don't want to. And I have dishes to do."

Giovanna shook her head. "When you're older, you learn,"

she said sadly. "There is no point to lose friendship over a boy. Boys, they come and go."

"Thanks, Giovanna," Janie said, lifting a heavy pot into the sink and turning on the water.

Giovanna was lost in memories. "I learn this the hard way," she said.

CHAPTER 16

The Cat

On Jin Lo's first day in her childhood house in China, in her haunted city, she sat cross-legged on the dusty floor with closed eyes, mentally paging through the Pharmacopoeia, recalling the pages she had memorized while working with the apothecary and his son. She was looking for a potion to summon ghosts, but she had found nothing.

On the second day, the striped cat she had seen in the street came to her, and she held it in her arms, stroking its soft fur. It was a tomcat with black and white stripes, and she named it Shun Liu, after her little brother: the willow tree that bends but does not break. In the afternoon, Shun Liu brought her a dead mouse, just as her old drooling black cat with the white nose used to do. The cat was concerned about her. It wanted her to eat.

She expected someone from the Party to come and turn her out of the house, tell her she had no right to be there, demand to see her papers. But no one came. She started a fire in the hearth and began to work. She still had a small vial of the Quintessence, from the tree the apothecary had forced to bloom three years ahead of schedule, back in London. That seemed long ago, longer ago than her childhood, which was vivid to her as she moved about her old house, talking to her family.

She tried to stay firmly rooted in time. This was the year of the Horse. They had forced the bloom in the year of the Dragon, when the tree was planning—if trees *planned*—to bloom in the year of the Sheep. Those flowers should have been sheep, white and fluffy and sweetly unnoticed. Instead they became dragons, doing combat with a fiery atomic ball of light.

The master to whom she had been apprenticed had never given much credence to astrology. He said it was a superstition for grandmothers. But he had been a Tiger, without question: fierce and powerful. And Jin Lo, born in the year of the Snake, had become silent and dangerous, quick and cold-blooded.

But here was a question: Would she have become so snakelike if she had stayed with her family—if she had kept her heart? She might have married the dutiful boy who lived up the street and wanted to become a doctor. She might have a fat, sweet baby of her own by now. But perhaps coldness had been her destiny. Perhaps it was in the stars.

She cooked a yellow resin from the tree that grew in the front yard until it turned to black ash. She steeped a bit of persistent ivy she'd found growing up through the floorboards for a bitter-smelling tea. She made herself a makeshift mortar and pestle from two stones, and she ground the brown thistle heads of weeds from the yard into a dry, beige powder.

The cat licked the corked top of her vial of Quintessence and mewed.

"Shh," Jin Lo said. "I'm working."

The cat rubbed its head against her leg.

"Stop!" Jin Lo said. "I need to concentrate."

She was no longer a child, but here she was still playing at "eluding the cat." She smiled. It was the kind of joke her father would have made. "Are you there, Baba?" she asked the air. "Are you putting your jokes in my head?"

There was no answer. She brushed the thistle powder into a pot at the edge of the fire, and heard a child cry. She turned. "Shun Liu?"

The cat mewed.

"Not you," she said. "Listen!"

Again there was a faint cry. She walked through the empty rooms and out the front door. She stood in the little yard where her family had faced the soldiers while she hid in the trunk, and her whole body started to tremble. She was shivering as if from cold, but she wasn't cold. She looked up and down the street, but it was empty. Was there a child next door? She would have heard it before now, she was certain.

"Shun Liu?" she said.

"He's gone," the cat said.

She looked down at the striped creature. "Did you speak?"

The cat mewed at her. Then it licked its fur.

"Let's go inside," Jin Lo said, her teeth chattering. She watched herself as if from a distance. If the neighbors complained, the Public Security Force might come.

Inside the house, she opened the vial of Quintessence, and the sweet smell filled the room. The Quintessence was the fifth element, the source of all life. It smelled like the first flowers of springtime, like honey and sunlight, like new grass after rain. The cat had licked the cork. Had it really spoken to her? Or was she imagining things? She tapped a drop from the vial into the cat's water bowl. Once she had been a serious chemist, conducting careful experiments. Now she was feeding a powerful substance to a cat for no scientific reason. She might be losing her mind. She was certainly losing control of her body, which would not stop shaking. She lay down on the dusty kitchen floor, near the fire.

The cat lapped up the water, then stretched and curled into the hollow of Jin Lo's body. She felt its warmth, its rumbling purr, the beating of its heart.

"You're right," Jin Lo said. "They're gone. I have no one."

"Not true," the cat said.

"I have you," Jin Lo admitted.

"You have friends," the cat said.

Jin Lo thought of the despairing apothecary, his frustrated son, the vanished Count Vili. "They've lost sight of our purpose," she said. "They've lost sight of our plan."

"Then help them to see," the cat said.

"They won't listen."

"Not if you do not speak."

"I'm too weak."

"Because you do not eat," the cat said. "You must eat."

"There's no purpose."

"There *is* a purpose," the cat said. "You must be the willow tree that bends but does not break."

"No," Jin Lo said. "That was Shun Liu. He's gone. And I am broken."

"*I* am Shun Liu," the cat said. "And you are strong."

CHAPTER 17

The Kiss

J anie slipped away during second period at East High, when she thought Mr. Magnusson's day at the office might be starting. She went into the dim and empty school auditorium, and stood looking at the stage where *A Midsummer Night's Dream* would be performed. She was proud of Raffaello for getting up there to audition, and for getting the part.

Then she sat in one of the worn, velvet-upholstered seats, which folded down with a squeak. She tapped a few grains of powder into a glass of water, watched them dissolve, and drank it down. She was supposed to contact Benjamin tonight, and the powder might not work then, but this was her best chance to learn something. She didn't know how long the effects of the few grains she'd slipped into the wineglass would stay in Magnusson's body.

She closed her eyes and thought about her roommate's father, the first day she'd met him, blond and red-faced from carrying Opal's boxes up the stairs. He had pumped her hand in greeting in the bare dorm room, blue eyes shining, and said she seemed like a sensible girl. Opal needed a sensible room-mate, he said.

Then she thought of him at dinner at Bruno's, jolly and imperious, slighting Opal out of habit and calling for more water, more wine, more bread.

Again, she had the sensation of darkness closing in all around her, and then the room grew lighter behind her eye-lids. She was in a modern office with tall windows, sitting behind a large, uncluttered desk. A hand reached out for a wooden box on the desk. The hand was pale and freckled and seemed enormous. It took a cigar from the box and cut off the end with a small knife, then dropped the end into a waste-basket. The cigar seemed to loom close to Janie's face. The hand produced a gold lighter, and spent some time getting the cigar lit. She thought she could taste the bitter tobacco. She had come at the wrong time. All she was going to see was Mr. Magnusson smoking a disgusting, stinky cigar.

Then a very pretty blonde in a pencil skirt and a green blouse walked into the office and wrinkled her nose. "I don't know how you can stand to smoke those things, first thing in the morning," she said.

"And I don't know how you can stand *not* to," Mr. Magnusson said. "That's what makes the world go round."

The woman sniffed.

"Don't pout, my love," Mr. Magnusson said. "It doesn't suit you."

"And cigars don't suit *you*."

Janie thought of the princess, Opal's mother. Did she know about this woman her husband called "my love"? Did Opal?

"Be happy for me, Sylvia," Mr. Magnusson's voice said. "My plan is working."

"And are you going to tell me what it is?" Sylvia asked.

"When it's further along."

"Is it to do with the mine?"

"Perhaps." He sounded pleased with himself.

"Will your wife approve?"

"She won't say so if she doesn't," he said. "She's not like you, full of opinions and contrariness."

Sylvia raised an arched eyebrow. "*That's* why you need me. Remember, it's her island."

"But it's my mine," he said. "I like the way that sounds. *My mine.* All mine." He clapped a hand on his knee. "Come sit on my lap."

"Tell me your plan first."

The picture was starting to fade. Janie concentrated harder.

"Oh, don't be difficult," Mr. Magnusson said faintly. "I want it to be a surprise." He exhaled a cloud of cigar smoke, and Janie strained to hear Sylvia's response, but the office vanished as the smoke dissipated. Sylvia was gone, and so were the desk and the enormous windows.

Janie was alone in the dark. She opened her eyes and saw the school stage and the empty seats. If only she'd started a minute later, she might have heard the plan and missed the cigar-trimming. It was so frustrating, not knowing when to try the connection. It was like picking up a telephone receiver and hoping the other party would *happen* to say something useful on the line.

Still, she guessed she could have found Mr. Magnusson in the bathroom, on the toilet. That would have been worse. She wondered if she should tell Opal about Sylvia, then quickly rejected the thought. Poor, tiny, frightened Mrs. Magnusson. She would never be able to compete with that spirited blonde.

Janie tried moving her head and didn't feel too nauseated, so she stood. The theater seat folded itself up with a squeak. She felt dizzy. Was it possible to lose your hold on your own world by spending too much time looking at other people's?

She'd think about that later: Right now she had to get to class. She turned and saw Raffaello in the aisle of the auditorium, smiling down at her. "Oh!" she said. "How long have you been here?"

"Just got here," he said. "What are you doing in the dark?"

"I needed to get away. To think."

"About what?"

"Everything. I don't know."

He shook his head, smiling. "You're so mysterious," he said. "I never know what goes on in your head."

"Not much, really." He was standing awfully close.

"I know *that's* not true."

"Um," she said. "Should we go to class?"

"They won't miss us."

"But we might miss some valuable information."

"I don't think there's anything that important."

Then his hand went to the back of her neck, under her hair. Benjamin had touched her like that, and it made her very confused. Raffaello's fingers sent a shiver down her spine. He leaned down and kissed her, tentatively. His lips were soft and warm. Then he pulled back to look at her, and there was a question in his eyes: Was this all right?

It was, and it wasn't. She ought to be pulling back. But there was something so tender about the kiss that she didn't. Encouraged, he kissed her again, with more confidence and sureness. But then she found her hand on his chest, pushing him away.

"I'm sorry!" she said.

Raffaello looked hurt.

"I'm sorry," she said again. "I can't—I don't . . . I have to go."

She ran past him toward the auditorium doors, stumbling a little, her face burning with embarrassment. What had she done? And why? She had kissed him and then she had shoved him, and she had to live in his apartment. She might have ruined everything.

"Janie!" he called after her.

She should stop now, and talk to him. But instead she pushed open the auditorium's door, her cheeks hot, and stepped out into the crowded hallway. The girls' restroom was across the hall and she dodged students to get to it. She splashed water from the cold tap on her face at the sink. She could still smell his skin. Raffaello. She looked in the mirror at her wet, miserable face.

"Janie," she said. "What are you *doing*?"

CHAPTER 18

Sidetracked

Benjamin was supposed to make contact with Janie at midnight her time, which was tomorrow morning for him. It was still evening, and the last of the light filtered through the obscenely lush trees overhead. But he couldn't wait. He needed to know what was going on.

It wasn't as if he hadn't met other girls in the last two years. But girls were more protected in the places he had been, and he had never been anywhere long enough to get to know any of them, or to earn their parents' trust. He'd been busy—working alongside his father, and making a code to send messages to Janie in case she needed him, and developing the powder that would let him see her. But now all the powder had shown him was that Janie hadn't been thinking about him in the same way. She'd met other boys in America, where everything was all free and easy, apparently. She was *living* with another boy. It was the last thing he had expected.

He had cooked the last of their rice and soup in another burned-out village, and his father had eaten distractedly while making notes about the medicinal plants of Vietnam.

Being forced to treat the murderous general had knocked his father out of his obsessive, despairing loop. They were going to Hanoi, where a steamer might take them across to the Philippines, where his father had a colleague. So at least they had forward movement. That was a good thing.

It would be mid-morning for Janie now. Benjamin went to the back of the hut, where his father wouldn't see him, and draped a mosquito net over himself so he wouldn't get eaten alive. Then he dropped a few grains of powder into the last of the water in his canteen. He drank it down, leaned cross-legged against the wall of the hut, and closed his eyes.

He thought of Janie as he had seen her in the mirror, with her new, older face. Then of Janie at fourteen in London, tapping him on the shoulder in the Underground when he'd been spying on her. He thought of the pain in her face when he'd told her, under the influence of the boiled truth-telling leaves, that he fancied Sarah Pennington.

Then a deep darkness descended on his closed eyes, and his vision brightened again, and he saw an office. It was a modern office, with a smooth, wide, pale desk and huge windows. A blond woman in a tight skirt and a green blouse stood in the middle of the room. Close up, a big, freckled hand held a fat cigar. It was the hand of a man. Benjamin nearly opened his eyes in confusion, but the woman was speaking.

"Will your wife approve?" she asked.

"She won't say so if she doesn't," the man said. "She's not like you, full of opinions and contrariness."

Benjamin looked for clues about where he was. On a cigar

box on the desk was a slim dagger with a wavy blade and a carved wooden hilt. It was a keris, a ceremonial knife from the Malay peninsula. Count Vili had showed him one in a market stall once and told him they were heirlooms, presented on important occasions, and that the Malays used to put arsenic on the blade so that their victims would die a slow death, poisoned from within. This one was small and delicately carved.

"*That's* why you need me," the woman said. "Remember, it's her island."

"But it's my mine," the man's voice said. "I like the way that sounds. *My mine.* All mine. Come sit on my lap."

The blonde was starting to fade. Benjamin was losing the connection. But why so soon? He'd just gotten here.

"Tell me your plan first," the woman said.

"Oh, don't be difficult. I want it to be a surprise."

But then the woman was gone, and Benjamin saw a dark theater. He wasn't with the big cigar-smoking man anymore, but it also didn't seem like the connection had ended. There was no vertigo, no nausea. He was looking at an empty stage.

He heard the squeak of the folding seat, and there was a blur, and then Benjamin was looking up into the adoring eyes of that kid with the curly hair. Janie was talking to him, but rage and panic flooded Benjamin, distracting him from what she was saying. He tried to figure out how to get her out of the situation. If he spoke, she wouldn't hear him, and he couldn't control her legs. He'd barely been able to move her finger half an inch the night before, with great effort. He watched help-lessly as the boy moved closer, and then disappeared.

The boy was kissing Janie.

"No!" Benjamin said, but they couldn't hear him.

Then the boy pulled back, looking—concerned? Or maybe just looking for encouragement. Janie didn't run away. The boy leaned in, kissing her again, and *she was letting him.*

Benjamin poured everything in his being—all his stubborn, formidable will—into Janie's left hand. He urged it to rise, bringing his own hand up. Then he shoved it into the boy's chest. It wasn't as hard a blow as he wanted, but it was a pretty definite push. The boy stepped backward in surprise.

"I'm sorry!" Janie said.

"Don't apologize!" Benjamin shouted helplessly, unheard.

Janie seemed confused. "I'm sorry," she said again. "I can't—I don't . . . I have to go."

Everything blurred as Janie ran past the boy and out into a bright hallway full of students. She forded the flow of distorted, hazy bodies and then she was in a bathroom over a sink, splashing her flushed face. She looked up at the mirror. "Janie, what are you *doing?*" she asked.

It was Benjamin's question exactly. The vision faded, and he was back in the jungle. The light was gone from the sky. Benjamin waited for the vertigo to pass, then went to find his father, who was working by the light of a small lantern.

"Let's keep moving," Benjamin said. "I have to get to Hanoi *now.*"

His father glanced up, confused. "Why?"

"I need to send a telegram."

CHAPTER 19

The Message

I n a newly built council house in the East End of London, the doorbell rang. The walls were thin, like those of all the houses that had gone up in a hurry to replace the city's bombed-out buildings. But there was new furniture, paid for by Pip's television salary. He was the lord of his household at sixteen, and had become insufferable.

"The *door!*" he called, although he was sitting in a chair right next to it, practicing a card trick that involved keeping one card pinned between his fingers on the back of his hand.

The bell rang again, and Pip's little sister, Tildie, scampered out of her room. She revered Pip, and was the only member of his family who wasn't mightily sick of his airs. She flung open the door to a boy about Pip's age on the stoop. He presented an envelope to her with an official flourish.

"What is it?" she asked.

"It's a telegram," the boy said, as if that was obvious. Then he whispered, *"From Indochina,"* as if it was a secret.

"A telegram!" Tildie said.

"Yup."

"Pip, it's for you! From Indoor China!"

The delivery boy leaned forward to catch a glimpse of the television star. The boy was small for his age, and wide-eyed like Pip. The only difference between them was that one boy had lucked into a job on the telly, and the other was delivering messages.

Pip stood, swiping the telegram from Tildie. "What are you staring at?" he demanded of the boy.

"Just makin' sure it's delivered."

"Well, it is."

"I 'ave a sister, too," the boy said. "We don't 'ave a telly, but we watch you at the—"

Pip didn't learn where the boy and his sister watched *Robin Hood*, because he had slammed the door in the boy's face. It was not a satisfying slam, the door being so light and flimsy. Their old place might have been a dark and filthy tenement building, but at least it had solid wooden Victorian doors that banged after a good swing. The sound took the edge off your anger. A slam here barely overcame its own wind resistance, and left Pip feeling as hollow as the door. He could hear, with perfect clarity, the boy's vivid curse from the other side.

Pip threw himself back in the deep chair, swung his legs up onto the arm of it, and tore open the envelope.

"Wot's in it?" Tildie asked.

"*What* is in it," Pip said. He had been studying the way the other actors talked, and had started lecturing his little sister on her pronunciation. Just sitting round the house, he spoke like he was reading the news on the wireless.

Tildie stamped her foot. "That's wot I *said*!"

Pip sighed and pulled out the telegram. It had come by means of electrical dots and dashes under the sea. That was really something, when you thought about it. The telegram said:

JANIE IN GRAVE DANGER. ITALIAN
RESTAURANT, GRAYSON, NEW HAMPSHIRE,
USA. CAN'T GET THERE.
CAN YOU? —BB

Pip dropped his feet to the floor and read the telegram again. What kind of danger was Janie in? It had to be important. Benjamin hadn't written in all this time. And Pip owed Benjamin and Janie. Meeting them in a juvenile lockup had gotten him his television job, which had gotten him everything: the new house for his family, the new life as a celebrity, even the beautiful Sarah Pennington on his arm—for a while.

The thought of Sarah Pennington gave Pip a pang. She had dropped him on some flimsy excuse, saying he had *changed*. Well, of course he had changed! That was the whole point! Who wanted to be a cockney pickpocket forever? And how *could* he be a cockney pickpocket, when his true love was Sarah Pennington, whose father was going to be an earl, if a third cousin ever died? Pip didn't know how healthy the third cousin might be. But the point was that Pip had changed for *Sarah*, and she had thrown him over. It was heart-stabbingly unfair.

But back to Benjamin's telegram. Pip's mind got off track easily these days, circling back to the pain Sarah had caused him, finding ingenious routes to get there. He had left St. Beden's so that he wouldn't come round the corner to find that dazzling crown of blond hair in front of him, those blue eyes assessing him coldly. But he couldn't stop his brain from poking at the memory of her like a bruise. He tortured himself with thoughts of where she might be now. Was she with someone else?

Sometimes he had found himself wishing for more of the apothecary's forgetting wine, to erase all trace of her. He wished he had kept the dregs of the bottle. He had been furious at the apothecary at the time, for stealing his memories, but it would be so sweet to drink the wine now and feel these painful thoughts melt away.

But the telegram. Janie needed him. Could he go to America? *Robin Hood* wouldn't start again for another month. He wasn't in school. But to get to America cost a packet, and his salary only went so far, with a whole family living on it.

He had a sudden sharp awareness, a sort of extra sense that he'd had in his pickpocketing days. The sense had grown fuzzy from disuse, but it told him now to go to the front door.

He pulled on the cheap doorknob and immediately ducked the thing that flew at his head. A mud clod burst open on the clean, new wall behind him with a spray of dirt and pebbles. The delivery boy was crouched and scowling by the gate, ready to fling another.

"Listen," Pip said. "I'm sorry about before. I was in a bit of a mood, that's all. If you take a message back, there's an autographed picture for your sister in it."

The wary boy considered the offer.

Pip held out his hand. "C'mon," he said. "Friends?"

CHAPTER 20

Theft

Janie stood in the steam at the sink at Bruno's restaurant, grateful for the absorbing task of the dishes. After spying on Magnusson, she had taken the powder at midnight to try to reach Benjamin, but it only made her throw up. The noise woke Giovanna, who made her lie down with a wet washcloth on her head. The next morning she had finally written to her parents, a complicated letter full of bland statements that were true, and omissions of everything else: *The weather is freezing. The Grayson basketball team seems good this year. The Winter Wonderland dance is coming up.* She had also spent two days making sure she was never alone with Raffaello, who looked increasingly hurt. But she hadn't sorted anything out in her mind yet. She liked Raffaello, and she needed him. Both her liking and her need were very clear to her. He was her only friend in a place where people were against her, and he was the only reason she had a roof over her head.

She also liked and needed Benjamin. Her idea of herself for the past year had been of someone who was in love with a boy named Benjamin Burrows. She missed him. She longed for him.

But if questioned under oath, by some hard-nosed prosecutor in her brain, she would have to admit that Benjamin Burrows was a boy she had known for three weeks, two years earlier, when she was fourteen. Three weeks! After that, she'd spent almost a year not knowing that he existed. And she hadn't seen him since. The sensible sixteen-year-old she had become couldn't call that "being in love." And the hard-nosed prosecutor in her brain would point out that the last time she'd seen him, he had drugged and abandoned her, destroying the links between two train cars to leave her behind.

And now she had the very vivid memory of Raffaello kissing her in the darkened auditorium. She had known Raffaello liked her. She wasn't stupid. But she'd thought he liked her as the household's new pet. Amusing and diverting, but not someone to kiss.

So she had pushed him away. She had done it instinctively, without thought—which must indicate something about how she felt about him. Right? It seemed an exhausting way to discover what you felt, to have to wait and see what you *did* about it. But it also seemed like a true measurement. In the actual moment, she had pushed him away. That was undeniable. But if she was honest with herself, she also remembered liking the kiss. A lot.

She blushed as she scrubbed out a pot. The noise of the kitchen went on around her, and she hoped no one could see her turning red. But maybe they would think it was just the steam and the hot water, the exertion of scrubbing.

Then, oddly, the noise subsided. The kitchen, which was never quiet, grew so silent that she heard a single clang of a pot on the stove, and then nothing. She turned, hands dripping, and saw Mr. Magnusson in the doorway. Everyone in the kitchen was staring at him. He was really an enormous man—Janie noticed it now that she saw him standing near the small Italian cooks in their trim white aprons. He was tall and broad-shouldered and ruddy-faced.

"So this is where it all happens!" he said in a booming, jolly voice, in the pin-drop silence. "My compliments to the chef! You've outdone yourselves."

Janie turned back to the sink so Magnusson wouldn't notice her, but the kitchen staff was frozen, and the movement caught his eye. She could feel his curiosity.

"Is that *Janie?*" he asked.

She didn't want to look up.

"I'd recognize that head of hair anywhere! What are you doing here?"

"Working," she said in a small voice, against her will.

"But what about your schoolwork?" He looked around, as if one of the staring cooks might have an answer. "Is money a problem? Why didn't you come to me?"

"I'm not at Grayson anymore," she said, squeezing her fingernails into her palms so she wouldn't fly at him, pound his chest, and demand her equipment back.

Again he looked astonished. "Not at Grayson? What

about your experiment? What about your brilliant scientific career?"

"They kicked me out."

"You? But that's outrageous. I'll speak to someone about it."

Janie was confused. Was this an act? Wasn't he behind it all?

"I have some influence at the school, you know," Mr. Magnusson said.

"Yes, I got that sense."

"Listen, give me your telephone number," he said.

"I don't have one."

"Then I'll give you mine." He grabbed a slip of paper from the little table by the kitchen coatrack and scribbled a number. "Call me in the morning," he said. "We'll sort this out. Does this mean you're not living with Opal anymore?"

"I'm afraid so."

"Why didn't she tell me?"

"Maybe she thought you knew?"

"But how would I know such a thing?"

"From . . . Mr. Willingham?" Janie ventured.

Mr. Magnusson's bushy white-blond eyebrows knit together. Then he roared with laughter, showing the pink inside of his mouth and startling the pastry chef, who jumped. "What—you think we have tea together? Your headmaster and me?" He roared again and wiped tears from his eyes, which had vanished into the folds of his red face.

Janie looked for a break in his act, trying to rethink everything. If Mr. Magnusson didn't know about the stolen equipment, then was the headmaster acting on his own? But Janie had spied on Mr. Magnusson, and he had talked about a plan! Was that just a coincidence?

Whatever it was, it was making the kitchen staff uncomfortable.

"Ah . . . ho . . . You aren't laughing," Mr. Magnusson said finally, recovering.

"I've been kicked out of school," Janie said quietly. "I don't find it very funny. And I've lost all my equipment, all my materials." She watched him.

He grew serious. "The school can't keep your experiment from you," he said. "It's yours."

"That's what I thought."

"I'm going to call that Wellington—Windermere—first thing in the morning," he said. "We'll get it back for you. You call me, all right?"

"All right. And it's Willingham."

"Willingham. Good to see you." He came forward and pumped her hand in farewell. And then he was gone, and everyone in the kitchen stared at Janie.

Bruno clapped his hands and said, "All right! Back to work!" in his usual kitchen voice, which was much too loud, without the usual kitchen noise beneath it.

Janie returned to the sink, trying to think. Could Mr. Magnusson really help her? Had she gotten everything wrong, and was he on her side? She allowed herself a little feeling of rising hope.

The dinner service ended, and she finished the mountain of

dishes, and then closed out the till for Giovanna. At the end of the evening, she took her peacoat from the kitchen coatrack and put it on, automatically feeling in the pocket for her little red notebook. But she felt only the smooth, satiny lining. She tried the other pockets—nothing. She froze, disbelieving. She was standing exactly where Magnusson had been.

She pushed aside the other coats and searched the floor in case the notebook had fallen out, but it wasn't there. He had known where she was living and working, and he knew the coat she always wore, and he had come to the kitchen for the one thing he hadn't already stolen: her notes. She realized with hot shame that she had tucked Benjamin's letters inside the notebook, too, to keep them safe. Magnusson had taken it all, while everyone in the kitchen stared at him. But when had he done it—when he first came in? While he fumbled for a slip of paper from the little table? Before he left the kitchen? Had he been a pickpocket before he became an industrialist?

But it hardly mattered *when* Magnusson had taken the notebook; he had done it. He had everything now.

PART THREE

Conjunction

1. the act of joining or the condition of being joined
2. (astronomy & astrology) an alignment of two planets or celestial objects in the sky
3. (alchemy) the turning point in the alchemical process

CHAPTER 21

The United States

Pip booked a cheap, last-minute, tourist-class cabin on the *United States,* the fastest ocean liner in the world. It would get him to New York in five days. A friend who had worked as a musician on the ship had told him what to do next.

The ship, Pip's friend explained, wasn't as glamorous as the *Queen Mary* or the *Queen Elizabeth,* but it wanted to be—bless the Yanks and their ambition. Most tables in the first-class dining room harbored a bored American teenage daughter, and there were never enough dancing partners. But the girls would report back to their friends about what sort of time they'd had on the *United States.* So the company needed boys to dance with the girls: glamorous boys, if they could get them.

That was a problem Pip felt he could solve.

The girls on board the ship in November would be slightly older than Pip, his musician friend told him. They would have finished Miss Porter's School or Spence. Girls usually liked older boys, but they would make an exception for a sixteen-year-old television star.

On boarding the *United States,* Pip made sure the steward had recognized him from the telly. They chatted in a friendly way about *Robin Hood.* There were two narrow bunks in the cabin. His cabinmate, a stranger, hadn't yet arrived, so Pip opened his single suitcase and tossed a dinner jacket and patent leather shoes on the bunk. It was the first dinner jacket in the history of his family, but he didn't let that show. He pretended that it was something he wore all the time, and had always worn. He noted that the steward had seen the dinner jacket, and then he said he thought he'd go out on deck, have a look round.

The tourist-class deck was crowded with men traveling alone, but Pip could see, above him, the first-class deck. A few young ladies were leaning over the rail up there, ribbons from their hats blowing in the breeze. *That* was where Pip wanted to be. He paced on deck as well as he could amid the crush, thinking about Benjamin's telegram, and then he went back inside.

There was a note on his narrow bunk saying that Pip had been moved to another cabin, which the purser hoped would be acceptable, and asking if he would care to dine in the first-class dining room at 8 p.m. Pip did a little jig of triumph. The dinner jacket had worked!

The steward had to lead him and his luggage to his new cabin, on the other side of the complicated architectural divisions between first and tourist class. The new cabin had a single bunk and a tiny bath and must have been the smallest first-class cabin on the ship, but it had access to that deck with the young ladies with the ribbons in their hats—*that* was what was important.

That evening, Pip went to the ballroom before dinner, resplendent in his dinner jacket, with freshly combed hair, and surveyed the people having drinks at the tables near the dance floor. He moved toward a girl in a lavender gown sitting with her father. Both of them welcomed Pip with smiles. The girl's name was Angelica Lowell, and she had eyes the color of slate. Her mother wasn't mentioned, but it was clear that Mr. Lowell's goal in life was to make his daughter happy. Pip regaled them with stories of life on the *Robin Hood* set and then asked Angelica to dance. She was warm and flexible in his arms, and they danced until it was time to go in to dinner. "I hope you're at our table," Angelica said.

But he wasn't. The maître d' steered him away, and Pip was placed with a family from Fort Lauderdale, Florida. The eldest daughter was named Deborah, and she wore pale face powder and a blood-red dress, with her dark hair pulled severely back. She had an odd, portentous voice when she ordered the Dover sole for dinner, as if she were announcing the future. Her tanned and lighthearted family seemed not to know what to do with her. She told Pip she was interested in astrology. The Dover sole arrived, as predicted.

Deborah didn't dance, but asked Pip if he'd walk on deck after dinner. They passed the Lowells' table and Angelica glared at them. Pip smiled apprehensively. He hadn't meant to get in trouble so soon.

It was cold on deck, but Deborah wore a black cashmere wrap and didn't seem to feel the North Atlantic wind. In his dinner jacket, Pip was freezing. In a pocket of calm at the stern, Deborah leaned on the rail and looked up at the dark sky with its scattering of stars. "Do you believe in fate?" she asked, in her fortune-teller's voice.

"Depends on what you mean," Pip said, pulling his jacket tighter.

"Do you believe things happen for a reason?"

"I believe you can make 'em happen," he said.

"Do you believe the alignment of the stars at the moment of your birth determines what kind of person you'll be for the rest of your life?"

"No," Pip said through chattering teeth. "I don't believe that." Every bone in his body seemed to be vibrating with cold.

"I do," Deborah said, her eyes burning with meaning. "I believe the stars align when two people meet who are meant to be together *forever.*"

Pip guessed that meant she wanted him to kiss her, but he was shivering too violently to do anything about it. He might bite her nose off by mistake. "I th-think I have to go b-back ins-side," he said.

On his way back to his room, he stopped for a hot lemon and honey.

"You look frozen," the bartender said. "Romantic walk on deck?"

Pip nodded miserably, but the hot drink helped, and he woke the next morning without a cold. He had bacon and fried tomatoes for breakfast in his cabin. In the afternoon, in the card room, he found a man with long white mustaches willing to play chess for money, and he made a nice little bundle. He didn't see Deborah anywhere. He went down to the pool, deep amidships, and found slate-eyed Angelica in a violet bathing suit. She kicked her legs in the shallow end and laughed while Pip tried to do handstands, the water sloshing against the tile sides of the pool as the ship rolled.

That night in the ballroom, an assistant purser steered him toward a waif from Connecticut named Clara, with colorless hair and a whispery, ghostly voice. He asked her to dance, and she felt like a wisp of smoke. He was seized with the conviction that she actually *was* a ghost, that he had been set up to entertain a dead girl, and that her family was watching closely to see how he behaved. But then Angelica entered the ballroom and gave him a betrayed look. And if Angelica could see her, then Clara couldn't be a ghost—could she? He thought she probably couldn't.

When Clara claimed exhaustion and spilled herself into a chair, Pip turned to see Angelica waiting behind him. The next song began, and she stepped into his arms.

"Why were you dancing with her?" Angelica asked.

"To be friendly."

"She has some terrible disease. She'll be dead within the year."

"Oh?" Pip said.

"Consumption," Angelica said. "Or pneumonia. Whatever Keats had."

"Do you know her?"

"I can tell just by looking at her. It might be catching. I'd keep your distance."

"Hm," he said.

"What will you do in New York?" she asked.

"Oh, have a look round."

"I wish it were summer. We have a yacht, and a plane, and a beach house in Maine."

"That rhymes," Pip said.

"I meant you could come with us."

"Might be a little cold."

"Maybe next summer," Angelica said, and Pip started to feel trapped by her small hand on his shoulder, and her other hand gripping his.

The next night in the ballroom, he met two cheerful girls in pretty frocks, Barbara and Maisie. They'd become friends on the crossing, and their families were dining together, and they were happy to share Pip with each other on the dance floor. Angelica was less happy, and she shot him a stormy look when he made the mistake of catching her eye over Barbara's or Maisie's smooth round shoulder.

She cornered him at the bar, where he was ordering lemonades. "Why are you dancing with them?" she hissed.

"They're nice girls," he said.

"They're awful!" Angelica said. "They cluck together like chickens!"

"Oh, they're all right," Pip said.

"I thought you had taste and discrimination!" Angelica said.

He watched her long blue gown swish away, and then he turned back to Barbara or Maisie, whichever it was, who came smiling to take the lemonade from his hand.

Pip wasn't used to his shiny black shoes, and had never danced so much in his life. He winced as he sat on his bed and peeled off his socks. The next morning, the steward brought him sticking plasters for the blisters.

"I've seen worse," the steward said. "One of my young men came back every night with his feet bleeding. Like a cursed prince in a fairy tale."

"Did he survive?" Pip asked.

"They all survive."

"None of them jumped into the sea?"

"Not one."

"I don't think they've met Angelica Lowell, then," Pip said. "Or Deborah the fortune-teller."

"Oh, they've met worse," the steward said.

When the *United States* slid into her berth in New York a day later, Pip tipped the steward handsomely from his chess winnings.

"I hope we'll see you on the return, sir," the steward said.

"I might swim back," Pip said. "Less tiring."

"You earned your cabin," the steward said. "Take care of those feet."

Limping down the corridor, Pip received a good-bye kiss from Maisie and Barbara, one on each cheek. At his last breakfast, he saw the ominous Deborah, and she passed him a folded piece of paper. It contained an indecipherable poem about celestial bodies meeting in the sky. Her cheerful father gave Pip his card and told him to look them up if he was ever in Fort Lauderdale. On the staircase, the ghostlike Clara, in a dove-gray coat, offered her cold little hand in farewell.

The crush of passengers and porters and trunks on the pier in Manhattan was overwhelming, and Pip struggled through it. Finally free of the pier, he stared up at the buildings. Everything here was different from how it was in London: the accents, the shouts, the smells, the traffic coming from the wrong direction, the sounds of the horns. It was winter, but the city seemed to generate heat: the men were ruder than in London, the crowd moved faster, the women were better dressed, sheathed trimly in wool. A man bumped into Pip on the sidewalk and told him to watch where the hell he was going.

Pip carried his suitcase along, staring at everything, until a chauffeur-driven limousine pulled up beside him on Forty-Sixth Street. Angelica Lowell leaned out the back window, shading her eyes in the sunlight, with a lavender ribbon in her hair. "Can we drop you somewhere?" she asked.

Pip hesitated. "I'm off to New Hampshire," he said. "Any clue about trains?"

"Penn Station," Mr. Lowell told the chauffeur, who was already out of the car, taking Pip's suitcase and stowing it in the front.

Pip got in beside Angelica. Her father faced them in the open backseat. Pip felt that trapped feeling again, the sense that he might never escape these people.

"I thought you were staying in New York," Angelica said. "You said you were just going to look around."

"I have a friend in New Hampshire," Pip said. He was struck by inspiration. "Her name's Janie. She's the *best* girl I've ever met, Janie is. She's smart, and loyal, and brave. She's American, like you. You'd like her."

Angelica stiffened. "I don't know that I would."

"Sure you would," Pip said. "Janie's great. She's a peach."

Mr. Lowell coughed.

Angelica gazed out the car window. Her back was so straight that she didn't touch the upholstery behind her.

"Penn Station," the chauffeur announced, stopping the car.

"Ta," Pip said, climbing out. "Don't get out!" Neither of them moved.

He took his suitcase from the chauffeur and swung it through the air as he walked toward the pillars of the enormous gray station. The bag seemed to weigh nothing. His feet no longer hurt.

"Wait!" he thought he heard Angelica's voice call.

But he couldn't be sure, so he kept walking. Pip had been released from juvenile lockups more times than he could count, and he recognized the elated feeling he had now: He was *free*.

And he realized something else, with a shock: He hadn't thought of Sarah Pennington all week.

CHAPTER 22

The Notebook

W hen Janie realized that her notebook and Benjamin's letters were gone, stolen by Mr. Magnusson or else vanished coincidentally at the moment he came into the kitchen, she went upstairs to the apartment fighting back tears. She didn't want to explain the theft to Raffaello, for fear he would try to comfort her, so she told him she was just tired and wanted to go to sleep. He gave her a stricken look, went into his bedroom, and closed the door.

When she was alone, Janie took out the glassine envelope Benjamin had sent, grateful that she hadn't tucked *that* into the red notebook. She tapped the last of the powder into a glass of water and drank it down. Then she sat on the living room couch and closed her eyes.

She imagined Benjamin in the dark on the deck of the *Anniken,* and was just settling into the memory when suddenly she saw blinding sun. Either she was getting better at this, or it was happening faster as more powder built up in her body. She was on a bicycle, moving through a chaotic city, dodging carts and cars and bicycles and motorbikes in the crowded street. Or no—she was in a kind of cart powered by a tricycle. A rickshaw. Someone else was pedaling. Benjamin must be a passenger. The images had trouble holding. She wished he would stop moving.

"Benjamin!" she whispered, even though she knew he couldn't hear her. She *thought* hard at him: *"Benjamin!"*

No response. They dodged an old man with two heavy bags slung over his shoulder. The man, bent nearly in half, didn't notice that he'd almost been hit. Where were they? What was this city?

Then they stopped in front of a shop with dusty bottles in the window. The world stopped breaking up and grew steady. The door of the shop said VINORAY APOTHECARY. Was Vinoray a name or a place? Had they found another colleague of his father's, part apothecary and part magician?

And how could she tell Benjamin about the notebook if she couldn't even get his attention? She thought of Magnusson standing by the coatrack, talking and gesturing and slipping her notebook into his pocket, and her cheeks burned with fury that she had let him trick her.

Then the apothecary shop started to disappear, and Janie had the disorienting feeling that she was moving again, but in a different manner. She wasn't on a bike, but in a car. She was in the deep, luxurious, leather-upholstered backseat, and a chauffeur was driving, and it was dark outside. In front of her, an enormous pair of pale hands flipped through *her red notebook*!

Janie was stunned, and then realized: She had been

thinking about Magnusson, not Benjamin. So now here she was, with him. His fingers pulled the folded letters from between the pages of her notebook. In a mumbling, meditative voice she hadn't heard him use before —nothing like his social booming—he read Benjamin's words aloud. "Dear J., How's all? Really beastly industrial nastiness, here. Can't help insulting natives, apparently." He didn't seem to make any more sense of it than she had the first time. He flipped through the notebook's pages, then stopped. She saw her note:

Benjamin! Are you in Vietnam? Point to answer:
YES NO

The hands moved the open page to show it to someone, and Janie saw that Mrs. Magnusson was also in the backseat of the car, nearly invisible in the corner, tucked inside her fur coat with her eyes closed.

"What do you make of this?" Mr. Magnusson asked her. "It's her handwriting. Look."

The princess opened her eyes and glanced at the notebook. "You shouldn't have taken that."

"*Look,* will you?" he said. "It's like one of those notes Opal used to pass around with her friends. 'Do you like so-and-so?' And it's in Janie's handwriting. But why the hell would she ask if someone is in Vietnam?"

"Because she wants to know," his wife said.

"But that's a crazy question, if she can show him the note! If she can show the note, then he's not in Vietnam!"

"Maybe she was going to send it to him."

"Send it *where?*" Mr. Magnusson asked. "She doesn't even know what country he's in."

"They must have a way of communicating," the princess said, unbowed.

Janie tensed, watching. They were getting warmer. What else did her notebook reveal?

Mr. Magnusson grew silent, thinking. "But how do they do it? Photographs? No. Unless they were using a telex machine. But for that she would need an address, a telex number."

"Maybe you can't know everything," his wife said, with evident satisfaction.

"The girl could tell me," Mr. Magnusson said.

"But she won't."

"I might *persuade* her to," Mr. Magnusson said. There was something menacing in his voice.

His wife said coldly, "You will not stoop to kidnapping."

"Oh, won't I?" he asked.

Janie's eyes flew open involuntarily, and she was back in the living room, heart racing with terror. She couldn't stay in the car with that man anymore, inside his body. She had the usual vertigo, and was careful not to move her head. She was sweating and afraid, as if someone were hiding behind the sofa, about to attack her. That was crazy, of course, but there *was* someone threatening her. She wasn't imagining it.

Magnusson knew she was communicating with Benjamin. Did he know who Benjamin was? It wasn't clear. But she knew she couldn't let herself be kidnapped. She wouldn't be able to keep Benjamin's secrets under pressure. That was why he and his father had given her the forgetting drug.

Again, she had the feeling that someone was hiding behind the sofa. She forced herself to look back into the terrifying shadows. No one was there. Just soft little puffs of collected dust.

She sat back down. It was all too much. She hadn't even told her parents she'd been expelled from Grayson. She pictured herself trying to explain to them why she'd been kidnapped. "But Mom, the glassware was really fragile and complicated, and it would have taken me *weeks* to set it up again."

No. She could see the whole situation from her parents'

point of view now, and it was simple. It was time to go home. She had money from dishwashing and could buy a bus ticket before Magnusson even knew she was gone. She crept downstairs to the telephone in the restaurant and asked the operator to reverse the charges. She'd be waking her parents up in Michigan, but there were times when it was right to wake your parents up.

Her father sounded groggy, but he sharpened when he heard the operator's voice, and he agreed to accept the charges. "Janie?" he said. "What's going on?"

It was all Janie could do not to burst into tears of relief when she heard his voice. She hadn't realized how much she had missed her parents, how much she wanted to be with them. "Dad," she said. "I'm coming home."

CHAPTER 23

Winter Wonderland

P ip took a train from New York to Boston and then a
two-hour bus ride to Grayson, New Hampshire. By
the time he got on the bus, he'd had his fill of the
American countryside. Out of boredom, he began a game of
low-stakes gin rummy with a man in a gray suit beside him,
but the man was a sore loser, so Pip arranged to lose until
they broke even, then returned to staring out the window. He
was already feeling nostalgic for the luxurious *United States*,
where he could wander about while the miles churned by, and
where the gamblers were more openhanded and gracious.

In Grayson, he left his suitcase in a bus station locker and
asked the solitary cabbie to take him to an Italian restaurant.
He thought he should next find a bicycle so he could check off
every possible type of American travel. Then a unicycle. Then
walking on his hands. Either there was only one Italian restaurant, which was lucky, or the cab took him to the right one first,
which was luckier. When he asked a waiter about Janie, the
man said, "You ask Giovanna," then fetched a bosomy Italian
woman from the kitchen.

"Janie went home tonight," Giovanna said. "In the bus."

"I just came from the bus station," Pip said. "She wasn't there." Had he come all this way just to miss her? Could he have walked past and not recognized her?

Giovanna shrugged. "That's where she went."

"All right," Pip said, trying to think. "Home where? To Los Angeles?"

Giovanna thought for a moment. "Mitchigan," she said finally.

"Mitchigan?"

"Is a state," Giovanna said.

"What city?"

"How should I know this?" Giovanna asked. "You ask my nephew. He is the friend of Janie."

"Is he here?"

"No. He is practicing for this play. This is Janie's fault also. I need my nephew to be a waiter. Later I thought he will be a big lawyer, like my brother in Boston. But now he wants to be an actor. Pfft. She causes a lot of trouble, your friend."

"Is she okay?"

Giovanna lowered her voice confidentially. "I think she has some fights with her roommate."

"Who's her roommate? Where?"

"At the Grayson Academy," Giovanna said. "A very beautiful girl. I think it is because of a boy."

"Where's Grayson Academy?" Pip asked.

Giovanna pointed. "Across the street."

So Pip used his feet, the simplest means of travel. The

campus was dark, but there was music and light coming from one of the buildings. Pip made his way there. It turned out to be a gymnasium, and a dance was going on. There was a folding table outside the gym, where a boy and a girl were taking tickets. The boy wore a tuxedo and the girl a white dress, and Pip wished he had known about the dance. His dinner jacket was in the bus station locker, and he could have blended in. Instead he wore ordinary trousers and a woolen jacket against the cold. He moved away into the shadows and found another door. A boy and a girl came out, laughing and moony, staring into each other's eyes, and Pip slipped inside before the door swung closed.

Inside the gym, silver streamers shimmered. Most of the girls were in white, and blue gels over the lights gave everything an underwater glow. The balcony had been garlanded with fluffy cotton to suggest drifting snow. The boys grinned nervously under new haircuts, faces scraped with razors. A fog of aftershave and cologne hung in the air, masking the gym's undertone of sweat, old basketballs, and disinfectant. The band was playing "Sh-Boom," and a pale, pomaded singer crooned, *Life could be a dream—if I could take you up— in paradise up above.*

Pip scanned the room. It was the first time he had seen a whole room full of American kids his age, and the girls were delightfully pretty. The boys were irritatingly tall. What did they *feed* these brutes in America?

Then a boy who wasn't tall moved toward Pip. He was round and wore a brown suit. He approached Pip and stuck out his hand. "Tadpole Porter," he said. "Dance committee."

Pip shook the offered hand. "I'm Pip."

"Do you have a ticket?" Tadpole asked. "You're a little underdressed."

Pip decided to address the last accusation only. "Forgot my dinner jacket."

"You're British, aren't you?" Tadpole asked. "I'm a big fan of English history. The War of the Roses and all that."

"Great," Pip said. "I'm looking for Janie Scott's roommate."

The boy narrowed his eyes. "Janie's your friend?"

"From London," Pip said. "We were in school together there."

Something dawned on Tadpole. "Hey!" he said. "Are you the friend in England she had a letter from? I thought it was from a girl!"

Pip shook his head. "I'm not much for letters."

"You know she got kicked out, right?"

"Of *school*?" It wasn't like Janie.

The boy nodded, then tilted his head. "Have I seen you somewhere?"

Pip didn't feel like having the *Robin Hood* conversation just now. "So where's Janie's roommate?"

Tadpole turned and surveyed the room. "Over there."

Pip followed the boy's pointing finger, and his mouth fell open. He forced himself to close it. Giovanna had been right that she was beautiful. "What's her name?" he asked.

"Opal Magnusson," Tadpole said. "She's mean, though. Don't get all excited."

The girl was standing alone in a simple white dress that

clung to her body, no fluffy rampart of a skirt like the other girls wore. She had smooth, bare, caramel-colored shoulders and hair like a sheet of silk. She looked up and saw Pip staring. He was standing close to her—somehow his feet had moved him nearer without his knowing it. "Hullo," he said. He was too dazzled to say more.

"Hi," she said coolly.

"You're Janie's roommate," he managed.

"I *was*."

"Why'd she get kicked out of school?"

Opal looked vaguely in the direction of the band. "I don't know about that."

If she had been a better liar, or if her rotten lying had been the result of nervousness, Pip thought he could have forgiven her. But she wasn't even *trying* to be convincing. That was how little she thought of him. He resolved to harden his heart. "She's a friend of mine, Janie is," he said.

Opal looked back at him. "Where are you from?"

"Mars," he said.

"Ha. You came all this way to find Janie?"

"In a spaceship, it's right quick."

"Did someone ask you to come?"

"What, I need an invitation? It's just a poxy school dance. Listen, I heard you two had a fight."

"Not really."

"Where is she now?"

"I don't know."

"She didn't really go home, did she?"

Opal blushed. "I don't know what you're talking about."

"You know where she is!"

"How dare you accuse me!" She glared fiercely at him, and he knew he was right. No one got mad like that unless they were hiding something.

Then a shadow fell across Pip's face, blocking the blue lights, and an enormous body loomed beside them. Pip looked up at the towering boy, who held two cups of punch in his oversized fists. "What's going on?" the monster asked.

"He's bothering me," Opal said.

The creature handed both cups to her and grabbed Pip's collar, but the boy in the brown suit yanked Pip out of his grasp. "Dance committee!" Tadpole said. "No fighting!"

"She knows where Janie is!" Pip said, struggling.

"I do not!" Opal cried.

"No ticket, no entry!" Tadpole said, with a forced cheerfulness, dragging Pip toward the gym doors.

Pip tried to twist free. "Let me go! I'll buy a ticket!"

Tadpole shoved him out into the cold night air. "You moron! You idiot! That guy could twist your head off."

"But she knows where Janie is!"

"So what? They're roommates!" Tadpole was breathing hard from the struggle.

"But Janie's in trouble!" Pip said.

"What kind of trouble?"

"That girl knows!"

"Well, you can't just pick a fight with her and her gargoyle date. That's really dumb, you know?"

"You got a better idea?"

They stood glaring at each other in silence. Inside the gym, the bandleader was singing in his saccharine croon, *"Fairy tales can come true, it can happen to you, if you're young at heart."*

"How long'll that thing go on?" Pip asked.

"The dance? Couple of hours."

"Where do Janie and that girl live?"

"Carleton Hall," Tadpole said, still winded.

"Show me their room," Pip said.

CHAPTER 24

The Game of Murder

By the fireplace in the empty house, Jin Lo broke two eggs into a pot. She had no card from the Party to collect rations, but the cat had led her to a nearby chicken coop, under cover of night. She had spoken quietly to the watchdog, who let her pass, and to the hens, who clucked to themselves but allowed her to gather a handful of warm, fresh eggs. The woman who lived next door had brought her some rice, and Jin Lo cooked that, too. The cat was right that she had to eat. Her wrists looked scrawny as she stirred the pot. She squatted by the fire because she'd lost what cushioning she'd had beneath her bones, and it hurt to sit.

On the other side of the fire was another pot, simmering gently. It wasn't food. There was something she was waiting for: a smell that would tell her it was ready. She couldn't describe the smell to the cat, because she didn't know what it was yet, but she would know it when it came.

She picked up her chopsticks and realized she was ravenous. She forced herself to eat slowly, and gave a piece of egg to the cat, who mewed in thanks. Soon her stomach was painfully full, and she set aside the rest of the food for later.

She had found a small shard of mirrored glass on her walk to the chicken coop, and she studied herself in its narrow reflection. Her black hair was stringy and unwashed. Her eyes were sunken and dull. She went to the neighbor, who led her silently to a bath. Dirt came off Jin Lo's body in gray sheets, and she had to scrub the bathtub when she was finished. Her hair felt lighter, as if she had halved its weight by washing it. The neighbor brought her a tunic and a pair of pants, and took away her clothes to wash them.

Jin Lo was startled by the woman's kindness. But of course the neighbor had been kind from the beginning. Jin Lo just hadn't gotten around to recognizing it and pointing it out to herself. She had so seldom *felt* kindness—she didn't let it through her hard shell to warm her.

But there had been times with Marcus Burrows and his son when she had felt warmth. The girl, Janie, had wiped the Oil of Mnemosyne from Jin Lo's wrists when it had given her such terrible memories. The boy, Pip, had brought them hot rolls in a paper bag for breakfast. The men on the *Anniken* had cheered Jin Lo for catching fish from the boat, and the old cook had brought the first fish off the grill to her.

And at Count Vili's house in Luxembourg, where she had rested with Marcus Burrows and his son, they had sat by the fire roasting chestnuts and playing a game in which one person was the detective and one was secretly the murderer, and the suspects made up stories about where they had been at the time of the crime. Count Vili was the best at the game, telling long tales about seeing an arm dripping with blood, hanging out of the dumbwaiter. He said he had seen Jin Lo washing something red off her hands in the pool.

"Red frosting," Jin Lo said, because she was not the murderer. "From cake."

"There was *cake*?" Count Vili said. "And no one saved me a piece?"

"Benjamin made it," Jin Lo said.

"Benjamin *bakes*?" Vili asked.

"Badly," Benjamin admitted.

"Perhaps this was the murder weapon," Vili said.

"Poison?" Marcus Burrows, the detective, asked.

"Eggshell," Vili said. "Left in the batter. Gets caught in the esophagus." He drew a fat finger across his throat. "No more birthdays, no more cakes."

They went on like that for hours, making things up, casting doubt on each other, becoming sillier. It was the first time Jin Lo had ever seen Marcus Burrows laugh. Benjamin, wrapped in a blanket near the hearth, laughed so hard he could hardly breathe. Count Vili grinned to himself, peeling hot chestnuts.

That seemed very long ago now. Vili had returned to Luxembourg in disgust after the Japanese fisherman died from the radioactive ash. And Marcus Burrows had become distracted, treating casualties of skirmishes in the jungle. Jin Lo had helped him as long as she could stand it.

"You heal these men and they fight again," she had told him, the night she left.

"Perhaps," he said.

"What about your plan?"

"My primary duty is to heal sickness," he said, touching his left eye to keep it from twitching. "You may go if you wish. This is my plan, for now."

In the end, she didn't know why she had left Vietnam. It might have been because she couldn't bear to see, any longer, what human beings were capable of doing to each other. The shrapnel, the bullet wounds, the blood. She had been drawn toward home.

The cat, curled by the fire, sat up and mewed. Jin Lo gave the green concoction a stir. The smell was the one she'd been waiting for—it still had the fecund stink of undergrowth, but it also had a sharp edge, as if it were just about to burn. She snatched the pot from the fire. Then she uncorked the vial of Quintessence and tapped in three drops. It sizzled and smoked, and let off that glorious smell, the smell of life. It brought back, unbidden, the smell of her baby brother's skin. Tears sprang to her eyes, and she blinked at the blurry pot. Then she stirred the simmering mixture, and the sweet smell was swallowed up in the smoky green funk.

She wrapped her hand in her long sleeve, picked up the pot by its wire handle, and carried it outside, the cat dancing at her heels. She tilted the pot to drizzle its contents into the flower beds of dead weeds along the front of the house, then along the side closest to the kind neighbor. She looked up and saw the neighbor watching her through a window, and waved.

Then Jin Lo rounded the back of the house, where her mother had kept a small kitchen garden of leeks and onions and leafy green vegetables. It was all dusty weeds now. She fed the green stuff from the pot to the empty garden, then to the beds on the other side of the house, then to the beds along the front gate where the soldiers had come into the yard.

She went inside the house and gathered her few possessions, tying them up in a handkerchief. The cat followed nervously.

"Don't worry," she said. "We have a little time."

They went outside and Jin Lo sat cross-legged on the ground, just beyond the gate. The cat climbed into her lap.

Green shoots first emerged from the winter soil along the front of the house. They unfurled their bright clusters of leaves and grew taller. The ones near the wall of the house climbed up it, twisting around each other for strength, reaching the window and running along the sill, then up the frame. The ones near the front path grew out in all directions like a carpet, covering the small yard. Vines grew across the door, weaving a lattice that was instantly obscured by waxy leaves. Moss climbed up from the ground over the peeling paint, making the walls furry and vibrantly green. The low fence around the house became a hedge. Long-dead bamboo shot up through the thick green web, spearing the eaves of the house as if it would simply push through the roof toward the sky. Then it did push through, with a creak and crack of dry wood.

A green branch broke through a window with a bright

crash, and snaked inside the house. A vine reached the roof, coiling tightly around the chimney.

Jin Lo watched. The cat mewed.

A branch came out through the chimney from inside. Long-dead sweet peas wrapped around the walls from the kitchen garden in the back. The house was being swallowed whole. It still had the shape of a house, with a chimney and windows, but the corners were softening. It would soon be a green mound.

And then she saw it: A shimmering shape escaped from the chimney. It was small, no larger than a fat one-year-old baby, and it danced and dissipated in the air. It vanished like smoke, but it wasn't smoke.

Then there was a larger figure, as tall as a man and shaking with laughter until it broke apart into the air. Then a lithe and feminine shimmer hung a moment in the air, before a breeze took it away. And finally a stout female shape that Jin Lo thought must be the brave Mrs. Hsu seemed to burst into freedom with relief. It vanished against the white sky.

Then there was nothing. The only sound was of the vines squeezing through cracks and wrapping around outcroppings, and the rustle of leaves. The house was gone, and could no longer be haunted. It had been seventeen years since Jin Lo had hidden in the trunk. She might have made a cake with her eggs, if she had not eaten them.

"No more birthdays, no more cakes," she heard Count Vili say.

Her family was free.

CHAPTER 25

Breaking and Entering

The girls' dormitory was silent and empty as Pip and Tadpole crept up the stairs. The leather soles of Tadpole's shoes slapped on each wooden step. "You doing a tap dance?" Pip hissed back at him.

"I can't help it!" Tadpole whispered.

"Put your foot down *soft*, that's all!"

Tadpole managed to lower the volume of his footsteps, but he still wasn't silent.

"I should've left you at the dance," Pip whispered.

"And found the building *how*?"

"Shh! Listen!"

They stopped, but if there had been a sound, it had vanished. The building seemed to be empty. They kept on, and Tadpole stopped outside a door on the second floor.

"How do you know this is theirs?" Pip asked.

"Every guy on campus knows which room is Opal's," Tadpole whispered. "Not that they've been inside it or anything. It's just, you know, a landmark." He tried to turn the doorknob. "It's locked, of course."

Pip had two thin metal rods in his pocket, one with a hooked end, just for such occasions. He was out of practice, and his fingers felt stubby and clumsy as he slid the first wire into the lock. But it was good to be back, sneaking about in the dark. He felt the satisfying clicks inside the mechanism as he maneuvered the hook. Was there a better feeling in the world? He wasn't sure.

He turned the knob and it gave easily. Access. That was all he'd ever wanted. *Robin Hood* had given him fame and Sarah Pennington, but it had taken away such deeply pleasurable moments as this.

The room was dim, but there was enough light from outside to reveal that it was a girls' room, long and narrow. It smelled of flowery perfume. There was a patterned carpet on the floor, and two beds along the long walls, one slept-in and one tightly made up.

Against the far wall were two wooden desks. One had books and papers spread across the surface. A puffy white dress had been tossed over the chair. The other desk was empty and bare.

Pip went to the messy desk. There was a pair of heavy black eyeglasses on the papers, and he looked through them. They seemed to be clear glass, no correction. He picked up a piece of paper and looked at it in the light from the window. It was math problems, with most of the answers marked wrong. At the top, it said *Please see me.*

Tadpole whispered, "This is making me nervous. I think we should go."

"Shh," Pip said.

"Seriously," Tadpole said. "I could get expelled."

"Quiet!"

Pip felt the underside of the desk for anything taped there, but found only the rough, unfinished wood. He checked the drawers and found pens and pencils, ink and erasers and scissors. There was a box of white letter paper embossed at the top with a golden dragon in the shape of a circle.

When he turned, he saw Tadpole dreamily touching the bodice of the puffy white dress. "Something sewn in the seams?" he asked.

Tadpole snatched his hands back guiltily. "Let's go."

"Not yet."

Pip felt under the pillow and mattress of both beds, but without much hope. Janie was clearly gone, and Opal didn't seem like the type to keep a diary. On her bureau was a picture of a girl, probably Opal, doing a split upside down on a horse. That was impressive. Pip pulled open the top drawer and found soft cotton and silky things, but nothing hidden beneath them.

The next drawer was full of sweaters. Pip's hands were plunged deep in fuzzy softness when he heard footsteps on the stairs. He pushed the drawer closed, grabbed the terrified Tadpole, and pulled him into the closet. They pushed past the hanging dresses to squeeze into the darkest, farthest corner. Pip reached up to quiet the clacking wooden hangers just as the door opened and light footsteps came into the room.

There was a short silence and then another noise Pip

couldn't identify. Was there an animal in the room? Did Opal have a cold? Then he realized: She was crying. The strange noise was her half-muffled, choking sobs.

Pip listened for a minute, and when the crying didn't stop, he started to push out of the closet, past the dresses.

"No!" Tadpole whispered, grabbing his shoulder.

Pip shook his hand off. "Stay here," he whispered. He stepped out into the room.

"Opal?" he said.

She was sitting at her desk with her face in her hands, and she turned to look at him. "What are you doing here?" she asked, through tears. Was she a little tipsy? Were those cups of punch spiked, the ones the gargoyle had brought?

"Looking for you," he said.

Opal laughed, but it sounded more like a sob. "No one cares about me."

"Sure they do." He wondered where her enormous date was. Far away, he hoped.

Opal sniffed and rubbed her nose with the back of her hand. "No," she said. "My father thinks I'm stupid."

"I doubt that."

"He really does."

"What makes you think so?"

She grew silent and very still. Even the sniffing stopped. Her eyes went to the math paper on her desk. "I called him tonight," she said.

"What did he say?"

"Nothing. He's gone."

"What do you mean, *gone?*"

She rubbed her nose again. "I think he went to the island."

"What island?"

"My mother's island. I think he took your friend."

"To an *island?*"

She nodded. "He thinks Janie's smart." Her voice broke again.

Pip pulled his chair closer and sat facing Opal. He gave her the clean handkerchief from his jacket pocket. "You've got to tell me what you know."

Opal clutched the handkerchief. "He wishes he had a daughter like Janie."

"So he just *took* her?"

Opal nodded and wiped her eyes. "He needed help with her experiment."

"Slow down," Pip said. "Pretend I know nothing. What experiment?"

"The one she was working on. Taking salt out of salt water."

"So he took her to an island?"

Opal nodded.

"And the island is where?"

"In Malaya."

"Ma-*what?*"

"In Southeast Asia. My grandfather is a Malay sultan. My father has a mine on an island there. He got the island when he married my mother, but he keeps it secret."

"Is it a gold mine?"

Opal shrugged. "How would I know? I'm stupid." Her

eyes were shiny and wet, her small nose was red, and her hair spilled over her pretty shoulders. She really was a staggeringly lovely girl.

"I don't think you're stupid," Pip said.

She laughed: an appealing little snort. "You don't know me."

"I have evidence," he said. He fluffed the puffy dress hanging on the chair. "First, you chose that stunner of a dress over this one, which would've made you look like a marshmallow."

She smiled a little.

"Second," he said, "you ditched that big dozy pillock from the dance."

"I didn't ditch him," Opal said.

"No?"

"He's waiting in the hall."

Pip's stomach grew cold, and he stared at Opal, who looked back at him with a runny nose and unsympathetic eyes.

Then she burst into laughter. "I scared you," she said.

Relief flooded Pip. "That you did," he said. "See, you're clever, whatever your dad says."

CHAPTER 26

A Confession

Y ou developed this substance on your own?" Benjamin's father asked. "Without telling me?"

They were in the apartment above the apothecary shop in Manila. They had joined the floods of people leaving Vietnam, or trying to leave. In Hanoi, they had found a small steamer going to a Catholic mission in Manila and talked their way on board, assuring the priest in charge that they had medical skills to volunteer for the journey, and only needed the passage. They had sweetened the deal with a packet of an extremely effective new painkiller, and finally the priest had nodded them aboard.

The Manila apothecary, Mr. Vinoray, had a shop on Calle Ilang-ilang, near the port. Vinoray knew about the work Benjamin's father was doing, although his own interest was in the treatment of cancer. He was small and round-faced and bald, and moved silently around the shop and the apartment, where he lived alone. He had gone out, but was returning soon to take Benjamin's father on a collecting expedition, to gather the local medicinal plants and to see a real ylang-ylang tree. A steel fan blew street smells in through the window. The smells of Manila were different from those in Vietnam, but the sweltering heat was the same.

"Why didn't you tell me?" his father asked.

"Because I knew you'd tell me not to do it."

"Yes, I would have!"

"That's why I didn't tell you."

His father sighed, and pressed his hand to his twitching left eye. "I see."

"You expect me to take over your work someday," Benjamin said. "But how can I do that if I don't *try* things? You made me read Geberus, who said that we have to experiment and perform practical work to attain mastery. So do you believe that or don't you?"

"I do," his father said. "But I would rather supervise your experiments, for now. Please explain to me how it works."

"I based it on one of the clairvoyance powders in the Pharmacopoeia," Benjamin began. "The ones you said affect the insula in the brain, and increase our awareness of other minds. I knew it would have to be taken in through the stomach. Empathy began as an awareness of other people's digestion, so we would know how not to poison ourselves. Right?"

"That's the theory," his father said, looking uneasy.

"But I changed a few things."

"All right," his father said.

"I wanted to create a substance that would let you connect with another person, if you both took it, no matter how far apart you were. It lets you see *as* that other person, through their eyes." It was the first time he had talked about the powder, and it felt exhilarating to explain it. "It only seems to work in one direction at a time, though. There are *incredible* possibilities, don't you see?"

"A spying powder," his father said, his voice full of judgment.

"No!" Benjamin said. "A mental connection powder! An approach to telepathy!"

"You remind me of myself when I was young," his father said. "When I was so terribly excited about the possibilities. But you have no idea how dangerous it is, this creation of yours. And you've brought Janie into it. She's only a child."

"She's sixteen," Benjamin said stubbornly. The girl he'd seen in the bathroom mirror was no child. But his father was right that there were dangers. Seeing the boy kiss Janie had pierced Benjamin's heart like a piece of shrapnel, and he hadn't yet recovered.

"You're entering another person's consciousness," his father said. "This is not a simple thing to do, or without ramifications. It's not a thing to do lightly."

"I don't," Benjamin said. "I wouldn't."

"Has Janie told anyone about it?"

Benjamin hesitated. He didn't want to tell his father this part. But he had to admit the truth. "I think she's been using it to spy on someone else."

His father exhaled and grew very still. Other men might pound the table or stomp about the room, but his father was more frightening when he became utterly motionless. "How do you know?" he asked.

"I made contact with her when she was doing it, so I saw through his eyes instead."

"Who is it she's watching?"

"I'm not sure. I think, from what she said, that his name is Magnusson."

"And why is she watching him?"

"I don't know!" Benjamin said. "I always said we should take her with us, and not expect her to go back to school like a normal girl. She's not normal anymore."

"She had parents. She was fourteen."

"And she helped us in Nova Zembla!" Benjamin said. "That trip *changed* me, and it changed her, too."

"Well, she shouldn't be striking out on her own."

"But she is. And it's our fault."

"And who is this Magnusson?"

"I'm not sure. He has a mine on an island. And he has a Malay keris—a small, delicate one, a knife for a woman. And I think he got Janie kicked out of school. But I lost contact before I learned anything useful." Benjamin thought again of Janie and the boy in the dark auditorium. He felt his face grow hot, but his father didn't seem to notice.

"What are the side effects?" his father asked.

"You feel pretty awful when it's over," Benjamin said. "Dizzy, and like you might throw up, if you're the one doing the watching. But that doesn't last long. And if you take it again too soon, it makes you really sick, and doesn't work."

"Does Janie know where we are?"

"She knew we were in Vietnam. But she doesn't know we're in Manila."

His father frowned. "How do you activate the connection?"

"You think about the person. You both have to have taken the powder. Then you concentrate, and it just happens. It's hard to describe. I guess if everyone was blind, and you tried to describe vision to them, it would sound crazy and made up. The idea that you know *exactly* what's across the room without going over and touching it—it would seem like magic, for people who'd never done it before. This is just like seeing, only you can do it across oceans instead of across a room." He could feel himself getting excited again.

His father sighed. "You've surpassed me in inventiveness, in what you can do. But you don't consider the consequences. How do you know that this Magnusson isn't now watching *us*?"

"He couldn't," Benjamin said, taken aback. "He doesn't know how to do it."

"But people learn, as you have demonstrated. Would you know if he were seeing through you?"

"Yes!" But honestly, Benjamin wasn't sure. He probed in his mind for any sign of a big cigar-smoking man, but what would that feel like?

"He could be watching Janie," his father said. "For all you know."

"Why would he want to spy on a couple of kids?"

His father's voice rose, a thing that almost never happened. "Because you *aren't* just a couple of kids, as you were reminding me just a moment ago!"

"He doesn't know that."

"He might suspect."

"There's no reason he would."

"I don't want you to use it again."

"But I'm just learning how it works! And she might be in trouble!"

"She'll be in more trouble if she knows we're in Manila. It's much safer for her to know nothing. Do you understand me, Benjamin? I forbid you to use it again. For Janie's sake."

Benjamin frowned. The thing that really worried him wasn't the cigar smoker. It was the boy in the dark theater. Janie could be kissing him right now. He didn't want to see that, but he also couldn't stand not knowing. His father was wise, and could advise him about so many things: dissolution, separation, calcination, the manipulation of matter, the closing of wounds. But he couldn't advise him about this. If Benjamin tried to explain his stabbing jealousy, his father would look baffled and then stammer out something embarrassing about adolescence and hormones. A stray breeze came through the window, cooling the damp sweat on the back of Benjamin's neck. A car horn blared in the heat outside the window, and men were shouting in Tagalog at someone who had stopped a cart in the middle of the street. Benjamin understood their curses and commands with no effort. That seemed unremarkable now.

"There's a boy," he blurted. "With Janie. She's staying with him. I saw him kiss her."

His father looked startled, and then his eyes grew serious. "I'm sorry," he said. "That must be painful."

"It's awful!" Benjamin said, his eyes stinging.

His father sighed. "You have to leave her alone, Benjamin. Let her live her life, and be safe, if you care for her. It's the kindest thing you can do."

CHAPTER 27

Kidnapped

Janie packed up her few belongings while Raffaello was at rehearsal for *A Midsummer Night's Dream*. She said good-bye to Giovanna, who wasn't too sad to see her go, although Janie thought she might feel a little wistful when it came time to close out the till. She threw her duffel bag over one shoulder and her knapsack over the other, and walked toward the bus station.

She was thinking about how she had made the right decision, to go home to her parents, when a dark-windowed black limousine pulled up at the curb beside her on Kingsley Street. The back door opened, and strong hands grabbed her arms. Janie struggled, but she couldn't get free. She saw the white-blond flash of Magnusson's hair. She was yanked inside the car, and a bag went over her head. Everything was dark. She was pinned against the leather upholstery and she felt the car lurch away from the curb. Her heart raced with fear.

No one except Giovanna and her parents knew she was going to the bus station, and they all thought she'd be on the bus until tomorrow. No one would notice she was gone. The car was speeding along. Janie reached blindly to find the door handle, thinking she would throw herself out into the street, but a hand came over her mouth, holding something soft. A handkerchief? She had just enough time to notice a strange smell before everything faded away.

It seemed like a moment later when the blindfold came off, and she was in a different place. The room was bright with artificial light. As Janie's eyes adjusted, she realized she was in the office where she had seen Mr. Magnusson talking to his secretary. There was the sleek, uncluttered desk she had seen through Mr. Magnusson's eyes. Now she was in a chair near one of the plate glass windows and she was very groggy. The desk looked enormous from this new perspective. It dominated the room.

She remembered that Magnusson's office was in Boston, a two-hour drive from Grayson, but she didn't know how much time had passed. It was still night outside the big windows. Was it the same night? On one wall of the office was a giant map of the Pacific. She thought of Mrs. McClellan's roll-down maps in the history classroom.

Mr. Magnusson sat down on the edge of his vast desk, his enormous hands gripping the desk's edge. "Miss Scott," he said.

"Mr. Magnusson." Her tongue felt thick and her throat dry.

"I'm sorry I couldn't invite you here more politely. I didn't think you would come."

"You're breaking the law," she croaked.

"Yes, I am," he said. "Sylvia?"

The blond woman he had called "my love" brought a glass

of water for Janie. The cool water was soothing, and Janie looked at the woman over the rim of the glass. Sylvia wore a white silk blouse and a string of pearls, and her hair was softly pinned up. The look on her face was conflicted, and Janie guessed that she hadn't known that Magnusson's plan involved kidnapping.

"The thing is, Janie, I need your help," Mr. Magnusson said.

The water in Janie's stomach made her feel queasy. "My help?"

"I need you to set up a desalination plant for me. I've given your experiment to my engineers, but they don't seem to have the requisite . . . flexibility of mind, let's say. They don't think it can be done."

"It *can* be done," Janie insisted.

"You see?" Mr. Magnusson said, smiling. "This is why I need you. You have that can-do spirit."

"Why didn't you just ask me?"

"I didn't think you were very fond of me."

"I'm not."

"That's all right. I'm a man of business. I don't need people to like me."

"You're a criminal," Janie said. "A kidnapper."

"Oh, I've done worse, in my time," Mr. Magnusson said.

Janie wondered if she could stand up, but her legs didn't seem to want to obey her. Groggy, she was so groggy. There was a tingling feeling in her fingertips. Was Benjamin trying to control them? Was he here? Or was it just the effect of the chloroform?

Magnusson turned to the big map and ran his finger across the blue ocean. "This is where we're going," he said. "I always think the island looks a bit like a seedpod, with its two rounded ends. It is in Malaya, in my wife's homeland. It forms the uppermost point of a triangle between these two islands in the Celebes Sea, do you see?"

"My parents will come looking for me," Janie said.

Mr. Magnusson smiled. "Do you know how many girls your age disappear every day? They run away, or they simply vanish . . ."

"People look for those girls!" Janie said.

"Of course they do," Mr. Magnusson said. "But they don't find them."

"Magnus," Sylvia said.

"How are you going to get me to that island?" Janie asked. "Someone is going to ask questions."

"I have long been a believer in business aircraft," Mr. Magnusson said. "To get the important people in one's company around."

"But it's on the other side of the world."

"We take the great circle route," Mr. Magnusson said, unconcerned. "We refuel along the way."

"Is Opal coming?"

"*Why* would I bring Opal?" he asked. "Poor Opal. You should have seen her as a baby, the most beautiful child. Everyone adored her. But now she's become so stupid and bad-tempered. And besides, she's at your foolish dance, with a block of concrete masquerading as a teenage boy, drinking spiked punch from a plastic cup. We leave tonight. You will come quietly, I trust. I don't have to put you back to sleep?"

"No," Janie said quickly. She didn't have a plan, but she didn't want the chloroform again, the sinking, the dry and aching throat. "I mean yes, I'll go."

"Good," Mr. Magnusson said. "Such a sensible girl. So different from Opal. You're the daughter I should have had."

CHAPTER 28

Transport

When Benjamin lost sight of the office where Janie was being held, his mouth watered with nausea and he shivered in spite of the heat. He stumbled to Vinoray's tiny bathroom, the vertigo compounded with horror. He splashed water on his face, trying to think straight. Janie had been kidnapped by Magnusson while Benjamin was worrying about some skinny Italian kid.

He looked in the mirror, wet and disoriented. His father had told him not to use the powder anymore. But then Benjamin wouldn't have known she'd been kidnapped.

His father had gone collecting with Vinoray, and Benjamin had a few hours before they would return. He left the apartment in a panic, walked down to the port, and started hailing tied-up boats: steamers and cruisers and sampans and pleasure yachts. When the skippers would talk to him, he asked them to take him to an island in the Celebes Sea.

Some of the skippers laughed, and some shook their heads. One old French captain said, "This is cyclone season.

You don't know where you'll end up. Cannibals will cook you in a pot and eat your brains."

"That's not true," Benjamin said.

"Believe what you wish," the man said. "I have seen this."

An American couple on a sleek wooden yacht called the *Payday* seemed ready to listen to Benjamin out of sheer boredom. The woman was blond and tan in a black dress, with a gold charm bracelet dangling from her wrist. The man wore a pressed linen shirt, and had silver in his brushed-back hair. He poured Benjamin a ginger ale with ice.

"How old are you?" he asked.

"Eighteen," Benjamin lied.

"Eighteen!" the woman said. "Oh, to be eighteen again, with the world before you, where to choose."

"Here we go again," her husband said, squeezing a lime into Benjamin's glass. "Charlotte's in mourning for her lost youth."

He handed Benjamin the sweating glass of ice-cold ginger ale, and it tasted like ambrosia. Benjamin wasn't sure he'd ever had anything better. He held the cold glass against his neck. The man smoothed out a chart on the table, and Benjamin showed him where he wanted to go.

"You know cyclone season is starting," the skipper said. "Bad time to set out."

"I don't have a choice," Benjamin said.

"And why's that?"

"My friend is there."

"You paying for the charter?"

Benjamin hesitated. "How much would it cost?"

"Oh don't be petty, Harry," Charlotte said. "He's just a kid. It would be fun!"

"What's your friend doing in Malaya?" the skipper asked.

"She didn't tell me," Benjamin said, which was true. He didn't think it was a good idea to say that she'd been kidnapped.

Harry's eyebrows went up. "Ah, it's a *girl*friend."

"Well," Benjamin said.

"Listen, kid," Harry said. "If a girl doesn't tell you why she's going someplace, maybe she doesn't want you to follow."

"She might be a woman of mystery," Charlotte said.

"I've learned to avoid those," Harry said, giving his wife a wry look.

"It's *really* important that I get there," Benjamin said.

"Sorry, kid," Harry said, shaking his head. "I'm not taking my boat into a cyclone for some runaway girl."

Charlotte, who smelled like gardenias and coconut oil, tousled Benjamin's hair sympathetically, and they sent him over the side. He walked back up the dock, drenched with sweat and disappointment. He thought of Pip, who would've been able to talk his way onto that boat. Pip would be helping to take up the dock lines right now. He wondered if Pip had received his telegram and where he might be.

Despondent and hot, Benjamin dragged himself back to Vinoray's closed-up shop and let himself in with a key. It was no cooler inside, but at least the sun wasn't beating down on him. He closed the door behind him and looked round.

There was a fishy smell to the cluttered shop, and many of the jars held things from the sea: dried squid, dried sea slugs, dried octopus. There were bottles with cobras preserved in liquor, and bottles with scorpions, and bottles that contained both cobras *and* scorpions. The scorpions were black, the cobras coiled and gray. It wasn't anything like his father's shop in London.

He tried to think clearly and consider his resources. If he could get a small amount of gold, he could make an invisibility bath and stow away on a boat, but he had no guarantee that the boat would go to the right place. Most of what he'd learned in the last year had to do with closing wounds, fighting infection, and drawing out bullets. None of it was going to get him any closer to Janie.

Then he remembered that his father had a small amount of the avian elixir left. It was only enough to turn one person into a bird. Benjamin would become an English skylark with it—a strange and foreign-looking creature, in a land of bitterns and cormorants. And there were birds of prey here that would eat a skylark for lunch. He had seen them hunting overhead: white-bellied sea eagles and mountain hawk eagles, with great wingspans and talons for ripping apart their prey, and collared falcons and peregrines that killed with their beaks.

The sea winds, too, were treacherous and unpredictable. Cyclone season was starting, as everyone kept reminding him, and it would be dangerous to look for a tiny island on his own. He remembered his body changing back into human form over the freezing sea and plunging into the waves. The memory made him cold, even in the heat of Manila. But Janie had rescued him from that icy sea, and now she needed his help. If no one would take him by boat, he had no choice but to go by air.

He went upstairs to the apartment over the shop and pulled his father's satchel from under the cot where he slept. He lifted out amber glass bottles until he found the right one. Then he tore a page from a notebook and wrote to his father.

Dad—
Gone to look for Janie. I know you won't think I should, but please understand. You always say we must do what we can to right wrongs. I'm taking the avian elixir. PLEASE DON'T FOLLOW ME. I will be back when I can.

B.

He rolled up the note and put it in his father's bag. He made sure the window was open. Then he opened the bottle and drank the rest of the avian elixir.

It had the familiar, bitter, mossy taste. His skin began to tingle all over as if both arms and both legs had fallen asleep. His body tilted forward at the hips, and he felt his legs begin to shrink and lighten beneath him. Feathers burst from his prickling skin and his skull lightened. His nose and mouth drew themselves into a hard, pointed beak. His hands disappeared into feathered wing tips, and his toes into tiny talons.

He wasn't sweating in the heat anymore. His eyesight improved so much, it was as if he were looking through a telescope at the buildings across the city, and his hearing grew sharper. His human sense of regret at leaving his father seemed to lessen. He was a skylark, and wanted nothing more than to fly.

He hopped up on the windowsill, scanned the sky for danger, felt the air currents moving past him, and soared out into the blue day.

PART FOUR

Transmutation

1. the action of changing or the state of being changed into another form
2. (physics) the changing of one element into another by radioactive decay, nuclear bombardment, or similar processes
3. (biology) the conversion or transformation of one species into another
4. (alchemy) the process of changing base metals into gold

CHAPTER 29

Flight

The airplane was a 1952 Twin Beech, with two propellers. It had two pilots and six fairly comfortable passenger seats, but only three of the passenger seats were filled. Sylvia sat directly across the aisle from Janie, knitting something from pale blue wool. Magnusson sat in front of Sylvia, reading a biography of Teddy Roosevelt. Janie watched through the window as the Great Lakes went by beneath them. She thought of her parents, down there somewhere.

Over what must have been Wisconsin, the pilot started to circle and descend. Janie saw a narrow runway coming straight at her. They were landing sideways. She grabbed Sylvia's arm. "We'll crash!" she cried.

"It's all right," Sylvia said. "It's how they manage the crosswinds. He'll straighten it out."

Janie watched the ground hurtle toward the side of the plane. At the last second, the plane straightened toward the runway. It rattled and bounced to a stop, and Janie realized she hadn't been breathing. She unbuckled her seat belt and started to get up. She had to get out of this death trap.

"Oh, no," Magnusson said, his head touching the ceiling of the cabin as he stood. "You stay here."

"You're *joking*," Janie said.

"Do I look like I'm joking?" The pilot opened the door and Magnusson climbed out.

Janie turned to Sylvia in disbelief. "What am I going to do, run away? In a place I've never been?"

"We can't take the risk."

"*Please*, Sylvia."

"I'm sorry."

"You're going to jail," Janie said. "I hope you know that."

"We'll be in Canada soon," Sylvia said. "You can stretch your legs there."

Janie looked longingly out the window. She wanted to escape, but even more, she wanted to breathe the outside air. "I *promise* I won't scream that I've been kidnapped by evil people who should be arrested."

Sylvia smiled at her. "Sorry."

"Just let me off the *plane!*" Janie cried, desperate. "Please!"

"Canada," Sylvia said.

Refueled, they took off again, the plane shuddering with complaint as it regained its natural element. They flew over mountains, and the way the plane bounced and plunged in the changing air currents made Janie feel sick. Her stomach seemed to rise into her throat. She hadn't gotten seasick on the trip to Nova Zembla, so it didn't seem fair that now she got *air*sick. She wondered if the Pharmacopoeia had a good cure for nausea in its pages, and thought she would trade all the rest of the book for that one thing.

Neither Sylvia nor Mr. Magnusson seemed bothered by the turbulence. Mr. Magnusson wore shirtsleeves and a loosened tie. He was making notes in a notebook. Sylvia was curled up against the window of the plane, asleep under the pale blue blanket she'd been knitting, with just her soft golden hair sticking out.

They landed sideways again in Canada, at a tiny airstrip, and let Janie off the plane. "Where are we, exactly?" she asked, looking out at the empty plains.

"You don't need to know that," Mr. Magnusson said. "And the attendant is deaf, so save your breath."

"Let's go for a walk," Sylvia said, taking her arm.

Janie eyed the old man in a jumpsuit refueling the plane. Sylvia steered her smartly away, across the tarmac. The wind was blowing cold and clear. There was an airplane hangar, and the fuel pumps, but there was nothing else in sight. "Where do we land next?" Janie asked.

"Alaska," Sylvia said.

"And then where?" Janie asked. "The Soviet Union? They're protective of their airspace—I don't know if you've noticed."

"Magnus has many connections," Sylvia said.

"How can you work for him?" Janie asked. "How can you *love* him?"

"He's been very good to me," Sylvia said. "When my brother was killed in Korea, I fell apart. I don't think I would have made it through without Magnus. He's been tremendously sympathetic and understanding."

"He's using you," Janie said.

"He's not as bad as he seems."

"That leaves a lot of room for badness."

"You're going to be helping people, Janie," Sylvia said. "You'll be providing the miners with a source of fresh water."

"No, I'll just save Magnusson the expense of shipping water in."

"It amounts to the same thing."

"It does not!"

"Let's go back to the plane." Sylvia had a tight grip on her arm.

Janie felt a sudden panic rising in her chest. She couldn't

let them take her. "No!" she said, trying to dig in her heels. "Help!" The man in the jumpsuit didn't turn. Either he really was deaf, or her voice had been carried off by the wind.

"Janie!" Sylvia caught her by both shoulders and shook her, looking into her face. "Pull it together. If you don't, he'll chloroform you again. You don't want that."

Janie stared into Sylvia's eyes. Sylvia was right. She didn't want that. And she couldn't run. She was in the middle of nowhere, in another country, with no money and no way to get home. She wanted to weep, but her eyes were dry in the cold, arid air.

Back on the plane, Janie hugged her knees in her seat and made herself small. As they shuddered along the runway toward takeoff, she closed her eyes and imagined herself elsewhere.

First she imagined herself in the auditorium with Raffaello kissing her, but that memory was still confusing, so she pushed it away. Benjamin on the deck of the icebreaker was the safe memory, the appropriate and innocent one: her first kiss. There were no betrayals in it, no complications. But that memory didn't seem to have the power it had once had. It had lost some of its glow. Was that because she had kissed Raffaello? She longed for sleep, for escape. Sweet *sleep*. She willed it to come.

Then she dreamed it was bright day, and she was flying. Not in an airplane, but as a bird, as she had in London with Benjamin and Pip. She was over the blue ocean, but she could dip and soar in the currents, with the wind in her feathers, instead of bouncing and shuddering in a clumsy, noisy, man-made contraption. She was grateful for the escape, and she felt stronger than she had ever been as a robin. Her wings were sturdy and she could catch every updraft, every thermal. This was bliss! This was real flying. The Wright brothers might have been brilliant and bold, but their rattling invention was a pale imitation of the effortless glory that was natural flight.

In her dream, there were islands in the distance. The air was soft and tropical. The islands, as they grew closer, were white sand and lush green. She hoped the dream would take her down close to one of them. The sun gleamed silver on the blue water.

Then a shadow came over her head, blocking the sun, and a terrible blow struck her in the back of the neck. Was it a knife? It held her tight. It was something with claws, a flying thing with talons, lifting her upward, and she was helpless, caught. Her heart began to race, and she understood. She wasn't asleep. It wasn't a dream.

Benjamin. Something had snatched him from the sky.

She sat up on the plane and screamed.

CHAPTER 30

Alistiar Beane

The striped cat vanished, slipping away on the day Jin Lo's childhood house was swallowed up in greenery. Jin Lo sometimes wondered if the cat had ever really been there, or if she had imagined him out of loneliness. But she remembered his small, persistent forehead, his silky body, and his rumbling purr.

The woman next door made her a bowl of mushroom dumplings and a bowl of chicken broth with green vegetables in it. She didn't ask about the swallowed house, or the green mound where it had been. She treated Jin Lo with a wary deference, as if she knew there were no simple answers. She brought out Jin Lo's clean clothes, fresh and folded.

Jin Lo walked out of the city the way she had come, and saw shimmering ghosts at every turn: children playing in the street, women sweeping, men pacing. They were there, the lost people of her city. They were doomed to haunt it. She could do nothing for them, although some of them looked at her as if they knew she had set her own ghosts free. Father, Mother, little Shun Liu, Mrs. Hsu. They had left this place, and Jin Lo could leave it, too.

She arrived at the train station with just enough time to buy a ticket and board before the train began to move. She would go back to the town where she had been apprenticed to the master chemist, and where she hadn't gone to collect her mail for two years.

She slept in her seat on the train. When she woke, she ate a hard-boiled egg. Another passenger on the train gave her a ball of rice and a cup of tea, and she smiled in thanks. The muscles in her face were so stiff and unused that she felt like a statue grimacing, but the man didn't recoil, so she guessed she looked something like a human being.

At her station, she got off the train and walked toward the post office. The first time she had arrived here, she had been an orphaned child, walking double time to keep up with the long, purposeful stride of the missionary. She had twisted and craned her neck to look at the strange, intimidating sights around her. Now the town looked drab and gray, and very small. She wished she had the striped cat for company.

At the post office, her vocal cords felt dry and unused, but she made herself understood, and they gave her a sack of mail. She sat on a bench in a small park and began to sort through it.

There were letters from colleagues within China, some of them two years old, and a letter from the university in Beijing. There was a coded letter from Marcus Burrows, postmarked before she left for London to join him for the voyage to Nova Zembla—it was pointless to decode now.

That the mail hadn't been seized was a good sign. No one was tracking her. Then a thought made her freeze with an envelope in her hand: Maybe the authorities did know everything. Maybe they had left the sack of mail untouched so she would think they weren't on her trail.

She scanned the park, and saw no watchers. Jin Lo looked down at the pile of envelopes again and pulled free a small envelope with her address typed on the front. It was a telegram, and it was recent: dated two days before. She tore it open and read the typed message:

NEED HELP. PLEASE COME. SEND REPLY
WITH CONFIRMATION TO ALISTIAR BEANE,
151 CALLE ILANG-ILANG, MANILA.

Alistair Beane, deliberately misspelled as *Alistiar,* was the apothecary's code name, to be used in an emergency. To confirm that she had received the telegram, Jin Lo was supposed to reply with her own alias, which was Mrs. Josef Bankes, after the botanist and explorer Joseph Banks.

She held the telegram in her hand. She had set her family free. Now her friends needed her help. It seemed very simple. The telegram had been sent just in time for her to retrieve it. Perhaps the world was orderly after all, and not chaotic and random.

Either way, she had to make a decision. She sifted through the rest of the mail to make sure there was nothing else recent, and went back to the post office to ask where she could send a telegram.

CHAPTER 31

The Sea Eagle

Benjamin left Manila as a nervous skylark, keeping an eye out for hungry falcons, but after a while he settled into the pleasure of flying and the absorbing work of navigating in the empty sky. The sea was bright turquoise and deep blue, marked by reefs and depths and currents, the air shot through with lacy clouds. Benjamin caught thermals that let him rest his wings, and flew southwest along the coast of the Philippines, charting the islands along the remembered path in his head.

It was lonely, flying by himself. On the way to Nova Zembla, he'd had Janie and his father and Jin Lo and Count Vili for company. Count Vili, an albatross with a vast wingspan, had navigated. Now Benjamin had no one. He whistled to himself. He looked for fish, although he wouldn't have known how to catch one, and couldn't imagine swallowing it raw—bones and scales and all. He saw an ominous gray shadow beneath the waves, at least twelve feet long. It made his speedy skylark's heart race even faster, knowing he might change into a boy and plummet into the water.

The wind came up, surprisingly strong. The sky on the horizon was dark blue like a bruise, and it seemed to be moving toward him, fast. Benjamin tried to remember what he knew about cyclones, how they rotated in the same direction as the earth, how they strengthened as evaporated water from the ocean rose and condensed in the air, how the core was always the warmest part. But none of that helped him decide what to do as the storm picked up his tiny bird's body and whipped him across the sky. He couldn't see anything, with the wind and pelting rain in his eyes. When he stretched out his wings to ride the air currents, strange gusts caught him so hard, he feared his fragile bones might break. On and on the storm battered him. Sometimes he didn't know which direction was the ocean and which the wet sky. He had seen dead birds washed up on beaches after storms before, and he began to fear he might become one of them.

And then suddenly it was still and warm. There were other birds—exhausted, wet, and now flying weakly. He thought he might have lost consciousness, because the warm stillness had the surreal quality of a dream. He was in the eye of the storm, trapped in the center of it, being carried wherever it decided to take him. He considered fighting his way back into the swirling winds, but it seemed too dangerous. He didn't think he could survive that battering much longer. So he let himself be carried along with this bedraggled aviary in the strange warm core.

Hours later, or maybe days, he found himself huddled beneath a stand of trees, ragged and disoriented and missing feathers. As he rested there, he saw other windblown birds eating seeds off the ground. Benjamin was hungry, and drew nearer. The storm-tossed birds darted away, full of mistrust. There was something about his skylark form that made the real birds uneasy.

Benjamin ate the abandoned seeds as quickly as he could. But the other birds, starved from their ordeal, lost their fear and flew at him, pecking at his eyes and wings. They screamed in their tiny voices, and Benjamin ducked his head and flew away.

In a tree, he found some grubs: fat white worms waving their tiny heads blindly in the soggy air. The bird in him said they were good to eat, but the boy was revolted. He ate them anyway, knowing he needed strength, and they were salty, with the texture of grapes, the thin skin popping in his mouth. He swallowed as quickly as he could.

He flew on, not knowing where he was. He had a better intuitive sense of navigation as a bird, just as he had better eyesight, and he knew he had been blown east, but how far east? He was definitely out in the Pacific Ocean, well east of the Philippines. But he hadn't intended to go that direction, so hadn't studied the map carefully.

A series of small islands appeared. Benjamin was thinking about where they might fall on the chart when he felt a hard blow in the back of the neck. Then there was a searing pain as something dug into his skin, through his feathers.

Benjamin screeched and flapped, trying to free himself, but the pain grew worse as he struggled. There was a gust of air and a sound of heavy wings, and he realized it was another bird that held him. It was carrying him toward the nearest island as he fought.

Benjamin felt his skylark heartbeat start to slow, and his skin start to tingle, and he knew he was beginning to change. But he couldn't let it happen yet. Not now. He would break his legs, or even his neck, if he became a boy and fell with the giant bird to the island. He concentrated on keeping his bones light and birdlike, his pulse quick, his arms winged. But it was hard to concentrate on *anything* with knifelike talons seizing the back of your neck. He couldn't hold on to his bird shape much longer, and the beach was still too far below. There was a canopy of trees off to the right. If he could only steer his captor toward the trees, maybe the branches would break his fall.

He tried flapping in the direction of the trees with his ineffectual, trapped wings. The bird that held him screamed and squeezed harder with its talons. A lightning bolt of pain erased all thoughts and all willpower, and Benjamin started to grow, in spite of himself.

His bones stretched and thickened, and his skull expanded and grew heavy. His legs and feet took on weight and density. His feathers retracted into his tingling skin and his wing tips became fingers. Then the fingers were attached to featherless hands . . . forearms . . . elbows. His blood slowed, his heartbeat dragging in his ears.

The big raptor, his load growing heavier, screamed and let Benjamin go. The green of the trees flew at him and he crashed into the treetops. He hit one branch with his ribs and another with his shoulder, and then he grabbed a third with both hands and hung on. The world that had been so noisy and chaotic, all crashing and screaming, grew still. The clinging, stabbing creature was off his neck. But the ground was still far below his hanging feet. He took a deep, shuddering breath.

How to get down? He considered, then swung hand over hand down the branch until he could grab the trunk with his legs. He clung there like a monkey, arms shaking, feeling the relative safety of the solid tree trunk. He wondered what island this was, and how he would get off it. But right now he needed to concentrate on climbing down. Just do the next thing. That was his task. He reached for a shaky foothold, then for a finger-shredding new handhold. He groped blindly with his toes for a lower foothold, then another.

Finally he lowered himself to the ground and put a hand to his neck to feel the damage. He came away with spots of blood on his fingers, but the raptor didn't seem to have torn him to shreds. His ribs were bruised where he'd hit the first branch, and his hands were raw from climbing down, but nothing was broken. He'd been lucky.

He looked up, scanning the treetops, and saw a muscular white bird with a gray hood of feathers perched on a high branch. It glowered down at him, looking both confused and humiliated. A sea eagle. It had nearly been his death. He wondered: Would his bones have grown inside the bird's stomach? Or would he have stayed a tiny thing if he had died as one?

"Nice try!" he called to the sea eagle.

The bird ruffled its white wings as if shrugging off embarrassment, and gazed away into the middle distance.

"Nice try," a gruff voice said on the ground, and Benjamin looked to find a man standing near him. The man had dark skin and a faded red Coca-Cola T-shirt over a woven grass loincloth. He had appeared out of the trees, and he was smiling. "John Frum?" he asked.

"Oh, no," Benjamin said, putting up his hands to push the idea away. He knew about John Frum from their time on Espíritu Santo, where the Americans had set up a base during the war. The navy had brought trucks and food and radios, things the people of the island had never seen before. A legend had spread of a man named John Frum, who was supposed to come back to the islands in an airplane, bringing more supplies—more cargo. The people were still waiting for him, on more than one island group. "Not John Frum," he said.

"You come from sky," the man said.

"Yes," Benjamin said. "Well, sort of."

"You have cargo."

"No," Benjamin said, holding out his empty hands. "No cargo. See?"

The man reached and took Benjamin's rumpled shirt collar between two fingers and rubbed it reverently, inspecting the fabric. "I tell the people, belong this island, long time," he said. "They don' believe. I say, John Frum, he must come. He come from sky. He bring cargo."

"I only came from the sky because I was a bird," Benjamin said. It sounded outrageous, spoken aloud. But being a bird seemed more plausible than that he, Benjamin Burrows, was the long-awaited South Pacific hero, bringing Cokes and wristwatches and jeeps to the people. And it had the advantage of being the truth.

The man looked at him a long time. "John Frum come from sky."

"But John Frum has an *airplane*," Benjamin argued. The exact beliefs were different from island to island, but he knew that John Frum was usually believed to be a pilot. Sometimes he was said to wear a navy uniform.

"John Frum come from bird," the man said. So either the cult on this island was different, or the prophet was willing to be flexible. Prophecies were tricky. The outcome was all in the interpretation.

"No!" Benjamin said. "I'm Benjamin Burrows. What island is this?"

The man moved toward a gap in the trees and made a beckoning gesture. "You come, John Frum," he said.

Benjamin hesitated, but he had no choice. He didn't know where he was and didn't have any way to get off the island. He looked at the bird that had brought him, but it lifted its great wings to go look for easier prey. So he followed the barefoot man.

His father said that the cargo cults had started even earlier than the war, with the nineteenth-century missionaries who arrived on the islands. The belief had only been intensified by the astonishing wealth of the American navy. The navy had so many goods, but the men who brought them clearly hadn't made them. The men had no skills. They did nothing but sit in offices, moving papers, listening to voices that came over small boxes. When the boxes broke, the men sent them away to be fixed. So there must be a source, elsewhere, of all this magical *stuff.*

After the war, the navy had bulldozed a lot of equipment into the sea, to try to discourage the cargo cults and return the islands to their undisturbed existence. But there was no returning to an earlier time. Such wanton waste of trucks and goods had only convinced the islanders that the coveted objects were *infinite* in the land of John Frum—in the legendary land of America. More would surely come.

The man in the loincloth talked quietly to himself as they walked. *"Nice try,"* he said. *"Nice try."*

Benjamin realized that the man was memorizing the first words of the returning John Frum. It was so ridiculous. He had to make them see that he wasn't a god.

They reached a clearing and found two small boys crouched over a bowl, chewing. The boys were bare-chested, in loincloths, and they looked up with wide eyes and fat cheeks. They were making kava. Benjamin's father had studied the root, interested in its narcotic properties, looking for possible medicinal uses. It was a drink prepared by chewing the root of the kava plant, mixing it with saliva, and spitting it into a bowl. Then the chewed pulp was fermented. Only

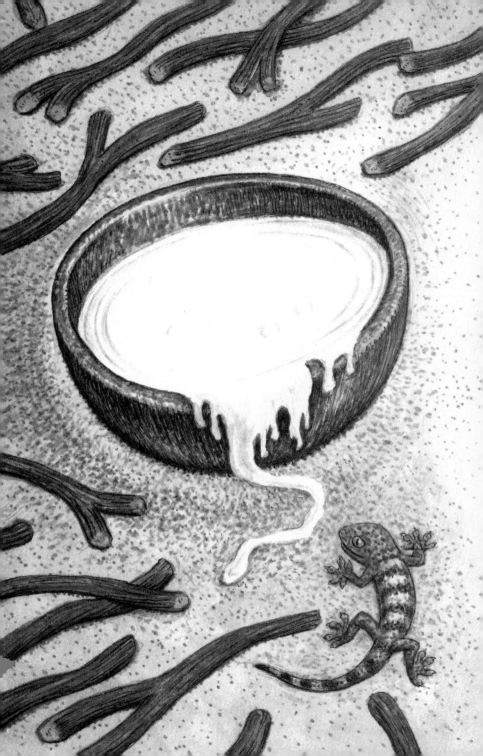

boys who hadn't reached adolescence or had any contact with girls could be given the task of preparing it. Once fermented, it became a powerful hallucinogen.

The man who had found him barked a command in a language Benjamin didn't recognize, and the smaller boy spit a glob into the bowl and dashed out of the clearing.

"Where are we?" Benjamin asked.

The man grinned at him. "Nice try," he said.

Two more men emerged from the trees a moment later, dressed in loincloths, but without Coca-Cola T-shirts. One had long, grizzled hair, and the other had dark hair cut very close to his scalp. They spoke with the prophet, and their eyes grew wide. The younger man put his hand on Benjamin's shoulder, bowed his head, and said, "John Frum."

"No," Benjamin said, and he started to explain, but the young man took his hand away from Benjamin's neck. There was blood on his fingertips. The three men seized Benjamin gently, with all the urgency and deference due to an injured god.

He was hustled into a dimly lit hut, and his bloody shirt was peeled off. He wished he had brought some of his father's blue paste, which would have healed the wounds instantly. He had no great hopes for the medical technology on this island. He hoped the water was clean, at least. The grizzled older man washed his wounds, and the younger brought Benjamin a bowl of white soupy goo.

"That's all right," Benjamin said, pushing the bowl away.

He had been curious about the visions people had after drinking kava, and the superhuman strength it seemed to give them. But he could only think about the fact that it was made with spit.

"Yes!" the prophet insisted.

The two other men held Benjamin's arms, and the bowl was pressed against his chin, the slimy contents tilting toward his mouth. Benjamin tried to protest, but when he opened his mouth to say "No!" it was filled with starchy, lukewarm kava. One of the men clapped a hand over his mouth so he couldn't spit it out, and pinched his nose so that he had to swallow to breathe. Benjamin gagged and shivered.

"That's disgusting," he said when they uncovered his mouth. "Let me up!"

But they were still holding his arms.

"Stay," the prophet said. "Good medicine." The bowl was pressed to Benjamin's mouth again, his nose held to force it down. He drank to avoid drowning, and then he sputtered and gasped for air.

"My father will look for me!" he said. He wasn't sure why he'd said it. It wouldn't mean anything to these men, but he was starting to feel desperate.

The prophet laughed. "John Frum has no father! He *is* father!"

"I'm *not* a father," Benjamin said. His head was starting to swim and his tongue felt thick. "I'm just a boy!"

"Boy John Frum."

"No," Benjamin said weakly. "No cargo." He could feel his hold on the room slipping. Shadows moved in the corners of his vision. Were they actually there? Had he asked that aloud? "No cargo," he said again, trying to be firm.

"Nice try, John Frum," the prophet said.

CHAPTER 32

Copley Square

Pip had a plan. He wasn't sure it was a good plan, but he had come all this distance to America, and he had to do *something*. And anyway, the plan was already under way. His first thought had been to go to Opal's mother for help, but Opal had said no.

"She's afraid of my father," she said. "She won't help. If anything, she'll just warn him."

So that left Opal's grandfather, the sultan. Sultans had money, he understood, and the ability to fly people places. Pip and Opal sent him a telegram as soon as the Western Union office opened, and then climbed aboard the bus to Boston.

"I've never taken a bus before," Opal said.

"It's not so bad."

Opal raised her eyebrows at the worn seats.

"Not what you expected?" Pip asked.

"I never thought about what a bus was like," she said, gazing out the dirty window through her clunky, pointless glasses.

It was a two-hour ride to Boston, and the bus swayed along. At the Copley Square Hotel, Opal went to the desk alone and booked a room on her father's account. Her family lived in Marblehead, outside the city, but she and her mother sometimes stayed in Boston when they went shopping. And her father stayed at the hotel when he was working late—Pip had some theories about *that*. While Opal checked in, Pip read a newspaper in the lobby. Then he trailed her up to the room. They made sure there were no maids in the hall before Opal unlocked the door. Now they just had to wait for word from her grandfather. They would be ready to go at a moment's notice.

The room had heavy curtains, blue-and-gold upholstery, and two identical beds under blue-and-gold bedspreads. "Did you ask for two beds?" Pip asked.

"Of course I did."

"That'll seem suspicious. You're just one person."

"I said I was going shopping, and wanted a spare bed to lay out dresses."

"And they believed you?"

"Of course. You'll have to sleep on top of yours, not in it. Otherwise the maids will know."

"How about you sleep on top of *yours*?"

She smiled at him and pushed her glasses up onto her nose. "Very funny."

Pip sat down on one smooth bedspread. "So," he said.

Opal sat on the other. "So what?"

"We wait for your grandfather's response."

"It's not like sending a telegram to a normal person's house," she said. "It has to go through attendants and translators. He doesn't even speak English."

"It's from the sultan's granddaughter. They'll get it to him."

"Maybe," Opal said. "If he's like my dad, he won't care."

"He'll care," Pip said. "And he'll send us a plane."

Opal made a skeptical face, then lay back on the bed with her hands behind her head and looked at the ceiling. Her hair spread out in a shining pool. Her legs in laddered blue tights hung off the end of the bed, warm skin showing through the runs. She kicked her legs. One scuffed shoe fell to the carpet.

"I'm bored already," she said.

CHAPTER 33

Nature Red in Tooth and Claw

J anie's first thought, stepping off the plane onto the small airstrip on Magnusson's island, was that she had walked into a wall of wet heat. The air was so dense and humid that her clothes stuck to her skin. She was weak from the long trip—they had stopped in *Siberia,* of all places, to refuel, and to take on a new pilot—and she was exhausted from the mental effort of trying to find Benjamin. She hadn't been able to make contact, and she tried to push away the idea that he'd been torn apart by sharp talons while he was trying to come to her rescue. Because he *was* trying to come to her rescue—wasn't he? He must have seen the office when Magnusson had shown her the island on the map. She should have closed her eyes so Benjamin wouldn't have known where to go. Then he would have stayed where he was. But she hadn't known he was there. And it's very hard to close your eyes when there's something interesting to see. She scanned for Benjamin overhead, but saw nothing but the oppressive glare of blue sky.

Magnusson, beaming with the pride of ownership, followed her gaze up into the air.

Janie tried not to look down quickly, which would look suspicious. "Hot day," she said. "Bright."

Magnusson studied her face. "It is," he said. "It gets that way."

The pilots were doing something with the airplane engine. The beautiful Sylvia looked tired and rumpled. Janie was rumpled, too. But what did it matter? A jeep came down a path through the trees and pulled up beside them. It was driven by a man in a green uniform who looked like military, although *what* military Janie didn't know.

They all climbed in, Janie feeling resigned. What else was she going to do? Run? Where? The jeep took them down a road of crushed seashells and past a pretty, sandy beach.

"Can I go for a swim?" Janie asked.

"You can swim in the pool," Magnusson said.

"I mean in the ocean?"

"Sure," Magnusson said. "If you want to be swallowed whole by a shark."

In Janie's demoralized mood, that idea didn't seem too alarming. "Whole is better than in two pieces," she said. "I might be able to fight my way out."

"Let me be very clear," Magnusson said. "You can't go in the ocean."

Next the jeep passed a pretty lagoon. It looked like a place for water nymphs to play. "What about there?"

"No," Magnusson said. "Very dangerous. Strange tides."

Then they were on the curving drive of a private villa: a

large white house with a blue swimming pool and a series of smaller cottages on a sloping lawn below.

"This doesn't look like a mine," Janie said.

"The mine is at the other end of the island," Magnusson said.

"So where's the desalinization plant?"

"It's not set up yet."

"You said you had a *plant.*"

"And I will, with your help."

There was something in his voice that bothered her. He sounded bored. He didn't care about desalinization. As they approached the villa, a high wire fence stopped them. A gate in the fence opened, and they continued down the drive. The big house had white columns, a terrace, and an oversized red door.

"What is this place?" Janie asked Magnusson. Something was still bothering her, buzzing in her mind.

"A very good place to wait," he said.

The gate closed behind them, the perimeter around the villa secure. "Wait for what?" Janie asked.

"For your friends."

Then the realization burst on Janie like the giant white blossoms opening on the hibernating tree in the Physic Garden, when the apothecary forced it to bloom. She had been too focused on her fears about Benjamin to see the truth: Magnusson had shown her the map *on purpose.* She felt sick. She forced herself to ask, "What do you want my friends for?"

Magnusson shrugged. "I collect talent."

"Talent?"

"Yes," he said. "That's how a good business works. You recruit the best minds. I have a hunch your friends can do remarkable things, as you can."

"So I'm the bait," Janie said, horrified. "In a trap."

"To put it crudely."

"They aren't coming," Janie said. She meant it as a bluff, but then realized it was true. If Benjamin was dead, then no one knew where she was. No one would come to her rescue.

"Where is your confidence, Janie?" Magnusson asked. "Your friends are more resourceful than you think." He put an arm around Sylvia. "Now, let's get this wilting flower a cold drink."

CHAPTER 34

Splintered

Jin Lo and Marcus Burrows were up all night in Vinoray's laboratory, grinding roots and measuring binding agents, trying to re-create Benjamin's telepathic powder. The Pharmacopoeia was open to the pages about clairvoyance, but there were no instructions for what Benjamin had done. They read, they thought, they argued, they broke their own rules of safety and methodical experimentation. They mixed concoctions, drank them down, and struggled to access each other's minds, but nothing worked.

Jin Lo finally lay down on Benjamin's unmade cot, exhausted from her journey to Manila and dizzy from drinking failed concoctions. As her head touched the pillow, she heard the tiniest crinkling sound. She reached carefully beneath the pillow, remembering the story about the princess and the pea, and came away with a small, square, glassine envelope with a little powder in it. She was too tired and too curious to get up and find a glass of water, so she put her finger into the envelope and put a few grains on her tongue.

There was a moment of recognition, of feeling that she

could taste every single thing that she and the apothecary had done wrong in the last twelve hours. She tasted their missteps and wrong turns. She was filled with admiration for Benjamin. It was like standing in front of a great work of art. That stubborn, willful, sometimes infuriating boy would do great things in his life. She closed her eyes to savor the great esteem and awe she felt.

And then she was reeling. The world spun.

She was in a room with a thatch ceiling and walls that heaved, as if they were breathing. A man in a loincloth and a faded red T-shirt stood nearby. He had the head of a sea eagle, and his long, curved beak was sharp and pointed at the end. He was saying something in a language Jin Lo didn't understand, and he raised his arms in excitement and screeched an eagle's screech. His arms became wings. Then his screech became a howl, and his head became the head of a wolf. He lowered his muzzle and smiled so Jin Lo could see his pointed teeth. He said, *"Nice try, John Frum."*

Then the wolf became a thin old woman with her belly spilled open. The wolf-woman tried to put her intestines back in as they slipped through her hands. It was like trying to stuff live snakes into a small bag.

And then the old woman really was putting snakes in a bag. They writhed and coiled around her wrists, which were no longer an old woman's wrists but a boy's again. One snake opened its enormous jaws at Jin Lo and hissed, flicking a long, forked tongue. And still the room spun.

Then the vision faded, and Jin Lo was back in the apartment

in Manila, on Benjamin's low cot. She sat up, swung her feet to the ground, and waited for the dizziness to fade.

Marcus Burrows was frowning at a Bunsen burner, his anxious brow lit by the blue flame, waiting for something to boil.

"I found him," Jin Lo said.

An hour later, they were poring over a map of the south Pacific spread out across the table. They had made a list of what they knew about different types of kava and their degrees of hallucinogenic power. They had a theory that the old woman was the one Benjamin and his father had saved in Vietnam, and was being remembered by Benjamin in the hallucination. It was statistically unlikely that there were *two*. They made notes about the location of cargo cults that believed in John Frum. They put pins in the map as markers. Jin Lo flipped through a book, an anthropological study of the Pacific Islands, with illustrations of the different types of clothing worn.

"In Espíritu Santo," the apothecary said, "the American navy cleared airstrips through the coconut groves that were the people's main source of survival. They mowed down the trees that fed the islanders. When there were fewer trees, the islanders' desire for cargo became more urgent. We brought them scarcity, and little squawking boxes, and longing for material things. And now they wait for John Frum."

Jin Lo turned the page in her book, looking for the woven grass loincloth she had seen in Benjamin's vision. She had gotten very comfortable being alone, with no one to speak to except the occasional cat. She wasn't used to all this talk. But she had noticed that the muscle in the apothecary's eye had stopped jumping now that they had a firm purpose again.

"There are splinter groups, of course," he said. "There are always splinter groups in any religion. People argue over doctrine."

Jin Lo turned another page and found a drawing of a man in a skirt or loincloth: a rectangular flap of woven grass in front, with a twist of cloth to secure it in the back. A necklace of red flowers hung around the man's neck. "This one," she said.

He leaned over to look. "You're certain?"

Jin Lo looked at her friend's mild, weary, lined face. Would she have said it, if she weren't certain? Did he not understand her at all? But no, he was only being very thorough and methodical, as always. "Yes," she said.

"Very suitable for a hot climate," he said, studying the loincloth.

"You want one?" she asked.

"I fear I don't have the figure for it," he said. He took a pin from the map, where they had last guessed Benjamin's island might be, and he moved it to the island of that particular loincloth. As a skylark, Benjamin could easily have been carried there by the cyclone.

"We go?" Jin Lo asked.

"We go," he said.

CHAPTER 35

A Dream

Magnusson woke from a terrible dream in which an old woman tried to stuff snakes into a bag. He was breathing hard and sweating. He was a strong believer in the predictive power of dreams, the idea that the unconscious mind knew something about the future. But what did it mean, the woman struggling with the snakes? And had they been snakes? He couldn't remember. He felt queasy, dry-throated and ill.

He had been thinking about Marcus Burrows and his son before he fell asleep. They would come for the girl, of course. They would feel responsible.

He had once seen two snakes fighting when he was a boy in Sweden. He had almost forgotten, but the dream had brought it back. They were huggorms, poisonous adders. But they didn't bite each other, their best weapon off-limits as if by mutual consent. One was defending a female who lay coiled nearby and watched with passionless, baleful eyes. The two males reared up in the air and tried to push each other to the ground. Magnus had thought of his own wrestling bouts with his cousins and felt grateful that he had arms to wrestle with. The snakes pushed each other's bodies and writhed and reared up while the female watched. Finally the intruder, exhausted, slunk away.

But what did it augur, this dream of the woman with the snakes?

There had been something else in it, he now remembered. A dark-skinned man in a loincloth, with the features of a South Sea Islander. But why wouldn't he dream of his own Malay miners?

He shook his head to clear it of sleep. Perhaps the vision he had seen was not a dream. It had a peculiar lucid reality to it, in spite of the hallucinatory strangeness. He knew the children had a way of communicating. Perhaps he had found the channel through which they contacted each other. But why would he be allowed access? Was it only because he was close, because Janie was sleeping in a nearby bedroom?

He struggled with the question, trying to make sense of it.

PART FIVE

Precipitation

1. (chemistry) the condensation of a solid from a solution during a chemical reaction
2. (meteorology) rain, snow, sleet, or hail that falls to the ground
3. the action of falling or being thrown down headlong
4. the fact or quality of acting suddenly and rashly

CHAPTER 36

John Frum, He Must Come

B enjamin found himself alone on a mat in a darkened hut. He didn't know how much time had passed. Hours? Days? Weeks? He felt weak, but he pushed himself to sitting and tried to stand. The room started to wobble, and he sat back down. The sour taste and the soreness in the back of his throat suggested that he had vomited, but when? He waited for the room to stop moving, then stood very slowly. His legs felt atrophied, and could barely support him. He looked down to see if they had shrunk. Dropping his head made the world spin as if his skull were a snow globe, his brain rotating freely inside. But his legs looked the same as they always did. He was wearing his khaki shorts and the shirt he had arrived in, filthy with dirt and kava and other things he didn't want to think about.

He had to get out of here.

He had come to a decision.

He took two shuffling steps toward the door, then two

more. Before he reached it, the door flew open, blinding him with bright sunlight. He jerked up his hand to protect his eyes and nearly fell over.

"John Frum!" cried the prophet in the faded Coca-Cola T-shirt, Benjamin's irrepressible discoverer and poisoner. "You sleep good!"

Benjamin cleared his throat. The way was clear. If he were John Frum, and acted like John Frum, then he might have some authority. He would be a god. He could get people to do what he wanted, and then they would stop seizing and drugging him and putting him in dark huts to hallucinate. He had to claim his rights, his destiny. Do the next thing. *Be John Frum*. He stepped outside and lifted his head painfully.

"I am John Frum," he said.

The man cried out with joy. "John Frum!"

"I am come," Benjamin said.

"He is come!"

"I will bring cargo."

"Cargo!" the man shouted.

"I have to throw up," Benjamin said, and he leaned into some nearby bushes. He wondered what the plants were, as he fed them the contents of his stomach. His father would know. They might be useful. He apologized silently to the plants, wiped his mouth, and straightened.

"Water," he said hoarsely to the man.

"Water, John Frum!" the man answered, and ran off into the trees.

Benjamin, left alone, stretched his legs, then shook them

out one at a time. He wanted to touch his toes but didn't trust that he would be able to stand up straight again. He did a little dance from one leg to the other. He held a tree for support and rotated each ankle. When he looked up, the prophet was back, holding a coconut shell. Benjamin reached for the shell and drank, feeling the water cool the back of his parched and burning throat.

The prophet watched with approval, then shifted from one leg to the other, rotating each ankle. He was imitating Benjamin's improvised stretching routine.

"What's your name?" Benjamin asked him.

"Toby Prophet," the man said.

At first Benjamin heard "Toby Profit," but then his mind got itself round the name as it must be intended. "Is that your real name?"

The man said a name so long that it would be impossible for Benjamin to say or remember.

Benjamin laughed, which made his ribs hurt. "Okay, Toby. Can I have some coconut meat?" he asked, pointing to the shell, and to a tree. "Fresh coconut?"

Toby Prophet disappeared through the trees and brought back a coconut. With a long curved knife, like a smallish machete, he stripped off the fibrous outer shell and chopped off the top. Benjamin thought of the delicate Malay dagger he'd seen on the cigar-smoking man's desk, and wondered where Janie was now.

"Drink," Toby said.

Benjamin drank the sweet coconut water. It wasn't cold,

but it was delicious. When the liquid was gone, Toby cut the shell in half with his sharp knife. He scraped out a strip of white coconut meat in demonstration, then handed the shell and the knife back to Benjamin.

Benjamin sat on the ground and tried it himself, awkwardly, unused to the curved blade, trying not to slice his thumb off. The coconut meat was soft and sweet, and he chewed happily. He was keeping food down, and they had trusted him with a knife. Things were looking up. He was going to get out of here. He just had to think clearly, and be godlike.

"Where are the boats?" he asked. He hadn't seen one on the island.

Toby Prophet looked blank.

"Boat," Benjamin said, and he mimed himself paddling a canoe, with the knife as a paddle. Then he held the coconut shell in his hand like a boat bobbing on the ocean.

"Far away," Toby said.

"Why far?" Benjamin asked. "You need to fish."

"Woman in boat is tabu," Toby said.

"Okay," Benjamin said, not understanding.

After a long explanation using Benjamin's coconut shell and some of his own language, Toby Prophet made it clear that women couldn't be in the same piece of water that a boat was in. It was part of their religion, a sacred prohibition, a tabu. But women needed to be in the water daily, for cleaning things, and therefore the boats had to be kept far from the place where women lived.

"Ah," Benjamin said. "Can I see one?"

"Woman?" Toby asked, with what seemed to Benjamin like false innocence.

"Boat," Benjamin said.

The man narrowed his eyes. "No boat."

"For cargo," Benjamin said.

"Cargo come," the man said.

"Of course it will," Benjamin said. "I just might need a way to—go get it."

But Toby Prophet was having none of this. His face shut down in suspicion: no more joyful smiles for Benjamin. "No boat, John Frum," he said.

Over the next few days, Benjamin grew stronger. He could turn his head without the world spinning, and his legs no longer felt like they might fold beneath him like a newborn colt's. He saw versions of his little leg-stretching dance everywhere he went. Men were trying it out, practicing, criticizing each other's technique.

Benjamin refused all offers of kava, and no one forced it on him. But he liked the two boys who made it, with their chewing and spitting. They looked no older than eight or nine, and they were sly and mischievous, not set in their ways. They were called Tessel and Salvation. They hadn't been alive during the war, when the navy brought jeeps and radios and Coca-Cola, so they didn't talk about cargo. Benjamin wasn't sure they even believed that he was John Frum. They ran free in the wonderland of their island, shinnying up trees for co-coconuts and swimming in blue water. What use did they have for squawking boxes?

The boys' ability to climb the coconut trees was so impressive that it seemed superhuman. Benjamin tried to climb one, and earned himself laughter for his un-godlike failure to get even a few feet off the ground. Both Tessel and Salvation could reach the top in a few seconds, like squirrels, and shinny down with a fat coconut tucked beneath one skinny elbow. They loved to be praised for their skill, and Benjamin's praise was real. They reminded him of Pip, in their agility. Pip could probably have climbed those trees.

The boys also spoke English better than any of the others. Missionaries and sailors had brought English to the islands long ago, and the boys' brains were like sponges. Benjamin found the two of them alone, drawing pictures in the sand. Tessel was an inch taller and the acknowledged leader.

"Tessel," Benjamin said casually. "You're a good swimmer."

"Very good," Tessel agreed.

"Are you good at paddling a boat?"

"Very good."

"Do you like to go out in a boat?"

Tessel eyed him warily. "Yes."

"Do you fish?" Benjamin asked, trying to deflect the boy's suspicion.

Salvation, still drawing in the sand, chanted, *"No boat for John Frum."* He sang it very quietly, as if reminding himself— and Tessel—of something they'd been told.

"Well, I understand that," Benjamin said, musing, looking out at the water. "But where are the boats hidden? I never see them. I mean, we have some *nice* boats where I come from. Sailboats, motorboats, canoes. I just wonder if yours are as nice."

"Very nice," Tessel said proudly, indignantly.

"Can't be as nice as ours."

"Yes. As nice."

"I'm not sure," Benjamin said. "I just want to see them. See if they're nice."

Tessel and Salvation looked at each other, some wordless communication passing between them. Tessel craned his skinny neck to see if anyone was watching.

"No boat for John Frum," Salvation repeated warningly.

But Tessel seemed less sure.

CHAPTER 37

Funny Business

Pip and Opal had been holed up in the Copley Square Hotel for two days, waiting for her grandfather to summon them. They ordered eggs Benedict and lemon meringue pie and root beer floats from room service. They read magazines, and Pip taught Opal the principles of blackjack. She was good at it.

"This is math, you know," he said.

"I'm terrible at math," she said.

"You're actually not."

She had stopped bothering to wear her heavy glasses, and he loved to look at her. Sometimes they even kissed, and that was nice. But there was no word from her grandfather, and Pip was thinking about trying to get a chess set when there was a pounding at the door.

Opal stared at Pip, her eyes deep wells of terror.

"Ask who it is," he whispered.

"Who is it?" she called.

"*Police*," said the voice.

"Play dumb," Pip whispered. Then he rolled off the bed and slipped into the closet, pulling the door closed after him.

"Just a minute!" Opal called.

Pip could see through the slats in the closet door that she had hooked the chain before she unlocked the door, so it could only open three inches. He saw a policeman's uniform through the gap.

"Is something wrong?" Opal asked innocently.

"You've been out of school for two days," the officer said.

"The first day was a Sunday," Opal said. "And I wasn't feeling well on Monday. I had a headache. I called and told the school that."

"You told them you were with your mother."

"Have you met my mother? She's no cure for a headache," Opal said, with a smile in her voice. She was flirting with the cop just the right amount.

"Well, you can't just run off and stay in a hotel," the officer said, softening.

"Why not?"

"How about you come with us, and we'll go see your mother."

"I need to make myself presentable first," she said.

"For your mother?"

"*Especially* for my mother," she said. "I'll meet you in the lobby in fifteen minutes."

A pause. "Okay. We'll be downstairs. No funny business."

Opal closed the door and made a little panicked squeaking noise.

Pip crawled out of the closet. "You were perfect!" he whispered.

"*Now* what?" She hopped a little, as if to shake off the fear.

"We go out the back way."

"I *told* you my grandfather wouldn't send for us."

"It'll be fine. Just stay calm."

Pip studied the fire escape plan and found the staircase that led to the back of the hotel. He looked out through the peephole and saw no one. They crept out silently, down the lushly carpeted hall, and past the elevators to the emergency stairs. Then they ran down three flights to the exit.

"Just walk out casually, like nothing's wrong," Pip said.

"Okay," Opal said.

He pushed the heavy door open, feeling the cold air on his face, and stepped outside, with Opal following. Behind the door, as it closed, were two policemen. One of them grabbed the back of Pip's collar. The other caught Opal by the arm. "No funny business, sweetheart, remember?" he said.

"Go!" Opal shouted. "Run!"

Pip shrugged out of his jacket, leaving it in the policeman's fist, and ran toward the street. At the corner he turned and headed for the river. He could hear the heavy footsteps coming after him. What was ahead of him? A subway station. He might duck down there, but what if no train was coming? He cleared the hotel and kept running, the gray brick wall of a library looming to his left. Should he run in there? Get lost in the books? He might stay the night in the stacks, if he kept out of the coppers' way. Most of the books Pip had read in his life were because libraries were good places to hide. But the policeman would see him going in. So no library. The sidewalk was full of people. He dodged shoppers and idlers and ran past a florist, a jeweler, a diner, a typewriter repair shop.

Then the crowd seemed to part, revealing an enormous policeman who snatched Pip out of the air, tucking him under his arm as if catching a rugby ball. Pip struggled, but the man had him tight, and you didn't want to hit a copper. He relaxed under the policeman's arm, and as he did, he saw Opal standing on the sidewalk up ahead. She was talking to a tiny woman in a fur coat and high heels, with tightly coiled black hair. Her mother, the princess.

The enormous copper set Pip down and pushed him into a waiting police car.

Opal and her mother turned, and Opal looked like she'd been crying.

"Don't cry," Pip called, and he waved. His tour of America wouldn't be complete, after all, until he sussed out the inside of their jails.

CHAPTER 38

The Gap

Jin Lo was impatient to get to Benjamin, but the apothecary refused to move fast. He had already made the avian elixir, but he said he wanted to be prepared for every possible outcome. He was fussing and measuring in Vinoray's laboratory, turning pages in the Pharmacopoeia, squinting at labels written in Spanish, Chinese, and Tagalog.

"We lose time," Jin Lo said.

"When you are in a hurry, dress slowly," the apothecary said.

"This means what?"

"It's a Zen Buddhist saying. It means that when you rush, you make mistakes."

"When I am in hurry, I dress *quickly*," Jin Lo said. "I make no mistakes."

"Yes, but you are a supremely competent human being," the apothecary said. "I am a mere mortal, and I'm taking no chances."

"What chances? We fly, we go."

"You saw my son fall from the sky."

"So?" she asked.

"So it could happen to us. We must guard against every circumstance we can predict."

"Then I know what will happen," Jin Lo said.

"What?"

"The circumstance we *do not* predict."

The apothecary sighed. "Well, at least we'll have eliminated the others," he said. "Our work is an ongoing struggle with unintended consequences. We must try to narrow the gap—which is sometimes a gulf—between what we *intend* and the results we *achieve*." He held a beaker of cloudy liquid up to the light and watched it swirl. "This solution will allow us to breathe underwater if we fall into the sea."

"Unless we are dead."

"Well, yes," the apothecary said. "We might be stunned by the fall, certainly. But if we can breathe underwater, we have a better chance of survival, and a better chance of reaching Benjamin."

Jin Lo had always wanted to be able to swim beneath the waves, like a fish. She reached for the beaker, but the apothecary pulled it away.

"Let me try it first," he said. "It might not be safe."

He drank some of the liquid, held the beaker and stood very still, looking thoughtfully into space, as if analyzing a fine wine. Then he said, "It's not as malty as it sight've been."

Jin Lo frowned. "Malty?"

"No, oh," he said. "I santed to way *salty*."

"Salty," she said.

"Yes," he said. "Sike the lea."

Jin Lo understood that something was wrong in the way he was speaking, and that she should be able to decode it, but English always took some effort for her. She had learned it from American missionaries, and the apothecary's vowels were different from theirs. Now his consonants were different, too, and she couldn't follow the scrambling.

The apothecary shook his head in frustration. "I'm baying things sackward."

"Backward?"

"Swell, witched," he said. "It's a soblematic pride effect." Then he brightened. "Mait a winute!" he said. He rummaged in his black leather medical bag, came up with a jar of dried mushrooms, unscrewed the lid, and handed a piece of mushroom to her. "Thew chis," he said, and he put one in his own mouth and chewed.

Jin Lo put the dried mushroom in her mouth and tasted the familiar earthy fungus. They had used it in Vietnam to acquire the language faster, before she left them.

Meanwhile, the apothecary filled a deep sink with water. He plunged his face in and held it underwater a very long time, until Jin Lo wondered if she should pull him out. Then he came up dripping, triumphant.

"Wit irks!" he cried, and she understood him: *It works!*

But with a problematic side effect. He could survive underwater, but he couldn't talk straight.

"As wirds we bon't be table to alk anyway," he rationalized.

Jin Lo nodded. It was true. Once they were birds, they would be relying on looks and gestures and avian understanding. She wondered if their birdcalls would be affected. She drank the salty liquid and concentrated on saying "Not so bad," but it came out "Bot no sad."

Then the apothecary drank the avian elixir, and she watched him greedily. She loved being a falcon, fierce and beholden to no one. She watched his head shrink and his shoulders tip forward and his legs sprout sharp talons. Snowy white feathers sprouted all over his head, and then they seemed to flow down the front of his body, downy soft to absorb sound so he could fly unheard. His eyes grew large and yellow, and his nose and mouth drew out into a sharp and dangerous beak. His arms spread out into broad wings for floating, and he lifted his powerful shoulders, articulating the complicated joints. When the transformation was complete, he rotated his head to test the vertebrae, and shook his whole body, ruffling each immaculate feather into place.

Where the apothecary had been was a large white owl, staring at Jin Lo with depthless golden eyes. She would never get over the wonder of it.

CHAPTER 39

Floating

Magnusson posted a guard outside Janie's bedroom at night, but she caught the guard sleeping and crept out into the silent house, searching for some clue about why, exactly, Magnusson was trying to lure her friends, and what he knew about them. There was a telephone in the kitchen and she picked up the receiver, wondering if she could call her parents in Ann Arbor. But a finger came down to end the connection. Sylvia was standing there in a blue silk nightgown. "Go to bed, Janie," she said. "Please don't make this harder than it is."

In the morning, at breakfast, the telephone was gone. Janie fired questions at Magnusson, but he ignored them and went off in the jeep. She guessed he was going to the mine.

The guards were Americans, and none of them was particularly smart or especially kind. Another guard was posted outside her room that night, but she had more reason than he did to stay awake. When he finally fell asleep, she crept outside. There was a guard on patrol around the perimeter and she waited for him to pass, then ran silently, barefoot, for the fence, intending to climb it. As soon as she touched the wire, it threw her back on the grass, where she lay stunned, her hands stinging and one ankle aching. The guard hauled her off the ground and dumped her back in her room. Sylvia brought an ice pack and explained that the wire was electrified, and that Janie's weight had been on her right ankle when the electricity passed through her body, seeking the ground.

"Yeah, I figured that out," Janie said.

"I wish you wouldn't fight so hard," Sylvia said.

"You mean I should give in and be like you?"

"I mean you're just hurting yourself."

"What does Magnusson know about my friends?"

"Just what he told you. He's interested in what they can do. And he knows you have some way of communicating."

Janie spent the rest of the night searching for Benjamin, hoping to catch even a tiny glimpse that told her he was alive. But she found nothing.

In the morning, she put on her swimsuit and dived into the saltwater swimming pool. The water tasted like blood on her lips as she swam, or like tears. She started to cry for the first time, underwater where no one could see her, and imagined she was filling the pool.

After that, she spent most of her time in the pool. She wasn't sure sometimes, as she floated on her back, where her own body stopped and the water started. Maybe everything was connected. Maybe her lifelong conviction that she was Janie

Scott, independent person with independent thoughts and control over her own destiny, was all an illusion. She was just a salty, water-based extension of the pool, in a black tank suit.

The sun shone pink through her eyelids. When she opened her eyes a millimeter, she saw bright stars refracting through the droplets of water on her eyelashes. Her winter skin was getting tan. Her fingertips pruned in the water. But she didn't get out. The pool was the only place she could forget the sharp talons sinking into Benjamin's neck.

Sylvia appeared on the pool deck, wearing a white cover-up and a worried expression. "Janie," she called. "Come have a lemonade."

Janie dropped her hips so she sank beneath the surface, her hair floating around her head. She blew out all her air. If she stayed on the bottom, Sylvia couldn't talk to her. But eventually she would have to breathe again. The apothecary should work on a way to breathe underwater. *That* would be useful. She rose to the surface and put her head up into the world where everything had happened.

Sylvia wore cat-eye sunglasses and yellow mules. Janie pushed herself out of the water, imagining that she was a sea lion, or a mermaid, and sat on the tiled edge.

"Osman put mint in it," Sylvia said, handing her the lemonade.

Janie stirred the bright green leaves with a straw. Osman, the cook, wasn't that much older than Janie. He had been a cook in the sultan's household before Magnusson brought him to the island, and he grew mint and herbs and vegetables in a little patch of carefully tended soil outside the villa's kitchen.

Sylvia kicked off her mules and dangled her legs in the pool. "You can't stay in the water all day."

"Why not?"

"Well, it's hell on your hair, first of all."

Janie twirled a strand of wet hair around her finger and brought it in front of her eyes. It looked the same as always. Brown. Wavy. *American*, Benjamin had said. She wanted to get back in the pool and drown the pain in her chest. "Looks all right to me," she said.

"The salt water dries it out," Sylvia said.

"What a tragedy." Janie let the strand go and sipped her lemonade, which was cold and sweet. She kicked her leg to see the little ripples in the water catch the light.

"So much sun will be bad for your skin, in the long run," Sylvia said.

Janie looked up. "The *long run*? Are you serious?"

"When you're my age, you'll care," Sylvia said.

Janie tucked her leg up to turn toward the secretary. "You've kidnapped me," she said, "and taken me to an island in Malaya. No one knows where I am. My best friend in the world is almost certainly dead, and if he weren't, you would have some terrible plan for him. And your boss, or your boyfriend, or whatever he is, has told me that no one will ever find me again. You really think I'm worried about the *long* run? About *wrinkles*?"

Sylvia frowned.

Janie turned back to face the pool and concentrated on her lemonade—the cold feel of it on her tongue, on the back of her throat, going down her esophagus.

"Magnusson was good to me after my brother died," Sylvia said.

"Yeah, you said that," Janie said.

"I still miss him every day."

Janie looked sideways at Sylvia, who had a faraway look. "How was he killed?"

"He went to Korea in 1950. They sent him with almost no training. It was terribly cold, and they were short of weapons. The Chinese came in overwhelming numbers, in warm, snow-camouflage uniforms. They'd been trained to fight in the mountains, and they killed our boys as they ran for their lives. My brother came home dead."

"I'm so sorry," Janie said.

"I think about him all the time. How funny he was, and handsome, how he walked into a room and people wanted to be near him. And how cold he must have been, and how afraid. Three years the war went on, boys like him dying every day. President Truman should have used the atomic bomb to stop it."

Janie was startled. "You think so?"

"All those boys would be alive now, and home," Sylvia said. "The North Korean army killed everyone with any education, in the occupied areas. They just shot all the professors and teachers and leaders so there would be no one to stand against them. We could have ended the war so easily, and ended a terrible government."

"But we would have killed people who had nothing to do with it," Janie said.

"We did that anyway," Sylvia said. "My brother had nothing

to do with it—with a made-up border across a country we didn't understand. None of those boys did."

Janie looked at Sylvia's pretty face, contorted with anger, and with the desire for atomic revenge. There was some connection here. "Why does Magnusson want my friends?" she asked.

Sylvia sighed. "I honestly don't know, Janie. He keeps parts of his business secret from me. I'd tell you if I knew."

"But you know how far back this goes. How did Opal happen to be my roommate?"

Sylvia hesitated. "I'm not sure."

"*Don't* lie to me," Janie said. "You owe me the truth. Did Magnusson get me into Grayson?"

"I'm sure you would have got in anyway."

"So the answer is yes."

"He did get you the scholarship."

For a moment, that almost seemed worse than everything else. Janie hadn't gotten the scholarship on her own. "What if my parents had made me go to Michigan with them?" she asked.

Sylvia glanced around the empty pool deck.

"No one's listening," Janie said. "Just tell me."

"He's very intuitive about people," Sylvia said. "He knew your parents would let you go to Grayson, if there was money for it. They think of you as very exceptional. Which, I mean—they're right to think that, of course."

Janie stared at her. "So he was counting on my parents' vanity about me."

"I'd call it their pride in you."

"What else does he think about them?"

"I don't think we should be having this conversation."

"What harm can it do?" Janie asked. "Here we are."

There was a pause. "Well, he knows about their political troubles," Sylvia said. "Not that anyone thinks they're really Communists. But points of vulnerability are always of interest. You're their primary point of vulnerability, and the political trouble is secondary."

Janie looked at Sylvia, with her methodical categories, her primary and secondary points of vulnerability. So much of her had gone into taking care of Magnusson and his affairs. It would be hard for her to walk away, even if she knew he was doing wrong.

"What about me?" Janie asked. "What's my point of vulnerability?" She thought of her tender, witty mother, and her father's goofy laugh. She thought of Benjamin, with his copper-flecked eyes.

Sylvia blushed. "We shouldn't be having this conversation."

"*Tell me,*" Janie said.

"Well—it's your ambition."

Janie was startled. "That's not true."

"Yes it is."

"Not Benjamin?" Janie asked. She'd been careful not to name him before, but it came out, in her surprise. "Not my parents?"

"No," Sylvia said. "You're *their* point of vulnerability. But they aren't yours."

"Are you sure?" Janie asked. It was dawning on her, slowly. To lure Benjamin, they'd taken Janie. To lure Janie, they'd taken—her chemistry experiment. Was Magnusson right?

Had she become so single-minded that her point of vulnerability was a bunch of glassware and a titrating apparatus, and not the people she loved?

Sylvia gave her a look of sympathy. "It's okay to be ambitious," she said. "It's hard for women to make a mark. You have to be determined."

"But *people* are more important."

Sylvia nodded. "I think so."

Janie hadn't told her parents that she'd been kicked out of school and moved in with strangers. She hadn't told them anything, so she could keep working on her chemistry experiment. And she had reached out to Benjamin only when they took her experiment, *because* they'd taken her experiment. And now Benjamin was dead. The thought flooded her with sadness. "The way you think about your brother every day," she said, "I think about Benjamin."

"Except that you'll see him again," Sylvia said.

"I don't think so," Janie said. "You didn't ask me who Benjamin was. Because you already knew."

"Yes."

"How much does Magnusson know?"

"A lot. He knows about Benjamin's father."

"So what does he want them for?"

"I couldn't tell you. Even if I knew. But I promise you I don't."

There might be more questions to ask, but Janie couldn't stand to have Sylvia looking so *sorry* for her anymore. She put her lemonade glass down, lifted her hips off the tile, and slipped feet first back into the pool.

CHAPTER 40

Sprung

The police dumped Pip unceremoniously in a holding cell at the Boston police station, and he picked himself up and grabbed the bars. "What am I in here for?" he demanded.

"Kidnapping a socialite," said the officer.

"I didn't kidnap her!"

"Her mother says you did."

"Well, her mother's wrong. Your mum ever been wrong about you and a girl?"

"You were in a hotel with her."

"I was *leaving* a hotel with her. That's no crime!"

"We were trying to question her," the officer said. "You ran."

"You were chasing me!"

"Seems like her roommate disappeared, too. Jane Scott. You might've had something to do with it."

"That's crazy! I haven't even *seen* her roommate!" Pip was trying not to get riled, but the accusation was ridiculous.

"We'll see what the detectives say."

"I get to make a phone call."

The cop hesitated. "Make it fast."

Pip thought about his options. There weren't many people he knew in America. He took a gamble, and asked the operator for the Italian restaurant in Grayson, New Hampshire.

"Which Italian restaurant, sir?" the operator asked.

"I forgot what it's called," Pip said. "Something with a *B*. Wait—*Bruno's*."

"Just a moment, sir."

Pip hoped Giovanna, the woman from the restaurant, would answer the telephone. She'd said she had a brother who was a lawyer. But instead, a waiter with a young voice answered. "Do you know a girl named Janie Scott?" Pip asked.

"Yes!" the kid said, and his urgency came straight over the telephone line. "Where *is* she? Are you the one who talked to my aunt?"

Jackpot. Pip grinned. The kid had a lawyer uncle, *and* he had a crush on Janie.

Two hours later, the kid turned up with his uncle the lawyer, who spoke perfect English, wore a nice suit, and made a big fuss about how the police had no actual charges to bring against Pip. He said that Pip was a celebrity, a television star, a *national treasure*—Pip liked that one—and the British consulate was going to be unhappy if the police didn't let him go.

Pip studied the nephew while the negotiations went on. He was handsome in that soft way girls liked, with black curls falling loose across his forehead. Pip started to wonder about

Benjamin's reasons for sending him to rescue Janie. Then Pip was free, and the uncle left, telling the two boys to stay the hell out of trouble after this.

It was cold outside, and Pip hugged his jacket to his body. He'd thought America was going to be so bloody glamorous, but it was *freezing* here, and the jails weren't much nicer than in London.

Raffaello said, "My aunt told me that some short English kid came looking for Janie right after she left."

"I'm not *that* short," Pip said.

"You're pretty short."

"Why weren't you at the dance at Grayson?" Pip asked.

"I don't go there. I had a rehearsal for a play at my own school."

"You're an actor?"

"Well, I don't know. I'm in a play. It's not like being on television or anything."

Pip was surprised by how unimportant being on television seemed now—except in that it had helped get him sprung from jail. He decided he trusted Raffaello. "So listen," he said. "I went to that dance, but Janie wasn't there. Her roommate, Opal, thinks she's on some island in Malaya."

"Malaya?"

"That's what Opal thinks. We sent a telegram to her grandfather, who's a sultan. I was hoping he'd send a plane for us."

"Where's Opal now?"

"She was with me when I got arrested, but they didn't bring her in. They probably took her home."

"So what do we do now?"

"We try to help Janie."

"In Malaya?" the kid said. "Do you know how far *away* that is?"

"So let's get started!"

They stared at each other a minute, then Raffaello shook his head and said, "I can't. I have a shift at the restaurant tonight."

At the word *restaurant,* Pip's stomach grumbled. He was cold and hungry, and almost out of money. He had no boat, no plane, no car. The restaurant sounded cozy and warm. They could go there and eat, and he would figure out how to get to Malaya tomorrow.

So they climbed onto the same worn-out bus Pip had taken to Boston with Opal for the two-hour ride back to Grayson. Raffaello got out a dog-eared paperback script to study.

"What's the play?" Pip asked.

Raffaello showed him the cover: *A Midsummer Night's Dream,* by William Shakespeare.

"Any good?" Pip asked.

"Sure," Raffaello said. "I think so."

"Are the girls in it pretty?"

Raffaello blushed. "I guess."

"Best reason to be an actor, in my opinion," Pip said, settling into his seat. "Loads of pretty girls. You in love with Janie?"

The boy's blush deepened. "Who wants to know?"

"My mate Benjamin, I think."

"It's none of his business."

"I'd say that means *yes.*"

"Look, I got you out of jail because you're Janie's friend," Raffaello said. "You made me late for work, and I haven't learned my scenes. What else do you want from me?"

"Nothing," Pip said. "Want help running lines?"

"*No.*" Raffaello frowned in concentration and started mouthing the words silently, and Pip left him to it.

In Grayson, they stepped through the back door of Bruno's restaurant into a bright, warm, busy kitchen. It smelled of delicious things to eat: grilling steak and tomato sauce and sizzling butter. The room was full of cooks and busboys in white, but there were also two people in dark overcoats, a man and a woman, talking to Raffaello's aunt on the other side of the room. Something about the two of them tugged at Pip's memory.

Giovanna waved Raffaello over, and the couple turned. They had worried, intelligent faces, and Pip recognized them at the same moment they recognized him. They were Janie's parents, Mr. and Mrs. Scott. Their faces brightened: hope mingling with despair.

Those looks made Pip think he was no actor, not really, because he could never fake an expression like that. It was how it looked when someone was the whole world to you, and was lost, and you would do anything to get them back.

CHAPTER 41

Escape

A great feast was held on the island, to celebrate the coming of the magnificent John Frum. An island pig was roasted, and there were bananas and yams, breadfruit and coconuts. Benjamin was served first, as a sign of honor. He ate everything that was given to him, knowing he had a long journey ahead. But he didn't drink the kava. He tossed the contents of his bowl into the bushes when he was sure no one was looking. He had no desire for more visions, or for more retching. His fellow banqueters had a better tolerance for the stuff than he did, but still they got drunker and wilder as the feast wore on.

Through the firelight, Benjamin caught Tessel's eye. The boy was eating roasted yam, scooping the soft orange flesh into his mouth. He nodded to Benjamin, clear-eyed and sober. Tessel's father was a master navigator and the boy was his apprentice, which was going to come in handy.

The other boy, Salvation, was alert and watchful, too. While one of the island's leaders gave a long speech in the language Benjamin still couldn't understand, Salvation trailed away into the darkness. Then Tessel vanished, too.

Benjamin waited, as agreed, taking thirty slow breaths. Then he stood, casually.

Toby Prophet, beside him, caught his arm. "Where you go, John Frum?"

"To—you know, relieve myself," Benjamin said. "To take a piss."

"Ah!" the prophet said, laughing. He clapped Benjamin on the back. "You drink too much kava, John Frum!"

No, *you* drink too much kava, Benjamin thought as he slipped away into the trees. The firelight had made him night-blind, so he made his way carefully in the direction of the hidden boats, waiting for his eyes to adjust. As he walked, the ground became clearer, the trees more visible. The water sparkled beyond the shore.

Tessel and Salvation had a small wooden boat, about sixteen feet long, waiting in the hidden cove. Benjamin waded into the water and then swam out, trying not to splash. Tessel helped haul him up, and Benjamin sat dripping in the cockpit. They hadn't had much opportunity to talk or plan. "You have food?" he asked. "And water?"

"Yes," Tessel said. The tone of his voice said that of *course* they had food and water. Did Benjamin think they were idiots? Or children?

But they *were* children, of course. These small boys were his guides, his rescuers, his hope. Benjamin looked to Salvation, hoping to gain confidence from the boy's solemn face, but the child in the stern wasn't Salvation. It was a girl, with her hair in short pigtails. The night was dark, but Benjamin was quite sure it was a girl.

"Who are you?" he asked her.

"Efa," she said.

"You speak English?"

She nodded uncertainly.

He looked back to Tessel. "Where's Salvation?"

"He stays," Tessel said.

Benjamin had gotten used to the idea of fleeing with Tessel and Salvation, but this was new. The punishment would be worse for a girl. "We must take her back," he said.

"No!" the girl cried, then she clamped her hands over her mouth. "Please," she said more softly, between her fingers.

Tessel's face was jumping with nervousness. "She is in boat now," he said. "It is tabu."

Was this a bluff? Benjamin understood that girls weren't supposed to be in boats, or even to be in the water with them. But would the islanders hurt her for it? He didn't know. "If she goes back *now*, they won't know," he said.

"She wants to sail," Tessel said. "To learn."

"Yes," Efa said, pleading.

Tessel took her hand. "I can't make kava now," he said. "We go."

Benjamin looked at the children's linked hands—the girl defying the tabu for a life at sea, the kava-maker despoiled by contact with a girl—and realized that they were not here to help him escape. They were escaping themselves. He was not being rescued; he was aiding and abetting runaways.

Tessel had already raised the sail, and the breeze picked up briskly, as if commanded by a god. The sail filled and tightened, and the boat slid away from the island. Tessel adjusted the lines, watching the top of the sail. Efa watched him work. Then she looked shyly at Benjamin and patted a bundle by her side. "Food," she said.

He nodded, resigned. The end result was the same: They were getting away.

Tessel studied the stars for their position and pushed the tiller to catch more wind. The three fugitives headed out of the hidden cove through a gap in the island's protective reef, to sea.

CHAPTER 42

Bird People

As morning broke, a falcon and a snowy white owl flew over the island where they had determined that Benjamin must be. They had been flying by night, to avoid the notice of hunters and fishermen. The white owl wore a small leather canister on his back, attached with a clever harness that kept the canister clear of his wings. It had been designed for carrier pigeons by a German apothecary, to deliver medication to a sanitarium, and Marcus Burrows had adapted it for his own use.

The morning sun glinted pink on the water. The air was soft and expectant, not yet shimmering with the full day's heat. The two birds, with their extraordinary vision, capable of seeing a mouse ear twitch a mile away, scanned the thatch huts for a sandy-haired boy sporting a nasty sunburn, but the island was still asleep.

They saw signs of a recent feast: a smoking fire pit, the carcass of a pig stripped bare, kava bowls made from coconuts abandoned on the ground. The island seemed to be suffering a hangover from the night before.

So the birds didn't expect
the swift arrow that shot out
of the glowing, sleepy morning. It
whizzed, unlooked-for, through the air
and pierced the owl's snowy wing. He gave a surprised cry
and began to plummet toward the ground, tilting helplessly.
The falcon screamed. The owl tried to right himself, but his
wing was shot through.

Crashing into the canopy of trees, he grabbed at a branch
with his talons, but the weight of the leather canister tilted
him backward. He tried to fly, but there was no space between
the lush branches to spread his good wing.

The falcon swept between the leaves, her wing tips clearing the branches by a hairsbreadth, and followed him down.

The owl landed heavily on the ground and began to grow.
A man in a loincloth and a faded red T-shirt came out
of the trees with a bow in his hand and stood over
the helpless white bird, whose legs were getting longer. Jin Lo perched on a branch, out of sight. The
straps of the owl's harness snapped as his body
grew, as they were designed to. The owl's skull
was growing larger, his feathers retracting,
his wings becoming arms.

The man with the bow retrieved
his arrow and watched the
transformation. His shirt
said *Coca-Cola*. He

was startled and interested, Jin Lo thought, but not astonished. Possibly he had already seen this thing happen to Benjamin. Jin Lo breathed slowly, to keep her mind and body calm. Stress, fear, and pain caused the avian elixir to wear off too soon, and for now she was more useful as a falcon.

The apothecary sat on the ground in his simple cotton clothes. His left arm was bleeding through his shirt where the arrow had gone through his wing. He held his good hand up for protection.

"Please," he said to the man. "Shon't doot me."

"You birdmen," the man said, without seeming to notice the apothecary's scrambled words. There was hot rancor in his voice. "You come from sky. You say John Frum, you say cargo. I very happy. Then you steal boat, you steal kava boy, you steal girl, you go. You tricky bad. This boy is not John Frum."

"No," the apothecary said simply.

The man looked at him with curiosity and the faintest trace of hope. "You John Frum?"

"No," the apothecary said.

The man looked forlorn. "He *must* come."

The apothecary clutched his bleeding arm. He could say nothing that the man wanted to hear. He could barely say anything that the man—or anyone else—could understand.

The man pointed to the leather canister. "What is this?"

"Medicine," the apothecary said.

"Poison?"

"No."

"Give me."

The apothecary hesitated, but when the man pulled out a curved knife, he handed the little leather canister over.

"You come with me," the man ordered.

The apothecary stood awkwardly, one-armed, and glanced up at the falcon, then allowed himself to be marched at knife-point through the trees. Jin Lo moved from branch to branch overhead as she followed. She tried not to become agitated. It would do no good for her to tumble from the trees as a woman.

In a clearing, two other men seized the apothecary by the arms. He cried out, but they ignored his injury and tied him with rough twine to a tree in a small clearing. The man in the Coca-Cola T-shirt slid the glass vials from the leather canister out onto the ground. He called to some women, who hurried off on a task that Jin Lo didn't quite understand. She had missed a few words.

Jin Lo caught herself, with a start. *She had missed a few words.* Otherwise she understood what the people were saying. She had read a description of the island's grammar in her book, and a translation of some vocabulary, but that was all. The mushroom the apothecary had given her to help with his scrambled consonants had amplified her small knowledge of the language so that she could assemble meaning. She paid closer attention.

The man in the red T-shirt said that the birdman was not John Frum. John Frum would come from the sky, but *in an airplane*—everyone knew that. The boy had tricked them, and now this second birdman had come to do the same. They would not bring cargo. They would only bring poison. At this, the man took a heavy rock and crushed the glass vials. Jin Lo watched all of the apothecary's careful preparation spill out on the ground, muddying the dirt among the glass shards. So much for dressing slowly.

But the man was still talking. The bird people would steal the island's boats, he said. They would steal the island's daughters, and their best, most precious kava-makers. But the people, *his* people, knew what to do. It was ancient knowledge. They would take the birdman's power. They would revenge the theft of their children. And they would punish the bird people for daring to impersonate their god.

Jin Lo suddenly understood the words she had missed. The women had been sent for dry *kindling*, to make a *cookfire*. They were going to roast the apothecary over a fire, and eat him.

CHAPTER 43

The Mine

Janie lay in the dark in her room in the compound on the island. Her mind kept circling around the fact that she had found Benjamin and asked him to help her, and he had died trying to come to her rescue. She longed to be able to switch off her thoughts and go to sleep. But then she saw a flicker of something. The dark sea, near the surface of the water. A sliver of sail buffeted by the wind. Was Benjamin there? She couldn't tell. It was too dark. The whole scene was flickering, fading.

Janie waited, but the image was gone. She opened her eyes and felt dizzy. It *had* been Benjamin. It had been a feeble signal. But she was sure that Benjamin was alive, in a small boat. She sat up in the dark room, full of new resolution.

She took her shoes in her hand and pushed her bedroom door open. The hallway was empty. They must have decided she was too depressed and apathetic to need a guard anymore. She slipped silently down the hall in her pajamas. The front door of the house was locked, but the long windows on either side were open for the breeze. She took down one of the window screens, and was able to squeeze out through the gap.

She crossed the terrace to the lawn barefoot before putting on her shoes. She was sure the mine had something to do with the reason Magnusson wanted Benjamin and his father. She had to get there. But first she had to turn off the power to the electrified fence.

There were four white cottages that served as barracks for the guards, below the main house. If there was a way to turn off the fence, it might be near where the guards lived.

Silently, she made her way down to the cottages. A light came from one of the doors, and she heard voices. There was a card game going on: four men around a table.

The man with his back to the door had his hair cut short, but it grew in distinctive whorls behind his ears: Janie knew those whorls. It was the pilot they'd picked up in Siberia, who never spoke. But he was speaking now—not in Russian but in a drawling, plummy British accent.

Janie gasped as she recognized the voice, and the pilot turned and looked out into the dark. Janie drew back, pressing herself against the wall. It was bright in the barracks and dark outside, so he might not have seen her, but *she had seen him.*

He had a shock of short-cropped white hair in front, where he used to have soft brown curls. His face was older and more weathered than it had been when he was a Latin teacher, as if ten years had passed and not two. She couldn't believe she hadn't recognized him in all those hours on the plane. He had always worn his helmet and goggles, but had never seemed to be hiding himself. Or maybe she just hadn't been paying the right kind of attention. She had been too distracted and upset by the thought of Benjamin in the clutches of some giant bird.

The pilot returned to his card game. No one came outside to look for her. The men were talking about the hand Mr. Danby had just played, and about his damned luck. Because it *was* Mr. Danby. She'd been sure he was dead.

Danby knew how to fly a plane, of course, having been a pilot in the RAF in the war. On her first day in his Latin class, he had asked if she was an Isabel Archer or a Daisy Miller, as an American girl in England. Then he had betrayed his country and left her alone on the deck of a Soviet destroyer to be poisoned by the radiation from a hydrogen bomb. And now he was winning at cards in Magnusson's barracks.

"Ill met by moonlight," a quiet voice said.

She whirled and saw Magnusson standing behind her in the dark, wearing a dark red silk dressing gown. His blond hair was mussed, as if he had come straight from sleep. He motioned her away from the barracks and she followed, full of questions.

"Let's not disturb their game," he murmured as they walked away from the voices and the light.

"Why is Danby here?" she asked in a whisper.

"I was half asleep," Magnusson said, "wondering when you would try to sneak out of your room again, when I had the strangest dream. It was of a girl's hands, taking the screen from a window near the main door. And then I was walking down toward the barracks, barefoot. I woke and thought—what would an analyst say of this dream? That my feminine side is interested in the lives of the pilots? But then I thought, no. The analyst would be wrong. This is a practical dream, a useful dream, and I wasn't even truly asleep. The dream is telling me the answer to my question. It's telling me something that is happening *right now*."

They were at the equipment shed, and Magnusson threw a switch on the wall and motioned for Janie to get into a golf cart. She climbed in, determined to learn more about what Danby was doing here.

"I don't think that I have acquired psychic powers," Magnusson said as he backed the golf cart with its quiet electric motor out of the shed. "Not at my age. You must explain to me how it works. Did you slip me something? In my food? On the plane? Did Sylvia help you? Or Osman?"

Janie shook her head.

"Was it at the restaurant?" Magnusson asked, watching her face in the moonlight, and then he laughed. "Ah, of course! So long ago! I am a fool. I could have been using it all this time. I congratulate you. And I thank you for including me."

The gate in the electrified fence was standing open. They drove through, and it closed behind them. Janie found her voice. "Tell me why Danby is here," she said.

"There's something he wants," Magnusson said. "Why does anyone go anywhere? But please—what was it, exactly, that you slipped me?"

"A powder."

"And how does it work?"

"I don't know."

"I had another dream," Magnusson said. "Three nights ago, of snakes and intestines. Any idea what that was about?"

"Just your evil, unconscious mind at work."

"You flatter me," Magnusson said.

They were on the road outside the villa, and she could feel and smell water close by—the little lagoon. Then they were in the trees, on the narrow waist of the island. She wondered if there were animals here, and listened for noises in the brush.

Then the island opened up again, and Magnusson stopped the golf cart among a cluster of small wooden buildings. The buildings seemed sturdy, if very small, and they all looked the same. Company houses, she guessed, for the miners. But there were no bulldozers, and no earthmoving equipment. Magnusson climbed out of the golf cart, and she followed him.

They walked among the silent, sleeping houses, toward a larger building like a warehouse. She felt a humming coming from beneath her feet. Magnusson pulled open a garage door, and the humming grew louder. She followed him inside, and in the dimness she could see a bulldozer, a truck, two rows of long tables, and a simple steel kitchen against one wall. Magnusson led her toward two elevator doors. One was normal sized, and one much larger, like a cargo elevator.

Magnusson drew out a key and turned it in a switch. Janie heard cables moving as the smaller elevator rose to the surface. When it opened, they stepped inside.

"I'm so pleased that you've come," Magnusson said as they

descended. "It's very frustrating to own a remarkable thing and not be able to show it off."

Then the elevator door opened again, and Janie stepped out into the worst place she'd ever been. It was hot and dark and strangely lit, below the ground, and there was a smell of dirt and gasoline. Narrow train tracks ran in both directions. Two carts with open-topped bins stood on the tracks. Janie thought the whole area beneath the village must have been excavated. It looked so little like a mine from above. There were pipes running along the rough ceiling, which must carry water—and maybe air?

"It's quite something, isn't it?" Magnusson asked.

"Why is it hidden?"

"So that people won't see it."

"What are you mining?"

"Uranium, of course," Magnusson said. "We do the milling beneath the ground, also. It's a remarkable feat of engineering, this mine, and the mill. A little tricky to dispose of the tailings."

"Is it radioactive?"

Magnusson laughed. "*Uranium?* Yes, that's the whole point, my dear." He frowned comically. "Don't tell me I've made a mistake, thinking you intelligent."

"But isn't it dangerous, to have everything enclosed underground?"

"Oh, if you were down here year after year, I suppose," he said. "But not for a quick tour."

"Do the miners know it's dangerous?"

"Perhaps. They are not men with many options."

"So they're slaves?"

"No, no!" Magnusson said. "I simply mean that we are each born to our station in life. And we make the best of it." He took two hard hats from hooks and handed one to Janie.

Janie looked at the yellow helmet. "The thing Danby wants," she said. "It's the uranium, isn't it?"

"Put that hat on," Magnusson said. "Protect that clever little head."

Janie wondered if this was her chance to run. There was no key switch to go up in the elevator, just a call button. But Magnusson was strong and determined, and right beside her. She'd never make it. She put on the hard hat and followed him. Her mind tumbled over the new information, putting it together.

"Who's the uranium for?" she asked. "Not for Russia. They have their own. And not for the U.S. or England. Danby already betrayed them both."

"Perhaps he's trying to win them back," Magnusson said jauntily.

"But they have their own uranium, too."

"How does a schoolgirl know so much?" They were walking down a tunnel, along a narrow railroad track.

"I read the newspaper, that's all," Janie said.

"Because you were trying to figure out where Benjamin and his father were? And with *which* nuclear test they were trying to meddle?"

Janie nearly tripped over her own feet, but she forced herself to keep walking. She wondered if *now*, if she turned and ran, she could make it into the elevator before Magnusson caught up with her. Magnusson might be slower than she was, but not by much. "I don't know who you're talking about," she said.

Magnusson laughed. "Ah, Janie," he said. "You are the most terrible liar. It's very charming."

"What do you want with Benjamin?"

"Oh, come. You haven't put it all together?"

They had stopped near an old elevator cage of some kind. It must once have lowered men deeper into the mine, but now it was unused and parked on a ledge. Magnusson pulled open the door, studying the rust on the hinges, listening to them creak. Janie's mind was racing through everything she knew: that Magnusson was mining uranium, that he had kidnapped her to lure Benjamin and his father, that Danby was on the island, that he had been alive all this time . . .

Suddenly her arm was twisted behind her back and she was being propelled, hard, into the elevator cage. She stumbled, trying not to go down on her face. It all happened before she could struggle free, and Magnusson slammed the door and slapped a padlock on it.

She was locked in.

But that fact was mixed up with what she finally understood. The two thoughts were like transparencies laid one over the other, with the bright light of awareness behind them. She grabbed the sturdy bars of the cage. She couldn't squeeze out between them. It made a perfect prison cell. Did she see *nothing* coming?

No: She saw one thing, very clearly.

"Danby wants uranium for a new bomb," she said. "And he wants to get rid of Benjamin's father so that no one can stop it."

"Wrong," Magnusson said, smiling.

"Wrong?"

"Mr. Burrows has colleagues all over the world," Magnusson said. "Drop him off a cliff, and another will spring up just like him. My sources tell me that the Chinese girl went home to Nanking, and the fat Hungarian count is still at large. I have also heard that Andrei Sakharov has been doing some troubling experiments, after seeing what your apothecary did to his bomb. He might be joining their number."

Janie ran through the facts again. It was like the mystery puzzles her father used to pose for her on the drive to King's Canyon—*the lights go out and the patient dies*—but those were for killing time in the car. This was about killing people, and she couldn't figure it out.

Then it came clear. "He wants to apothecary-proof the uranium," she said, stunned by the simplicity of the answer. "He wants an unstoppable bomb."

Magnusson beamed at her. "Very good," he said. "*A*-plus! You are the brightest student. I knew you were."

"Mr. Burrows won't do it. He would never do it."

"We'll see what he will do."

"And anyway, he isn't coming," she said, although she wasn't sure about that anymore, not since she'd seen the flicker of Benjamin's sail.

"We'll see about that, too," Magnusson said. Smiling, he turned and left her in the poisonous heat of the mine.

CHAPTER 44

The Swamp

Jin Lo, still a falcon, watched helplessly from a tree as the islanders prepared a fire to cook Marcus Burrows. They had a system for rotating a spit, supported by forked branches thrust into the ground, but it was designed for roasting the small island pigs. A large woman in a yellow cotton dress said the spit would be too low. Men knew nothing about cooking! She demanded new, longer, stronger supports, to raise the body higher off the coals. The men went off to find the right branches. Jin Lo guessed that cannibalism wasn't a customary thing here, but was a disused ritual of revenge.

When the islanders were occupied, the falcon flew down to the tree to which the apothecary was tied. She hoped he would understand what she was doing. He seemed sluggish and sleepy from the pain and shock.

She began to tug with her beak at the knots that bound his wrists. The twine was made from bamboo, and was very strong. Threads of it came free as she pecked and pulled, without diminishing the strength of the main cord. She felt the apothecary stir.

"Lin Jo?" he whispered. He was still talking backward, but she understood him.

She answered by tugging harder at the knots.

"Go!" he whispered. "It's doo tangerous."

She got a whole strand of twine free: a triumph. She looked to make sure no one had noticed, and kept working.

"Bave Senjamin," Marcus Burrows whispered. "Please."

She pecked sharply at his hand. It was a spiteful, falconish thing to do, but she couldn't help it. It was just *like* him to give up at a time like this. She wanted him to stop talking and help her.

Then she felt a hand around her feathered neck. She screeched, but the strong grip cut off her air, and her cry trailed off. She heard a woman's voice announcing that *she had another birdman!*

Jin Lo struggled and kicked and tried to scratch with her talons, but the grip was tight. She could see her captor as she twisted: It was the bossy cook in the yellow dress, who could easily snap her neck. Her feathered scalp prickled. She knew what that meant, but scarcely dared to hope. The rushing blood slowed perceptibly in her veins. The light, hollow bones of her wings felt heavy and dense. Her skinny bird legs began to stretch painfully, the sharp talons retracting into feet and toes.

Jin Lo regained her human head and her long hair, and the woman shouted in astonishment, still gripping her neck. But Jin Lo had a sharp elbow now, not a falcon's wing, and she jabbed it into the woman's startled face. She got the woman's neck in a choke hold, then kicked her legs out from under her and dragged her, struggling, toward the apothecary's tree.

A small girl approached them, and Jin Lo shouted, "Stop!" in the islanders' language. The girl froze.

If she spoke one word at a time, Jin Lo could make herself clear. With her free hand, she tore impatiently at the knots that still bound the apothecary. "Pull!" she said.

The apothecary tugged his hands free.

"Knife!" she said.

The apothecary picked up a large knife with a curved blade lying on the ground.

"Run!" Jin Lo said, and he did, toward the densest trees. Jin Lo followed, dragging her hostage.

When they reached the edge of the trees, Jin Lo shoved the stout woman into the two closest girls, who automatically reached to catch her fall. Then she raced away. Within a hundred meters, she and the apothecary were in a swamp, mud pulling at their shoes.

And they were alone—no one had followed them. Jin Lo wondered why. It was a tidal mangrove swamp, the high tide marked on the tree trunks. They waded in until the water was up to their knees. It was murky, and the trees blocked the sunlight. The dimness seemed menacing. Then the water was up to Jin Lo's waist.

"Mollow fe," the apothecary said, and he ducked beneath the water.

Jin Lo expected him to resurface, but he didn't, and she

remembered. They had prepared for this. She lowered her head beneath the murky water and crouched there. Light filtered down from the surface and made the water yellow-green. The apothecary had already moved away. Jin Lo followed. She wasn't taking the water into her lungs, to extract the oxygen there. She must be taking it in some other way—through her skin? She simply had no need to breathe. She should have asked the apothecary how it worked, but she had been too impatient to get to the island.

She held on to roots and rocks beneath the water, and she blew out the air in her lungs to make herself less buoyant. It felt like a dream, gliding silently underwater, between the stumps of trees and the strange gloomy plants that grew up from the bottom of the swamp. She wanted to catch up to Marcus Burrows, to share the pleasure of it.

But where *was* he? They would need to clean his arrow wound. This swamp water couldn't be good for it. She made her way forward, still holding to the bottom, looking for him in the cloudy green depths.

And then she stopped. A nose was inches from hers, but it wasn't the apothecary's nose. It was reptilian, above a vast, uneven row of teeth. Two blurry catlike eyes looked into hers. She pulled back slowly, beneath the water. The thing was a monster. Its giant head must be two feet across. If she had been breathing to begin with, she would have stopped. It was a crocodile, so close it could crush her head in its jaws simply by opening and closing its mouth.

But it hadn't attacked, and Jin Lo thought it was trying to decide what she was. Humans didn't move silently beneath the water with no bubbles, and fish didn't wear clothes. She backed slowly away from the terrible jaws, and felt the trunk of a tree in the water behind her. It was a mangrove, with multiple trunks all woven together. If she could get a foothold, then she might be able to climb up into the air, to safety. But would the crocodile snap out of its trance and take her leg off? The bark was smooth and slippery. It wouldn't be easy to climb.

Words from her childhood came into her head: *We be of one blood, ye and I.* The master words of the jungle, from a copy of Kipling's *The Jungle Book* in the Reverend Magee's library at the mission.

She tried to move slowly. She lifted her head above the water, and the crocodile raised its eyes up to watch her. She could see it clearly now, the ridge of its armored back. Was it twelve feet long? More? She told herself to be calm. She breathed the tropical air in the usual way. She tried to concentrate on speaking clearly. Her life might depend on it. *"Please,"* she said softly. *"Be we of one blood, I and ye."* She reached up into the tree—slowly, slowly, trying to grab the highest handhold she could. *"Klease don't pill me."*

The crocodile burst out of the water like a rocket shot from a cannon, seized her arm, and yanked her from the tree, rolling her over beneath the water. Jin Lo gasped instinctively, forgetting that she didn't need to breathe. She tried frantically to *think*. There must be some way to gain the upper hand, get a finger in the animal's eye, get an arm around its enormous head, find a vulnerable soft place beneath the scaly armor. But the crocodile had her upper arm in its teeth, and its huge body lay on top of hers. There was no way to gain leverage.

She realized she was going to die here, on this strange island, so far from home. She thought of her parents and little brother. It was time to join them: That was all. She had lived many years that would have been taken from her if her father hadn't hidden her in the trunk. She had been given an unexpected life. Who would have thought that a crocodile would be the collector of that debt? She heard something in the water: splashing, footsteps. A search party. Rescue, maybe. But they moved past.

After a minute, the grip on her arm released and the huge weight slid ominously off her chest. She prepared herself for the great jaws, but they didn't come. She rose to the surface and took a breath of real air, and she heard voices, but now they were beyond her in the swamp.

She saw a long curved knife raised in the air: Marcus Burrows, dripping swamp water, stood ready to stab the crocodile.

"No!" she cried in a half whisper.

He stayed his knife, confused. The voices of the search party receded. The crocodile moved away in the other direction, a long, sinuous gray curve at the surface of the water. It turned its head to give her a reptilian glance before disappearing beneath the surface. She understood.

The master words of the jungle had worked. The crocodile had saved her life. It had hidden her from the search party with their knives and their cookfire. Now it would lead her out of the swamp. It wasn't time to join her family yet. There was a murky future still ahead.

CHAPTER 45

Babysitting

P ip sat at a table in Bruno's restaurant with Janie's parents, eating a giant plate of spaghetti and meatballs. He had always liked the Scotts, but they were in a bad way now. Mrs. Scott was pale and seemed to be in shock, and Mr. Scott was seething. They explained how Janie hadn't arrived at home when she was supposed to. The bus had been the fastest way for her to get home, and she had insisted that it was safe. But then she just disappeared. They met the bus in Ann Arbor, and the driver said he'd never seen her. So they drove all night from Michigan to New Hampshire. At Grayson Academy, the headmaster told them Janie was staying with a doctor aunt in Concord. But she didn't have a doctor aunt in Concord! Or any aunt in Concord! And they still didn't understand how Janie could have been kicked out. She didn't need to cheat at math. She could do math *circles* around that headmaster.

Pip let them talk. Adults, especially parents, never knew what to do with full information. They overreacted, and they failed to strategize. They wanted to challenge authority directly, when every kid knew that a frontal attack just made authority dig in. You could circumvent a powerful opponent or you could launch a sneak attack, but it was no use bashing your head against him.

"I'm calling the police as soon as we finish dinner," Mr. Scott said. "I also want to contact that roommate's parents. What's her name? Jewel? And I'm going back tomorrow to that ludicrous headmaster, Willington."

"Willingham," his wife said.

"Willingham," he said. "He's going to wish he'd never seen me."

Pip wanted to explain that the police wouldn't know anything. And that the headmaster had to be in on the deal. Magnusson was dangerous, and connected. The Scotts would just get themselves and Pip in trouble, while Janie was still stuck in Malaya. Pip tried to think of *any* way they could be useful, before he got rid of them. "Do you know anyone with a private aeroplane?" he asked.

"Oh, sure," Mr. Scott said. "I'll just call up Jack Warner at Warner Brothers."

Pip was impressed. "Can you?"

"No!" Mr. Scott said. "That was a joke."

So they were really no use at all.

"I think Janie's in Florida," Pip said. It was the first state that popped into his head.

"Florida?" Mr. Scott said.

"I think she went looking for Benjamin."

"Who?"

Pip realized that the Scotts hadn't been at St. Beden's School, surrounded by people who had known Benjamin. So they hadn't had any reason to work at remembering him. They'd gone along with their lives, minus three weeks, and minus Benjamin Burrows, happily oblivious. "A friend of ours," Pip said. "She thinks he's in trouble."

"But why wouldn't she tell us?"

"Because she knew you'd tell her not to go."

"Well, of *course* we would have!"

"See?" Pip said.

"Where in Florida is she?"

"Fort Lauderdale," Pip said, because it was the only city in Florida he knew.

"Fort Lauderdale? Are you sure?"

"Pretty sure," Pip said. He hunted in his jacket pockets until he found Deborah's father's card, from the ship. He also found Deborah's folded poem about celestial bodies meeting in the sky, but he wouldn't give Janie's father that. Deborah believed in fate, and he was sending her a little dose of fate.

"It just isn't like Janie to run off like this," Mr. Scott said.

Pip wanted to tell him that it was *exactly* like Janie, who'd run off to Nova Zembla without telling them, but of course the Scotts didn't remember that. "This man can help you," he said, handing over the card. "He's a friend. Tell him I sent you."

Mr. Scott studied the address. "Will you come with us?"

"I can't," Pip said. "But I want you to follow any lead you can. Be observant. Listen for clues. Talk to the daughter especially." Deborah would tell the Scotts ominous, confusing things to keep them busy, and her genial family would keep them safe. And then they couldn't get Pip rearrested, or tip off Magnusson to the fact that Pip was coming. "And listen, Janie needs you. So you need to eat, all right? You're no good to anyone all starved and useless."

Janie's parents picked up their forks obediently.

"I wish we had any information that didn't come from a kid," Mrs. Scott said.

"If you don't mind my saying, ma'am," Pip said, "you could do a lot worse."

CHAPTER 46

A Squall

Tessel and Efa tried to teach Benjamin their language in the long hours on the sailboat. He had guessed they were eight or nine years old, but they weren't exactly sure. Their sense of time was different.

Their sense of space was different from his, too, and much, *much* better. Benjamin hadn't known what he was getting into, leaving the island—he just knew he had to get away. He hadn't understood how tiny the boat would feel, bobbing in the vast ocean. He never knew where he was. But Tessel knew. Benjamin had drawn a crude map of where they were going, and Tessel could rise from sleep, look out at a vast, unchanging horizon, and know instantly that they had veered half a degree off course. They had no instruments. Tessel had only the wind, the sun, and the stars, and some freakishly accurate gyroscopic compass inside his brain.

At least it *seemed* freakishly accurate, because Tessel was so confident. Benjamin guessed he would discover how good the boy's instincts were when they found Janie, or found Antarctica and penguins, or died of exposure at sea.

But it was clear that Tessel and Efa were tough and resourceful and devoted to each other. Tessel's kava-making career was over, and Efa had been made untouchable just by being in the boat, but she was learning to sail it, and she had grown cheerier the farther she got from home. She seemed wired for happiness, in general, and she found Benjamin's attempts to learn their language enormously funny. Tessel did, too. There was no question in their minds that he could ever have been John Frum. How could someone so deeply ignorant be a god? They called him Benjonfrum, and thought it a splendid joke. Their dark skin protected them better against the sun than Benjamin's did, and he was sunburned by the second day. Concerned and motherly, Efa rigged a sunshade from a spare sail.

"How is America, Benjonfrum?" she asked, as if asking about some distant, magical planet.

"I don't know."

Efa was startled. "Why?"

"I've never been there," Benjamin said. He'd seen glimpses of America through Janie, but he didn't know how to explain that to Efa. He'd seen a room with flowered curtains, a boy actor, a dark auditorium, and two different bathroom mirrors. Not much of an American tour. "I come from England," Benjamin said. "It's an island. Like yours."

"Not like ours," Efa said.

"Well, no. England has cities. Big cities, where many people live. And much smoke. And it gets cold there. People wear heavy clothes made of the hair of sheep, not just grass skirts and loincloths."

"You have tabu?" Efa asked.

"Not the same ones as yours."

"You have a god?"

Benjamin wondered how to explain a country of mostly Anglicans but also Hindus and Muslims, Sikhs and Buddhists, atheists and agnostics, Catholics and Jews. "There are so many people that they have different gods," he said.

"You see them?"

"No. Only statues and paintings."

"But they will come?"

"I don't think so," Benjamin said. "Some people say their god is coming back, but a lot of people don't."

Efa studied Benjamin's face. He could see her trying to imagine this far-off place with many clothes, many gods, and no *waiting*, no endless anticipation of the return. "People pray?" she finally asked.

"They do."

"For cargo?"

Benjamin thought of Father Christmas with his bag of loot over his shoulder. "They do pray for cargo, sometimes," he said. "For things they want. They pray for other things, too. For safety, for peace, for good weather. For people who are sick to get better. For love."

"It comes?" she asked.

"I don't know, Efa," Benjamin said. "Sometimes the things we want come. Sometimes they don't."

Efa nodded, absorbing that.

Tessel complained that he couldn't see over the sunshade, and when they lifted it, the sky behind them was bruise-colored and ominous. Another cyclone, or at least a really nasty storm.

"Oh, not again," Benjamin moaned.

Tessel said something with dread in his voice, and set about reefing the sail. Efa deftly rigged the sunshade as a sluice to collect water in their emptying casks.

"What should I do?" Benjamin asked. "To help?"

Tessel clambered over him with furious concentration and said, "*Pray, Benjonfrum.*"

CHAPTER 47

Underground

W hen morning came, the work of the mine began. Janie sat in the padlocked elevator cage in her pajamas, where Magnusson had left her. The miners looked at her when they passed by, and she looked out at them. They were all Malay, all coated with sweat and dust. The older men were leaner, their faces more hollow. She thought she had never seen any group of people work so hard. Her father had sometimes said of certain writers, with admiration, that they worked like hard-rock miners. If she ever saw her father again, she would tell him he was *wrong*. But would she see her father again? It was looking doubtful. She had studied the heavy padlock and yanked on it, and it wasn't going anywhere.

She wished she had some of the apothecary's sweet-smelling Quintessence to absorb the radiation from the air. She leaned back against the bars of her cage and thought about that lovely smell, the smell of hope and sunlight.

It was impossible to tell what time it was, underground, but it might have been the middle of the day when Osman, the young cook, brought her a sandwich wrapped in waxed paper and a bottle of lemonade.

She scrambled to her feet when she saw him. "Osman!" she said. "Can you get me out of here?"

He glanced back up the tunnel. Janie saw one of the green-uniformed guards waiting there. Osman passed the sandwich and the bottle through the bars of her cage. "I'm sorry," he said.

"Have you seen Magnusson?" she asked. "Is he going to leave me down here?"

"I don't know," he said. "I have to go."

"Listen," she whispered. "My friend Benjamin is going to be looking for me. But it's dangerous for him here. Maybe you can help him."

The guard barked, "No talking!"

"Wait!" she said. "Osman, please!"

"I'm sorry," he said, backing away.

When he was gone, she felt lonelier than ever. She opened the waxed-paper parcel and found a chicken salad sandwich inside, cut diagonally in half, the lettuce crisp and fresh. Her stomach grumbled in anticipation, and she took a bite. It was delicious and mustardy, with chopped-up bits of some crunchy vegetable from his kitchen garden. It made her think that Osman really was her friend.

A little later, Magnusson came and looked into her cage. "Did you get the sandwich?" he asked.

"What, are you expecting *thanks*?"

"Yes, in fact I was," he said mildly. "Danby wants to see you, but I've told him he can't. I don't trust him."

"You think he'll kill me?"

"He might, in anger. He bears a grudge. And I need you alive, to summon your friends."

"They won't come."

"We'll see about that," Magnusson said, smiling. And he left her alone.

As soon as he was gone, she spread out the waxed paper that had been wrapped around her sandwich. With the last of the lemonade, she made a little mud with dirt from the mine's floor. There was a tiny chance that Benjamin could see where she was. Painstakingly, with her finger dipped in the sticky mud, she wrote a message on the paper:

BENJAMIN—DON'T COME.

CHAPTER 48

A Sail

Jin Lo and the apothecary, arms bandaged with strips torn from their clothes, waded silently along the island's swampy northern coastline, keeping an eye out for venom-spined rockfish and angry islanders. They were looking for one of the island's boats to borrow. Marcus Burrows was usually opposed to stealing, but he seemed to relax his moral stance with people who had tried to roast him on a spit.

Jin Lo's biceps ached. Her arm was bruised, the skin broken. The crocodile might have had good intentions, but even the gentlest crocodile bite left a mark. He could have taken the arm right off, if he'd wanted to.

They made their way through tide pools. Little fish darted away from their feet.

"Is it possible to become fish?" she asked. "Like birds?" They could talk normally now, which was a relief.

"No," Marcus Burrows said. "There's a note in the Pharmacopoeia from a previous owner. I don't know the handwriting, but it certainly predates my grandfather. The writer believes it is *possible* to become a fish, but unadvisable, as fish are so often eaten. So he provides no instructions."

"I see."

"There's also the question of freshwater or saltwater fish—it's very complicated."

"Yes."

"But I now believe that part is manageable."

They had rounded a rocky point and saw a trim, elegant yacht, about sixty feet long, anchored off the island. Two white people were visible on the yacht: a man struggling with a dinghy on the stern, and a woman in a black bikini shielding her eyes. They hadn't seen the castaways yet.

"Can you swim, with your arm?" the apothecary asked.

Jin Lo nodded. But it was a longer swim than it seemed, and difficult with their wounded arms and the need to breathe air. When they came alongside the boat, treading water, the skipper jumped and swore with surprise. "Where the hell did you come from?"

"The island," Marcus Burrows said.

"Do they have ice there?" the woman in the bikini asked. "And rum, and bananas? And maybe some nice bacon? We're running low on provisions."

"I don't think you should go to the island," Marcus Burrows said.

"Not even for *ice*?"

"If you help us aboard, we'll explain."

"How do we know you aren't pirates?" the man asked. He had silver in his hair.

"Do we look like pirates?"

"Yes, in fact, you do."

"We're wounded," Marcus Burrows said. "We have been attacked by the islanders. I assure you that we mean you no harm."

The woman looked at her husband. "Oh, perfect," she said. "Hostile natives. And you have no idea where we are."

"Well, we wouldn't be here if you hadn't been too *bored* to stay where we were!" he said. "In a perfectly safe harbor! In cyclone season!"

An arrow whistled through the air. It splashed into the water behind Jin Lo. Two archers in loincloths stood at the edge of the shore.

"They're firing at us," Marcus Burrows said. *"Please."*

The man hurried to the stern of the boat and lowered the swimming ladder. "Get in!" he said. "Quick! Charlotte, the anchor!"

"Oh, God, I hate the anchor!" Charlotte said. With her long limbs, she reminded Jin Lo of a stalking waterbird as she moved toward the bow.

Jin Lo climbed the ladder first. Her arm ached. An arrow splashed closer. She heard the boat's engine start, and the grinding rattle of the anchor chain. The man and the woman were shouting at each other, half in fear and half in anger. Jin Lo hauled herself dripping onto the hot teak deck, then reached to help Marcus Burrows with her good arm. He pulled the swimming ladder up after him just as the couple brought in the anchor. An arrow passed so close to Jin Lo's head that she felt the air displaced by its flight against her ear.

The woman in the bikini swore colorfully about those rude and unwelcoming savages, and the fact that they *still* didn't have any ice.

Jin Lo sat in a salty puddle in the cockpit, her arm throbbing. She kept her head down, to avoid both the arrows and the couple's shouting.

The skipper turned the boat, showing the archers its stern, and they motored away, as fast as the sleek hull would go.

PART SIX

Corrosion

1. the process of damaging or destroying metal, stone, or other materials by chemical action
2. damage or weakening caused gradually, as to ideals or morals

CHAPTER 49

At Sea

Benjamin sat at the tiller of the little boat, sunburned and windburned, his lips so chapped that bits of them were flaking off. The mast had broken, and the squall had left him hopelessly confused about where they were. Tessel had worked out a new course, and they had rigged up the mast again, laying the two parts over each other and lashing their sunshade around them, but it could hardly take any sail. Benjamin was trying to stay on the course that Tessel had set for him, but the wind had gone, and they barely had steerageway. He remembered reading that sailors whistled to make the wind come up, and he tried, through parched lips.

The children were asleep like two puppies in the bottom of the boat, exhausted by the storm. Efa laid her head on Tessel's arm and tucked her knees up against the boy's rib cage. Their lips were as chapped as Benjamin's, and their hands, like his, were raw from working the salt-roughened lines. They had run dangerously low on drinking water, in spite of refilling their casks in the squall, and their last meal had been the raw flesh of a flying fish that had landed mistakenly in their boat. It was bony and unsatisfying.

Tessel was a preternaturally good navigator, but he hadn't seen the charts Benjamin had seen. Were they really on course? They might be run over by a cargo ship, or taken by pirates. They might drift along forever. And even if they *could* find the island where Janie was, what then? Benjamin would be taking the children from the dangerous sea to a dangerous island.

He saw a dark ship on the horizon and stood and waved his shirt, but the ship was miles away, and grew smaller as he watched. Birds overhead eyed him. He waved his shirt some more to show that he wasn't wounded, wasn't even close to dead. And neither were the children.

The birds flew on, and Benjamin fought sleep, his eyes drifting closed and then snapping open as he shook himself awake. The sun was relentless. The sky was an endless blue. He wondered if he had imagined everything else in his life, if he had always been here, drifting, baking in the sun.

Then something hard and swift jostled the side of the boat beneath the water.

Benjamin grabbed the gunwales, awake, looking into the fathomless blue.

A fin broke the surface of the water, a little farther off, and was gone again, ghostlike. Tessel had made a spear by tying a short-bladed knife to the end of a long pole with a strip of bamboo. They had tried fishing with it, without much success. Benjamin picked up the spear now and waited.

Another bump, harder than the first, rocked the boat, too fast for Benjamin to react with the spear. The thing was trying to knock them into the water. Tessel stirred, blinking.

"A shark," Benjamin said. He said it again in Tessel and Efa's language. They had seen other sharks, though not so close, and it was a word he felt confident about.

Tessel was alert, kneeling in the bow and peering out. He held out his hand for the spear like a surgeon awaiting his instrument, then cocked his arm and waited, scanning the water, but nothing surfaced.

They were so preoccupied that they didn't see the sailboat until it was almost upon them. A woman's voice called, "Hullo, you! What're you spearing? Dinner?"

It was a wooden sloop, steering toward them. There were two women perched on the bow. One was Charlotte from Manila, deeply tanned in a black bikini, shielding her eyes with one hand.

The other was waving wildly and grinning. She wore loose cotton clothes, and had a bandaged arm and a black braid snaking over her shoulder. Benjamin nearly fell into the bottom of the boat with surprise when he recognized Jin Lo.

A third figure came to the bow, also with a bandaged arm: Benjamin's father. He was grinning, too, and didn't look distracted, or preoccupied, or deep in thought. He looked like he had never been happier, although his eyes were full of tears. Benjamin felt his own wind-chapped face cracking in an enormous smile of gratitude.

When the battered little boat was tied behind the *Payday* and the three fugitives had clambered aboard, Benjamin's father hugged him so tightly, he thought his weakened bones might break. He couldn't remember the last time his father had hugged him.

"I told you not to follow me," Benjamin said.

"I know," his father said.

He wanted to sink in relief onto the deck. "I'm glad you did."

There were explanations and introductions. Tessel boldly shook hands with everyone, though Efa shied away. Benjamin's father and Jin Lo had been to their island.

"Your powder," Jin Lo said. "Is brilliant."

"Are they angry about the children?"

She nodded. "Also about John Frum."

"Now, who wants a cold drink?" Charlotte said. "Your nice dad made us plenty of ice, out of nowhere. I wish I knew how he does it!"

Benjamin looked at his father, who shrugged. They didn't usually do party tricks like making ice. Maybe his father was planning to give Charlotte and Harry the wine of Lethe and make them forget everything. Benjamin decided that was true. Otherwise it would be impossible to talk about anything. The boat was too small for secrets. "I'll have a ginger ale," he said. "And I'd like to see your charts."

They all leaned together over the chart table. The skipper put his finger on a spot of blue on the map. "I took a noon sighting with the sextant, and I think we're here."

Tessel frowned. He squinted at the sun, which was setting in that sudden equatorial way, and at Venus, which had just become visible in the twilight. He pointed to a spot on the chart just east of the skipper's finger. "Here," he said.

Charlotte burst out laughing. "I trust the kid," she said. "Harry never gets the same sextant reading twice."

"It's a good thing I don't," her husband said, indignant. "That would mean the earth had stopped moving. I'm a perfectly capable navigator."

"Yes, and I'm Shirley Temple."

Benjamin pointed to an island that formed the top of a triangle with two others. "This is where Janie is," he said. "I think there's a mine there."

"Wait, hang on," Harry said. "I have a guidebook."

"I'll get the drinks," Charlotte said.

When they had both gone below, Benjamin said, "Did you bring the little packet of powder?"

His father shook his head.

"I think Janie's trapped underground," Benjamin said. "The powder's worn off almost completely, but I get tiny flashes. I just wish we had *anything* useful!"

Charlotte brought drinks up from below, her charm bracelet clinking against a glass. Benjamin eyed the bracelet. "Are those charms real gold?" he asked.

"Of course!" she said. She set down the drinks and turned each charm over, baring the inside of her sun-browned wrist. "The racquet is from the tennis team at Farmington. The pair of dice is from Monaco. The elephant is from India. The gold anchor was supposed to make me better at setting our anchor—but it didn't work. The shoe is kind of silly because I never wear shoes anymore."

Benjamin nodded, as if that was all important information. "Could we borrow a few of the sillier ones?" he asked.

CHAPTER 50

The Materia Medica

Jin Lo had been trained early in the *Pao zhi* of Chinese medicine. At twelve, the master to whom she had been apprenticed told her that she would not always have a laboratory with everything she needed arranged in neat glass bottles. To teach her to work with scarce resources, he sent her out on scavenger hunts, giving her assignments for which she had to scrounge weeds and bits of rock and metal, and improvise: *Make your hand turn blue, then change it back. Trap a whisper in a jar of oil, and release it later. Move a book across a table without touching it. Paralyze a cricket, and then set it free.*

Luckily, their hosts on the *Payday* were scavengers themselves. They were not clever people, Charlotte and Harry. But they had been all over the world, living a lonely, nomadic existence. Like those greedy, lucky black-and-white birds called magpies, they had taken bright things that pleased them and tucked them away in their floating nest. Jin Lo scoured the boat for these souvenirs, then sat at the table in the yacht's saloon with Benjamin and the apothecary, considering the impressive array:

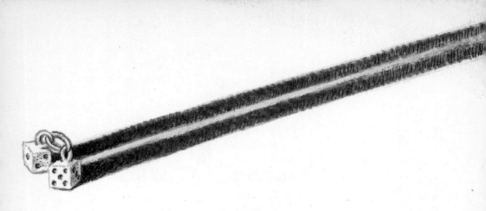

—An intricately carved red box made of what she knew in China as *jindan,* which Charlotte called cinnabar, and the apothecary called mercuric sulfide. It could be roasted to make quicksilver, which might not bestow eternal life when mixed into the Golden Elixir, as the early Chinese alchemists believed, but was extraordinarily useful anyway.

—Three charms that Charlotte was willing to give up from her bracelet: the shoe, the dice, and the skull. "The skull is to remind you that you'll die someday," Charlotte had said. "And I don't need to be reminded of that."

—A small jade carving of a frog.

—A piece of purple quartz.

—A jar of very high quality ylang-ylang oil from the Philippines, which Charlotte had bought as a perfume.

—A set of six silver teaspoons.

—A healthy aloe vera plant growing in a terra-cotta pot.

—A sickly fern in another pot.

—Aspirin, quinine, rubbing alcohol, mineral oil, and a bottle of iodine from the medicine cabinet. Also a

decongestant called Dristan, Pepto-Bismol, calamine lotion, smelling salts, and Unguentine First Aid Spray for sunburn, which Charlotte had tried to use on the back of Benjamin's neck. He had waved her away.

—A small amount of high-grade opium, which Harry insisted was for toothaches.

—A bottle of powdered talc with a gardenia scent.

—Several graphite pencils and one grease pencil.

—A smooth yellow stone, surely sulfur, which gave off the stink of rotten eggs.

—Three hen's eggs, still reasonably fresh.

—A vase covered in a bright purplish blue glaze, which Jin Lo believed to be *gu,* or cobalt, though she would need to grind it up and burn it to be certain.

—The guide to the islands that Harry had promised: a mimeographed booklet written by a sailor he had met in Manila. It was called *Captain Marty's Sailing Guide to Malaya.*

—A mortar and pestle, a decent cooking knife, and a hammer.

All in all, it wasn't bad. Jin Lo had worked with less. She could hear her old master's solemn, gravelly voice. *Consider the properties of each substance, but do not be limited by what you already know. It is the union of opposites that is important: hot and cold, wet and dry, acid and alkali, solar and lunar. They are separated, they join together. The work is a flowing river from which you divert a stream.*

So it was time to divert a stream. She picked up the pretty carved box, placed it on a wooden cutting board, and hit it hard with the hammer. It broke into several pieces, and she took the smallest piece and hit it again, crushing it.

"Oh!" Charlotte cried. "I'm not going to watch this."

Jin Lo had forgotten the woman was there. Charlotte's long legs disappeared up the hatch. She would distract herself by teasing and tormenting her husband, who was sailing the boat with the help of the two island children.

The magpie, *xi que* in Chinese, was the bird of married happiness, but not for its own sake. It was because the magpies in an old legend made a magical bridge to unite two separated lovers. If Charlotte and Harry could bring Benjamin and Janie together, maybe that would be their contribution to the world's happiness, since they had so little happiness of their own.

"You said you figured out how to talk to animals, right?" Benjamin asked.

"Perhaps," Jin Lo said. It was possible that she had been losing her mind, and only *thought* the cat was talking to her. But she was fairly sure about the crocodile.

"Maybe we could get some dolphins to help us sneak onto the island," he said.

Jin Lo looked up at Benjamin. He was not so many years younger than she was, but he was a romantic, which made him more of a child than she had ever been. He could imagine himself riding a heroic pod of dolphins to rescue his princess. "Animal with less intelligence is better," she said. "Does not have so much own mind, own plan."

Benjamin frowned, thinking. "Sea turtles?"

"Giant squid is better," she said, and she was rewarded with a look of disgust and horror.

"*Squid?*" Benjamin said.

"Squid has complex brain. This is good. But does not have *plans.*"

"Don't they eat people?" Benjamin asked. "Like the kraken?"

"Sometimes."

"And they're slimy?"

"Yes."

"I don't think I want to ride on a giant squid."

"The *Aidos Kyneê* is our best option," the apothecary said, turning a page in the sailing guide. "We have the necessary gold, and invisibility is the safest, surest thing."

"Invisible solution will stay on body?" she asked. "In water?"

The apothecary looked thoughtful. "That's a good question. It might not."

"And does not work on clothes. We want to be naked and visible, on island?"

"*No,*" Benjamin said.

"So no animals, no invisibility," she said. "Too complicated."

The apothecary was reading the sailing guide. "I found Janie's island," he said. "Listen to this."

The island is believed to possess a geological oddity in the form of an underwater tunnel between the southern point of the island and a small lagoon near the island's center. Formerly, the island was the ignored property of some Malay potentate, and there were rumors of pearl divers with enormous lung capacity reaching the open sea from the secret lagoon, like mermen. Now the island is privately owned. Very stern NO TRESPASSING signs warn off the curious sailor looking for a placid moment on a sandy beach. A pompous white villa has sprung up like a wart on the pristine island's face, near the mermen's lagoon. Apologies to the island's owner if my little book finds its way into his hands and he reads this opinion. But your humble guide maintains that he has taken from the world one of its loveliest spots.

He looked up from his reading.

"If we can get through that tunnel," Benjamin said, "we can get close to the villa, and no one will see us!"

"I believe that's so," his father said. Then his brow furrowed with concern. "You do know how to swim, Benjamin?"

"In school, we went to the public baths every Wednesday."

"Ah," his father said. "Well, that's a relief."

"That might be a thing a father would know," Benjamin said.

His father pushed his spectacles up onto his nose. "I realize that I was too distracted by my work, in those years."

"Too distracted to know if your son could swim?"

Jin Lo was impatient with the same old argument. She wanted to remind Benjamin that he *had* a father, a very good one, better than most. "So we swim through tunnel," she said. "We breathe underwater."

"But we have to consider the unfortunate side effect," the apothecary said. "The language centers of the brain are affected."

"We talk funny," Jin Lo said. "This is okay. Better than naked. Agree?"

"Yes," father and son said together.

"Okay," she said. "So we begin."

CHAPTER 51

Underwater

Harry and Tessel brought the *Payday* as close to the island as they dared, in the moonless dark of early morning. The skipper had grown dependent on Tessel as a first mate. They whispered a word or two, but barely needed to speak. The plan was to pretend to tack badly, slowing the boat, while Benjamin and his father and Jin Lo went into the water on the far side, away from the island. That way, if a lookout saw the white sail, it wouldn't seem threatening. Charlotte said they had lots of practice tacking badly.

"You're not abandoning us with your stolen children?" she whispered to Benjamin.

"No," he said. He spoke in one-word sentences so they wouldn't become scrambled, but also because he was nervous about swimming underwater without breathing.

"I fear we're a bad influence on them," Charlotte said. "So don't run off for good." She smiled, and ruffled Benjamin's hair. "Good luck."

"Good luck, Benjonfrum," Efa whispered.

If there had been sun, the water might have seemed

inviting, but in the dark it was inky and forbidding. Benjamin wore Harry's swimming trunks, and a diving mask and fins they had pulled from a locker of gear. On his back was a knapsack containing their jars of provisions, wrapped carefully in his clothes and his father's.

"Ready about," Harry said in a normal voice, at the wheel. "Hard alee." They began to stage their failure. The boat turned into the wind, slowed, and stalled.

Jin Lo went into the water first. She had made an underwater light, some kind of phosphorescent glow, and she had wrapped it in oilcloth to shield it from sight. She also wore a knapsack and mask and fins. But even so, she entered the water without a sound, dropping in like a knife blade.

Benjamin rolled in next, feeling the water swallow his arms and legs, trying not to think about sharks—their bumping noses, their many teeth.

His father climbed awkwardly down the swimming ladder in his mask and fins. His spectacles were in Benjamin's knapsack, and he couldn't see well without them.

They swam at the surface, keeping their bearings by watching the dark silhouette of the land. When they reached the island's southern point, Jin Lo nodded and dived beneath the water. Benjamin and his father dived down after her.

Jin Lo uncovered her phosphorescent light, and they saw coral beneath the water, shaped like globes and trees and fans. Fish darted between the coral branches.

Benjamin used to win his breaststroke races at the public baths by swimming the whole length of the pool underwater.

Some people said it was cheating, but it was just physics. If you broke the surface, the friction slowed you down. If you could hold your breath long enough to make use of the advantage, why shouldn't you? But not to breathe *at all* was a thing he had only dreamed of. He glided through the water, following Jin Lo's eerie yellow glow, never feeling that urgent need to take new air into his lungs or burst.

The tunnel entrance was right where the sailing guide said it would be. Jin Lo swam into it. The swell nearly shoved Benjamin into the spiky coral protecting the entrance, and he kicked away. But once they were inside the tunnel, the coral was gone. Only sponges that needed no sunlight grew on the rock walls. Jin Lo's phosphorescence illuminated startled fish that shot away into the dark like lightning. Benjamin wondered if his father could see them without his glasses. The swell pushed them forward, and they kicked along with it, and then the surge reversed direction, and they held on to the rocky bottom to avoid being pulled back out to the open ocean.

The tunnel seemed to go on forever, and Benjamin began to worry that the rumor of the pearl divers wasn't true. He didn't want to get stuck down here when his ability to go without breathing wore off.

At last they saw starlight above. They surfaced in the lagoon, dripping wet, like Captain Marty's mermen. Jin Lo extinguished her light. They climbed out, then unpacked their clothes and dressed quickly in the predawn darkness. Benjamin's father put his spectacles back on with relief.

The villagers fighting the Vietminh had taught them how to crawl on their bellies, silent and unseen. Benjamin was better at it than his father was. His father was pushing forty, after all. Jin Lo moved like she'd been a jungle fighter all her life.

When they reached the villa's wire fence, Jin Lo warned them against touching it. It gave off an electrical buzz. Benjamin brought out their jar of Alkahest and poured it on a section of the steel wire. It wasn't *actual* Alkahest, the universal solvent the old alchemists had sought—it wouldn't dissolve gold. But it was effective enough to be given the name. Benjamin knocked away what remained of the corroded wire with the glass jar.

They climbed through the hole in the fence. Benjamin's father brushed his leg against the electrified wire and swore softly under his breath, a thing Benjamin had almost never heard him do. His meaning was clear even though his consonants were still mixed up from the underwater breathing.

They slipped into the densest greenery near the main house, looking for a place to hide. Dawn was breaking, and at this latitude the sun came up fast. They found a kitchen garden, planted in neat rows, surrounded by fruit trees and trellised vines. They crouched there, hidden from the house and from the grounds as the sky lightened.

Benjamin's father looked round the garden. After a moment, he said, "The hardener gere is a mood gan."

"What?" Benjamin whispered.

"Good," his father said, and then he paused. "Man." He paused again. "He'll help." Alliteration made the sentence come out clear.

Benjamin looked at the neat rows of plants, which told him nothing. He was suspicious of the idea that a garden could reveal that the gardener was a good man. He looked to Jin Lo, who shrugged. They had no other evidence to go on. So when a skinny youth came outside with a watering can, Jin Lo grabbed him, covering his mouth before he could call out, and pulled him into the fruit trees.

Benjamin looked into the kid's frightened eyes and prepared himself for one-word communication. In a low voice, he said, "Janie." The kid stared at him. "Safe?" Benjamin asked.

The kid's eyebrows knitted together.

"Benjamin," Benjamin said, pointing to himself. He waited a safe length of time, then gestured to his father and Jin Lo. "Friends." He waited. "Janie."

The kid nodded, in spite of how little they seemed like his friends. Jin Lo carefully took her hand away from his mouth, and he didn't shout for help. "I am Osman," he said, in low, precise, accented English. "Janie is locked in the mine."

"Locked?" Benjamin asked.

"In a cage."

"Exits?" Benjamin asked.

"Two."

"Where?"

"One near the miners' houses. One near the sea."

"Guards?"

"Yes," the kid said. He was quick. Benjamin liked him. "Near the houses, but not always by the sea."

CHAPTER 52

Alkahest

From her cage beneath the earth, Janie talked to the miners whenever they came by. Mostly they ignored her. At the villa, she hadn't wanted to talk to anyone. But at least people had talked to her. She realized now that there was companionship even in ignoring people, and she missed it.

One of the miners brought her a small blanket, and another a pillow, and that made her cage a little more comfortable. She told them that the radiation would poison them slowly, and that they outnumbered the guards three to one. But they hurried away, their faces full of mistrust. She guessed they had children to feed, in the houses built over the mine. She could hear her father saying, "Now you're a labor organizer, Janie?"

Out of boredom and frustration, she strained to reach a rock outside her cage, bruising her shoulder against the bars. When she had the rock, she struck it against the heavy padlock, but it was hopeless. It crumbled against the steel.

She heard footsteps and hid the remains of the rock behind

her, but it was only Osman, with a guard. She grabbed the bars. "Osman! You have to help me! I'm going crazy in here!"

"I have food," he said. He thrust a waxed-paper package through the bars of the cage, into her hand. Then he set a bottle of lemonade on the floor. He looked uncomfortable.

"I don't want a sandwich!" she said.

"It is important to eat," Osman said, looking her in the eye and nodding to emphasize his words. "Not drink but eat."

"I don't want to eat! I want *out*!"

"It is important," he said. Then he was gone, back up the tunnel with the guard.

Janie almost hurled the sandwich after them in frustration. Instead, she put it down with the lemonade and turned away in disgust. She didn't want food. She didn't want lemonade. She wanted out of this place. She curled up in the corner of the cage, wrapping herself in the little blanket and clutching the pillow to her ears to block out the noise of the mine.

CHAPTER 53

Camouflage

Benjamin waited under a tarp in the jeep, outside the mine's main entrance, while Osman delivered the sandwich and the bottle to Janie. He had asked to be smuggled into the mine, but Osman said it was impossible. There were too many people watching and spying. But Osman had to pick up a shipment of food at the pier, and he could hide one person in the jeep and leave him near the sea entrance to the mine. Benjamin insisted that he should go: Jin Lo and his father were both wounded, and he was strong. After a brief standoff, his father agreed, and stayed hidden with Jin Lo in the garden.

It was stifling under the tarp, and Benjamin barely dared to breathe. Finally the cook returned. "So?" Benjamin whispered.

The engine started. "It's a terrible place, the mine," Osman said.

"But she's all right?"

"She's all right."

"Did she understand?"

"I think so." He backed up the jeep. "The guard was there. I couldn't talk."

Benjamin felt mad with frustration. The jeep headed down a steep hill, taking sharp, slow turns.

"Get out now," Osman said quietly.

Benjamin slipped out from beneath the tarp and hid himself in the thick tropical undergrowth. The jeep continued down another turn to the pier. Osman called to a uniformed guard, who helped him load a stack of boxes into the jeep and cover them with the tarp. Then the guard climbed into the jeep beside Osman and they drove away, back up the switchbacks cut in the steep hill. Benjamin flattened his body to the ground as they passed.

He was alone, and could survey the pier built out into the ocean. A motorboat was docked alongside it. He guessed there must be a channel dredged in the reef, for boats to come in. He looked for the mine entrance, but saw only trees and the rocky hillside. He moved closer.

Slowly it all came into focus. It was like looking at an optical illusion. A wide door in the hillside had been painted to look like the rocks surrounding it. It was expertly done. A canopy of trees hung over everything, hiding the door from the water.

Janie was inside there somewhere. She should have been able to escape her cage by now. He moved closer, staying low.

He was still thinking about how to get into the mine when strong hands seized his arms on either side. He tried to break free, but two guards in camouflage uniforms, complete with brush on their helmets, held him tight.

CHAPTER 54

Aloha 'Oe

Pip had never been in an airplane before, and at first he found it delightful. He stared out the window at the clouds below and imagined falling into them, as into soft, white cotton. Angelica Lowell's father flew the plane himself. Angelica had a stack of American movie magazines, and Pip flipped through them twice, forward and backward. She didn't play chess, so he played against himself on a little travel set.

He had called Angelica in New York and pitched the idea to her as an island vacation, with the possibility of meeting royalty. Her father did anything she wanted, but he was also keen to test the capabilities of his new plane, which had been fitted with extra fuel tanks for longer distances. It had been shockingly easy to get them to go.

When they landed to refuel in Hawaii, Pip leaped off the plane, full of restless energy from being cooped up so long. Even on the airstrip, the air had the most incredible smell. It was sweet and warm and lush. Angelica noticed it, too.

"Why can't we just stay *here*?" she asked.

"Too many people," Pip said. "Where we're going, it's much more exclusive."

"But I like it here," Angelica said, gazing at the banks of flowers growing up the airport walls.

"We're going to a private island," Pip said. "Empty beaches!"

"I don't want an empty beach," Angelica said. "I want to see people. And I've run out of magazines."

"So we'll stay here," her father said.

"No!" Pip cried. "We'll get more magazines!"

But Mr. Lowell was already talking to someone, arranging to keep his plane at the airport.

"That other island is too far," Angelica said.

"But what about Janie?" Pip asked.

She frowned. "What *about* Janie?"

"Well, she might be on the island. That's all."

"Oh, then we're *definitely* staying here," Angelica said, heading after her father.

Pip wondered if he could steal another plane. But what was he supposed to do, pilot it himself?

Mr. Lowell ushered them both into a cab outside the airport, and kept saying how much he *liked* this place as they drove past palm trees on their way to the Royal Hawaiian Hotel.

Angelica glowed, having gotten her way as usual.

"I've seen so much of the world because of you, sweetheart," her father said. "Without you, I would have just stayed home."

Pip wanted to throw up. It was a hazard he should have anticipated. He'd tied his fortune to a girl who got her way in all things, but he had counted on her way being *his* way. He'd forgotten that she might change her mind.

So Janie was going to have to hang on a little bit longer, that was all.

CHAPTER 55

Another Ghost

Jin Lo lay on her stomach in the kitchen garden, looking out at the villa's vast lawn and the white cottages, wondering why the place gave her a bad feeling. Something about it felt corrupted, corrupting. She was trying to decipher the feeling when a golf cart came in through the gate. A man strode out of one of the cottages, in khaki pants and a white shirt. He was tall and thin with an unhurried lope. The way he walked was familiar.

"Look at this man," she whispered.

Marcus Burrows, who had been studying the cook's garden, crawled awkwardly over to peer out. The men in the golf cart wore camouflage, and one of them pushed a prisoner out of the cart. The prisoner's hands were bound behind his back and he had a shirt over his head, blindfolding him. One of the guards pulled it off, and Jin Lo saw Benjamin's sandy disheveled hair, his eyes wild and blinking and disoriented. His nose was bleeding; someone had hit him.

Marcus Burrows started to leap up, but Jin Lo grabbed his arm and held tight. "Stay," she whispered.

"Hullo, Benjamin," the tall man said. His voice was British and military and lazy all at the same time, and his hands were in his pockets. "You're looking rough."

"Mr. Danby," Benjamin said, and Jin Lo understood why the man was familiar. She had seen him in Nova Zembla climbing out of a helicopter.

"What *took* you so long?" Danby asked. "Feels like *weeks* we've been kicking around here, waiting."

"Sorry to inconvenience you," Benjamin said sarcastically.

"Where's your old dad?" Danby drawled. He looked around, as if expecting to see Marcus Burrows come waltzing out from behind a tree.

And the amazing thing was that Marcus Burrows did. He stood up and walked out of their hiding place, even as Jin Lo grabbed frantically at his pant cuff. It was the most foolish thing she had ever seen anyone do.

"Let my son go!" he called to the guards.

They all turned to look at this strange apparition.

"No!" Benjamin cried when he saw his father.

But the apothecary kept walking. "I'm the one you want," he said, in a commanding voice. "Take me instead."

CHAPTER 56

The Miller's Daughter

Magnusson came out of the villa with his arms wide in welcome. He was ruddy-faced with white-blond hair, and his smile was so broad and happy that his blue eyes disappeared into the folds of his cheeks. Benjamin wanted to spit at him, but he didn't. *Someone* had to have some self-control, if his father was going to do insane things like surrendering to their enemies. Everything had happened too fast, and it clouded Benjamin's brain with emotion—seeing Danby alive, watching his father walk absurdly across the lawn, and meeting Magnusson. He had to think rationally and figure out what to do next.

They crossed the island again in the jeep and went down the elevator into the mine, which was hot and dirty and suffocating. Benjamin's fingers had gone numb from having his hands tied behind his back. Guards walked on either side of his father. They walked past tunnels that seemed to descend into the depths of the earth, but Benjamin didn't see Janie.

Magnusson unlocked a heavy steel door, and they passed into an underground space that was surprisingly clean and cool and ventilated, with a concrete floor and white walls. "Welcome to our mill," Magnusson said, sounding pleased with himself.

"What kind of mill?" Benjamin asked.

"You haven't worked that out yet?"

"He's not as bright as the girl," Danby said.

"You've seen Janie?" Benjamin asked him. "Is she okay?"

"I don't know," Danby said, glancing at Magnusson. "I haven't had the privilege."

Benjamin didn't have time to wonder what that meant, because they had entered another clean, concrete-floored room that was nearly filled with neat rows of black steel barrels. A man in a white coat opened one to reveal a grainy yellow powder. There was a smell of sulfuric acid in the air.

Uranium. That was what Magnusson was mining.

"It's been milled," Magnusson said. "Now the object is for you to make it *effective,* so it can't be stopped by you or your friends."

Benjamin's father pushed his spectacles up onto his nose. "You know the story of Rumpelstiltskin?" he asked.

"The imp in the fairy story?" Danby asked.

"It begins with a miller. Who claimed that his daughter could spin straw into gold. The king locked the girl in a tower with a pile of straw, but of course she couldn't do it."

Danby smiled. "So you're the miller's daughter?"

"I was able to control the effect of an atomic explosion," Benjamin's father said. "It doesn't follow that I can make your uranium immune to such control. You see the logical error in the assumption? This is not my area of expertise. I can't do what you want any more than I could spin straw into gold. Or gold into straw."

"You're a man of great ability," Magnusson said. "If you put your mind to it, you'll find a solution."

"If I remember the story," Danby said, "the girl promises the imp her firstborn if he'll help her. Is that right? But this story's a little different. You sacrifice your firstborn if you *don't* do the spinning." He put his hand on Benjamin's shoulder, and Benjamin shook it off.

"You can't take my son as punishment for something I can't do," his father said.

"Shall we feed him to the sharks?" Danby asked. "Or lock him up and let him starve? Or drop him out of an aeroplane?"

"You must understand," Benjamin's father said. "I don't know how to do what you want. I've never considered it."

"Then I suggest you start," Danby said. "Think of it as an intellectual challenge. And no *pretending* to spin gold, Burrows—our engineer will test the uranium before we let you have the boy. We'll leave you to think." He pushed Benjamin toward the door.

"I need my son to help me!" his father said. "He's my apprentice, and he has outstripped me. He has a more inventive mind."

Danby and Magnusson looked at each other. Danby shrugged. "No harm in it, I suppose."

"You must unbind his hands," his father said. "And I'll need supplies. I don't know yet what they are. Paper and pen, to start. And I need to send a message, by radio or telegram. You may read it if you like. But I *must* consult with my colleague in Manila if I am to succeed."

Danby took a small leather-bound notebook and pen from his shirt pocket, and Benjamin's father scrawled a message and an address on a page. "We also need privacy, to concentrate," he said. "And please tell me when the message has been sent."

"Try anything funny and we kill the girl," Danby said. And they left.

Benjamin rubbed his freed wrists, bringing the blood back to his hands. His fingers throbbed, and his skin itched. "Janie should have escaped by now," he said.

"I can't do this," his father said. "Not ethically, not practically. I don't think it can be done. I don't think it *should* be done, even if it could."

"Good," Benjamin said.

"But I have to try," his father said. "What choice do I have?"

"Did you send for help in your note?"

"I asked Vinoray to take your packet of powder and consult the Pharmacopoeia. I swallowed half of what remained before we left Manila, so I might see the book through him if I needed to, in a case like this."

The idea was both brilliant and insane. "But you sent Vinoray some kind of coded SOS, too?" Benjamin asked.

"Your Mr. Danby would see through such a thing."

"Why is he *my* Mr. Danby?"

"A cry for help would only alarm Vinoray. He would have

no way of reaching us in time. I need him to be calm and purposeful, with no agitation of mind."

"You might've tried to tell him *something*."

"If you'll be quiet a moment, I need to think."

A guard returned and said the message had been sent. Benjamin's father gave him a list of supplies, and then plunged into the kind of deep contemplation that Benjamin remembered from his childhood. Occasionally he wrote something in Danby's little notebook.

Benjamin scratched his wrists and wondered how they were going to get any useful information from the Pharmacopoeia. They couldn't even tell Vinoray to stop on a particular page. And which page of the ancient book explained how to make an atomic bomb impervious to the antidote that his father and Jin Lo and Count Vili had invented? No page. The whole thing was hopeless.

Finally, his father said, "The message should have been delivered to Vinoray's shop by now. So I close my eyes and think about him, yes?"

"Once you find him, you can move his left hand a little, if he's right-handed," Benjamin said. "The less dominant hand is more open to outside control. You might be able to turn pages."

"Thank you," his father said. "I meant what I said about your having the more inventive mind. If you have any other ideas, they would be most welcome."

Benjamin watched his father sit down and close his eyes. He wondered what ideas he, Benjamin, could possibly have about their situation. Doing Danby and Magnusson's bidding went against everything they believed in. Peace was his father's calling, his vocation. Benjamin should have thrown himself down a mineshaft as they walked through the tunnel. That would have been the brave and noble thing to do. If Benjamin was removed from the situation, then there was no reason for his father to do this terrible thing.

But then he wouldn't be able to help his father escape. Or was that a rationalization? Did Benjamin only selfishly want to survive? His father looked vulnerable, sitting with his eyes closed, and Benjamin felt a rush of tenderness for him. He couldn't leave him alone.

Finally his father opened his eyes. "I can't make contact," he said. "I don't see anything."

Impatience replaced the tenderness, and Benjamin wished *he'd* been the one to take the powder and try. He was better at it.

There was another knock at the door, and two guards came in, carrying a card table piled with things the apothecary had asked for. There was a jug of water, a Bunsen burner, the knapsack full of supplies that Benjamin had hidden in the kitchen garden, a cylindrical container of salt, and two cooking pots, one large and one small.

The two guards stood looking at the list like removal men with the last of the kitchen furniture. They were Americans, a little thuggish, a little simple, probably men with few other options in life. Benjamin looked at the back of the nearest guard's thick neck and thought about throwing an arm around it, the struggle, the snap of vertebrae, the escape. He had craved a life of adventure when he was back in school, but after two years he knew something about adventure, and also something about what he was capable of. Killing a man with his bare hands wasn't one of those things.

The guards left—Benjamin's chance missed—and his father began arranging the table as a proper workspace. Then he began to work.

PART SEVEN

Germination

1. (of a seed or spore) growth and the putting out of shoots after a period of dormancy
2. the coming into existence or development of an idea or feeling

CHAPTER 57

The Confrontation

Janie sat up with a start in the elevator cage, throwing the pillow off her head and struggling out of the confines of the little blanket. She hadn't been asleep, but she had been startled by a sudden thought, an inspiration that was something like a dream.

There had been a meaningful look in Osman's eye when he brought her food, and she had ignored it. The sandwich! He'd kept telling her to eat. She grabbed the sandwich and tore off the waxed paper, looking for a key to the padlock.

What she found instead was a note. She unfolded it. *Janie*, it said.

DON'T DRINK from the bottle. Pour it on the lock. And don't get any on you, it's nasty stuff. There's a second exit from the mine, near the sea, that isn't guarded. It's our best chance. If you can make your way out, I'll meet you there.

Bx

Benjamin! He was on the island! She looked at the corked bottle. How much time had she wasted? Why hadn't she even *looked* at what Osman had brought? She pulled the cork. The liquid smelled sharp and burned her sinuses, and she flinched and blinked. She had a sudden, intense memory of Benjamin pulling away from her on a train, two years earlier, the connection between their two cars corroded. He had left her end of the train behind so she couldn't follow him. The drugged champagne had already started erasing her memories at that moment, but still the image was burned in her brain. It was the moment she'd lost him.

But now Benjamin was *here*! How had he done it? Were the others here? Did Magnusson know?

She tucked the note into the pocket of her pajamas and poured the liquid carefully over the padlock, her hands shaking. The steel sizzled and smoked so much that she thought someone might hear or smell it. She stopped and listened. There were no footsteps in the tunnel. She poured more of the liquid. When it stopped sizzling, she tapped the crusty metal with the side of the bottle. The lower part of the lock fell away. The curved bar now hung useless and free, and she tapped it out of the metal loop, freeing the hasp that held the door closed.

She listened again for footsteps, and then pushed open the door of the cage. The rusty hinges creaked. She wished Benjamin had sent more instructions. Where was the other exit? Which direction was the sea? She headed up the tunnel toward the main corridor, and the mine seemed weirdly deserted.

Then she heard voices, and she scrambled to hide herself behind a cart. She couldn't see who was coming, but she could hear them. One of the voices was Magnusson's. "It's very frustrating, to own a remarkable thing and not be able to show it off," he was saying, just as he'd said to her.

"I love what you've done with it." That was Danby's ironic drawl.

A third voice asked, "Where's Janie?"

She froze in her hiding place, heart pounding in her ears. It was Benjamin.

"Oh, she's stowed safely away," Magnusson said. "I'll see she's all right once I get you settled."

She crept silently forward to peer around the corner and watch them draw away. It really was Benjamin. He was taller now, and broader-shouldered, but that was his sandy hair. His hands were tied behind his back. She was sure the other man was his father, flanked by two guards.

Janie tried to think. Magnusson didn't know she had escaped, and he was coming to check on her. If he discovered the empty cage, he would raise an alarm and they would find her. She needed Magnusson to remain complacent and unworried. Especially now that they had Benjamin. She had to find a way to set Benjamin free.

As much as she hated the idea, she needed to get back in that cage.

She crept back down the tunnel toward her detested prison. Her foot dislodged a rock, but no one came running. Finally she was at the cage and let herself in, the rusty hinges creaking horribly.

She looked for the padlock, and found the curved bar on the ground, and the heavy casing for the lock itself. But how to reassemble it convincingly? She closed the hasp and put the curved bit through the loop, but the casing would never stay in place. She took her ponytail down and wrapped the elastic around both parts of the lock. It wouldn't quite hang straight. She would have to keep Magnusson from looking at it too closely.

After a few minutes, she heard his booming voice again, coming closer. He was in a good mood, laughing, and she heard the word *Rumpelstiltskin*. She moved away from the lock and told herself not to look at it and draw attention.

"Janie, my dear!" Magnusson cried. "I've brought your old friend Danby. He's been itching to talk to you."

"Let me out," Janie said, gripping the bars. "I'm not your *dear*."

"You see what a spitfire she is?" Magnusson asked.

Danby was studying Janie with interest. "You've grown up," he said.

"What did you expect? That I'd shrink?"

He smiled. He looked older, too. The shock of white hair was unsettling. "I asked once if you were a Daisy Miller or an Isabel Archer, as an American girl abroad," he said. "I've been through those conversations in my head many times, you know. You said you hadn't read the books. I suppose you have now?"

"Yes," Janie said.

"So you know that one heroine ends up trapped, and one ends up dead. That wasn't what I was thinking at the time. It was a purely ingenuous question then, when you were simply a new girl at school. But it's surprising how *apt* it is now."

"Why do you want an atomic bomb that can't be stopped?" Janie asked.

Danby laughed. "What a ridiculous question, Miss Scott. That's the whole *point* of an atomic bomb. If people aren't frightened of them, we can't have peace."

"Is it for the Russians?"

"No," Danby said. "My love for them has waned." He turned his hand over to consider his fingernails, as if looking for dirt beneath them, and Janie saw with horror that the fingernails were gone. The skin was healed over, but all of the nails had been pulled out. "My Soviet comrades didn't treat me particularly well, after your little escapade in Nova Zembla," he said. "But perhaps all youthful infatuations fade. Yours has faded for Master Burrows, I understand. I hear rumors of a handsome young waiter back in America, with dreams of the stage."

Janie blushed.

"So the rumors are true!" he said. "You always did turn a fetching shade of pink, Miss Scott. I'm happy to see you haven't grown out of *that*."

She wouldn't let him confuse her. "Is the uranium for the Americans?"

"Never. How vulgar."

"Who, then? For China?"

"I could never love Chairman Mao," he said. "And China is too large to need help from someone like me."

A woman's voice came from the end of the tunnel. "I know who it's for."

They all turned and saw Sylvia making her way toward them in a pencil skirt and high heels, aiming a pistol with a long, fat barrel at Danby. Janie was grateful to see the gun, but impatient with the outfit. Sylvia had a *purse,* of all things, slung over her shoulder. And did the woman own a single pair of flat shoes?

"Move away from her," Sylvia said.

The men both stared, as at an apparition, and didn't move.

"I love you, Magnus, I really do," Sylvia said. "But if you don't move now, I will shoot you both. I promise."

Magnusson and Danby backed slowly away from the cage. "Sylvia," Magnusson said. "Be reasonable."

"I kept trying to put it all together," she said. "And finally I did. Danby is buying the uranium for Kim Il-sung, in North Korea. I can put up with a lot. I *have* put up with a lot. But not with that. Not with helping the country that killed my brother build an unstoppable bomb."

She reached with one hand into her purse, producing a pair of handcuffs, which she tossed to Danby. Startled, he caught them.

"Put those on," she said.

"No."

Sylvia shot at the ground half an inch from Danby's foot, and he leaped away. The gun made a strange, muffled sound, and Janie realized that the long barrel was a silencer. "I grew up in Texas," Sylvia said. "I'm a very good shot. Put them on."

Danby did as she said. She tossed a second pair of handcuffs to Magnusson, who put them on also.

"Now move away from the cage. Over there." She handed a key through the bars to Janie.

"I don't need the key," Janie said, taking the elastic off the ruined lock. She opened the door and stepped into the protected space behind Sylvia.

Magnusson looked surprised.

"I told you not to underestimate the girl," Danby said.

"You two, inside," Sylvia said.

Magnusson lunged toward Sylvia, reaching for her with cuffed hands, and she shot him in the heart. Again, the odd, stifled sound from the gun. He crumpled to the ground: the great bulk of his body laid out, the ruddy face astonished, the blue eyes looking up at his mistress. "Sylvia," he moaned, blood beginning to pool.

Tears sprang to Sylvia's eyes. "In the cage, Danby."

Danby obeyed. Sylvia produced a new padlock from her handbag and handed the lock to Janie, who mentally apologized for thinking the purse ridiculous. It was a *very* useful purse. As she locked the cage, Danby grabbed her wrist, handcuffs clanking on the bars. "This isn't over, Miss Scott," he hissed. "I *promise*."

"Let her go," Sylvia said, and he did.

"I told Magnusson not to trust you," Danby said.

"Well, he did anyway," Sylvia said, her eyes still bright and wet. "Love is blind. I ought to know. Empty your pockets."

Danby didn't move.

"Empty your pockets and throw everything out, or I'll shoot you like I shot him," she said. "I'm not a sentimental girl. Maybe you've noticed."

Danby turned his pockets inside out, revealing a money clip and a gold pen. He threw them out of the cage, at Sylvia's feet. She swept them up with one hand and tucked them into her handbag.

"Now, where are the boy and his father?" she asked.

"In the mill," Danby said.

Sylvia started back toward the main corridor, negotiating the rough ground in her high heels.

Janie looked at Magnusson lying on the ground in a pool of blood. Opal had never been able to please him, and now she would never have a chance. Janie crouched beside him. "Opal was really smart," she said. "You just made her think she wasn't." But Magnusson didn't seem to be breathing now, and she didn't think he could hear her.

"Janie," Danby said.

She looked up. His hands clutched the bars of the cage.

"In Siberia," he said, "there is a tribe of people whose word for the future means 'to go back.' Their word for the past means 'to go forward.'"

"That doesn't make sense," Janie said.

"It does, because you can't see the future coming," he said.

"All you can see is the past. We stare at the past, we analyze it, we replay it, while the future sneaks up behind us, unseen."

"Okay," Janie said.

"I'm trying to make a better future for all of us, Janie. You have to believe me."

Janie looked at him, mesmerized by the thought of moving blindly backward into the future, and then she shook her head to clear it. She shouldn't be listening to Danby. He was slippery, and might talk his way out of the cage. She turned to run after Sylvia.

"Janie!" Danby called, but she didn't look back.

As they approached the mill, Janie saw billowing dark smoke coming out of an industrial-looking steel door. Two uniformed guards stumbled out, coughing and squinting, and ran toward the elevator.

Sylvia handed Janie her silk scarf. "Tie this over your mouth and nose," she said. "And stay low."

They crawled through the open door onto a clean concrete floor, the air heavy with acrid smoke. A man in a white coat lay dead or unconscious. The smoke was coming from beneath a second door. When Sylvia reached to open it, Benjamin tumbled through from the other side, dragging his father's body.

Janie felt her heart skip at the sight of Benjamin. He looked anguished. "Help me!" he said. "We need someplace he can breathe!"

Janie helped him carry his father out into the mine, but the body was lifeless and heavy. They struggled past the tunnel that led to Danby's cage, and two of the Malay miners emerged. One had bony cheekbones, but the other's face was soft. They must have seen Magnusson dead and Danby caged, so they would know that everything had changed.

"Please help us," Janie begged. Her arms ached and the smoke stung her throat.

The miners glanced at each other, then took up the burden, one lifting the apothecary's shoulders and the other his feet. They were strong, and carried the unconscious body toward the elevator as if it weighed nothing.

Janie and Benjamin followed, and she reached for his hand, which was sweating in the underground heat. She hoped it wasn't too late.

CHAPTER 58

The Count

The Hungarian had appeared in the Manila apothecary shop unannounced, and Vinoray feared that he was there to steal the Pharmacopoeia. Guarding the ancient book had made him anxious, and kept him from sleeping. He wished Marcus Burrows and his son would come back.

The Hungarian, in an expensive linen suit, asked a lot of questions and swung his blackthorn walking stick within inches of the rows of glass bottles, making Vinoray wince. But finally he got to the point. "Where are Burrows and the boy?" he asked.

"I have no idea what you mean," Vinoray said.

The Hungarian put a telegram on the counter. It asked the recipient to come to Vinoray's shop, and was signed Alistiar Beane. "It's from Burrows," the Hungarian said. "I had a hell of a time getting here. So let's not play this game."

"You are a true colleague of Marcus Burrows?" Vinoray asked.

"True as true."

"Then do something."

The Hungarian raised his eyebrows. "A party trick?"

"A demonstration," Vinoray said. "So I know you are no impostor."

The Hungarian frowned, then struck the tip of his blackthorn walking stick twice against the floor. Vinoray's open account book riffled its pages in an arc, and then the heavy leather cover closed. The book slid, untouched, across the glass counter.

Vinoray watched, amazed. He couldn't do that. "Come upstairs," he said.

They went through the things Marcus Burrows and Jin Lo had left behind, including a map tucked inside a book about the anthropology of the Pacific Islands. The count—for the Hungarian was Count Vilmos Hadik de Galántha, of whom Vinoray had heard many stories—unfolded the map and studied the pinpricks in it. "There must be a way to determine which pin was put in the map *last*," he said. "Which molecules of the paper were disturbed most recently. That might tell us where they are."

"Perhaps," Vinoray said.

The count picked up the book about the islands and let it fall open where it would, to a photograph of a man in a loincloth. He peered at the photo. "Now, that might be the last page that was held open, or it might just be someone's favorite page," he said.

The bell rang downstairs. Vinoray excused himself and received a telegram from a messenger boy. He took it back upstairs to show to the count.

The Hungarian glanced at the telegram and then ran down after the boy. He was very spry for such an ample man.

Vinoray, meanwhile, took the Pharmacopoeia from the wall safe behind the photograph of his mother and laid the book open on the table. He emptied the little glassine packet of powder into a glass of water, as instructed. There was not much powder left, but Vinoray hoped it was enough. He drank the solution down, sat before the book, and waited.

Nothing happened.

The count returned, pink from running up the stairs, and unfolded the map again. "The telegram from Burrows originated here, in Malaya," he said, pointing. He noticed the Pharmacopoeia, the glassine packet, the water glass. "What are we doing?"

"It's a sort of telepathy," Vinoray said, keeping his eyes on the book. "The boy designed it."

"Benjamin?"

"He wished to see the girl in America."

"I see," the count said. *"Mater artium necessitas."*

"Marcus Burrows now wishes to use it to read the Pharmacopoeia, through me," Vinoray said, turning a page of the book.

"How do you know you're on the right page?"

Vinoray had wondered the same thing. "I don't. It's an incomplete science. One can only see and hear in one direction."

"I see."

They waited. Nothing. No buzz of connection, but Vinoray had been warned that he might feel nothing.

The count said, "Perhaps we should just go to the island in my boat, and take the book with us."

Vinoray turned a page. "He needs to see it now. And the boat might capsize. The book is irreplaceable."

"Fortune favors the bold," the count said.

"I've been charged with a task."

The count sighed. "Oh, bloody hell."

Vinoray hadn't felt authorized to read the Pharmacopoeia before, but now he couldn't take his eyes from it. The page he was on contained instructions for making the human body invisible. He had always longed for that ability, and heard that it was possible, but hadn't come across the correct information before. He turned another page, trying to feel for any intrusion in his brain, any slight indication that he should stop on *this* page and not another. He felt nothing.

After a while, the strain of concentration grew too much, combined with his recent lack of sleep, and he felt his eyes begin to close. He snapped them back open. His colleagues needed help: the beautiful and brusque Jin Lo, who made Vinoray so shy that he could not speak, and the boy, Benjamin, and Marcus Burrows, who was supremely accomplished. Sometimes a bit pedantic, perhaps. But interested in the local plants, which was gratifying. Vinoray's eyes began to droop again. He must not fall asleep. He must complete his task. But he had slept so little, and he was drowsy.

In the darkness, behind his eyelids, he saw a small table laid out with a makeshift laboratory: a Bunsen burner, a series of glass jars. A pair of hands, where his own hands would be if his eyes were open, was grinding a yellow stone into powder. He heard the boy's voice: "I still think we should've called for help."

"Please, Benjamin," the voice of Marcus Burrows said.

"It's no use rehearsing what's been done. We must move forward."

"By helping our enemies?" Benjamin asked.

Burrows must have looked up, because Vinoray saw Benjamin sitting across the little table. "I would like to think that I could sacrifice your life for my principles," Burrows said. "But I find that I can't. You're my son, and you are all I have in the world, and I would appreciate your help keeping you alive."

"All right," Benjamin said, more impatient than a dutiful son should be. "Then I have an idea." The image in Vinoray's mind was starting to fade.

"For treating the uranium?" Burrows asked.

"For getting us out of here." The boy lit the Bunsen burner and the flame blazed up, like a spirit set free.

CHAPTER 59

Unintended Consequences

When Benjamin emerged from the mine, he saw Jin Lo running toward them, out of the trees. Benjamin was even more grateful to see her than he had been on the little sailboat, harassed by sharks. Sylvia brought up her pistol, but Benjamin pushed it down. "She's our friend!" he said.

Jin Lo kneeled and felt his father's pulse. "Weak."

"You have to help him!" Benjamin said.

"In the garden," Jin Lo said. "Everything is there."

"The golf cart," Sylvia said. It had been abandoned at an awkward angle near one of the houses.

The two miners eased the apothecary's limp body into the passenger seat. Jin Lo squeezed in beside him, and Sylvia climbed in to drive. The two miners clung to the back of the cart, and the electric motor strained. There was no room for more passengers.

"We'll follow," Benjamin said. "Just go!"

The golf cart drove off, the motor complaining about the weight.

Benjamin watched for stray guards as he walked with Janie through the trees, along the narrow waist of the island between the mine and the villa. He couldn't stop thinking of his father. It eclipsed the strangeness of being with Janie again. "I thought it was a good idea," he said. "It seemed like a good idea!"

"He'll be all right," Janie said.

"Remember the orange smoke Jin Lo made so we could escape from the bunker in London?" he asked. "I was thinking of that. I thought if I made something that created a lot of smoke, and put it out under the door, then they would have to open the door to see what was wrong. The smoke would mask us, and we could escape. But there was something wrong with it. It poisoned him."

"You couldn't have known."

"But I *should* have known! I should have!"

"Benjamin." She stopped and took his face in her hands. "He'll be all right. Jin Lo will help him."

And there in the trees, the world seemed to fall away. He leaned forward. He was kissing Janie Scott again. He could hardly believe it. Her lips were softer than he remembered. Even in dirt-smudged pajamas with smoke in her hair, her skin smelled fresh and sweet. He pulled back to see if she was really there.

"You're not going to vanish and fade away," he said.

"I'm not."

A sudden pain reminded him. "That actor," he said. "The one you were staying with."

"Raffaello," Janie said. "He helped me."

"I sent Pip to New Hampshire to rescue you from him."

"From *Raffaello*?"

"It seemed important. He kissed you."

"You *saw* that?"

"I didn't mean to spy—"

But Janie was kissing him again, and the pain in his chest turned into a sweet, flooding ache. She put her cheek to his and whispered in his ear, "You can't be jealous of Raffaello."

"Why not?"

"Because he's not you. No one else could ever be."

Benjamin's heart felt dangerously full, hearing that.

Then shouts came from the direction of the villa, startling them out of their reverie. They were acting like fools. Keeping their heads low, they ran along the edge of the road. When they got close to the villa, the gate in the electrified fence stood open.

"We have to get to the garden," Benjamin said. "Stay low."

When they rounded the corner of the house, they saw that the kitchen garden was growing. Vines entwined themselves among the fruit trees, making a green wall, and climbed willfully up the side of the house.

"Hey!" a voice shouted, and Benjamin saw two of the uniformed guards running toward them.

"Go!" he said. He parted the vines for Janie, who climbed through. He followed, forcing the branches apart. One of the guards grabbed his ankle, but Benjamin wrenched it free, and the entwining tendrils wrapped around the guard's torso and carried him upward as they grew. Benjamin heard a shout of fear from eight feet over his head, then ten, then twelve. The gap he and Janie had climbed through had already filled in, dense and green. Benjamin saw the ragged edges of grape leaves in the wall, and the long, smooth leaves of vanilla vines.

Jin Lo was inside the protective green cave, hunched over Benjamin's father, who lay on his back, unconscious. The two miners were there, too. The plants were still growing. Jin Lo had opened the apothecary's shirt, and his bare chest rose and fell with his labored breathing.

She looked up at Benjamin. "What is in this smoke?"

He told her, and her face darkened with disapproval.

"I had to find a way to escape," he said.

"So you make poison."

"I didn't mean to."

"And Danby?"

"He's in a cage in the mine," Janie said. "And Magnusson is dead."

Jin Lo raised her eyebrows. "You feel his pulse?"

"Sylvia shot him in the heart. You can ask her."

"There are others?"

"There was a man in a white coat," Benjamin said. "An engineer. But he was poisoned by the smoke."

"You feel his pulse?"

"We were in a hurry," Janie said. "And he was unconscious, like Mr. Burrows."

Jin Lo was impatient. "Mr. Burrows has many substance in body. He is bird, he is shot with arrow, he is breathing underwater twice. He is not young. Human body can support many transformation. But many transformation, plus wound, *plus* poison, this is difficult."

Benjamin looked at his father lying helpless on the ground. He hadn't thought of all the ways his father might be weakened—all of them in the service of finding Benjamin.

"So," Jin Lo said. "Situation is this. You poison father. You leave number-one enemy Danby alive in cage. Also Magnusson—maybe dead, maybe not. Also engineer, alive, to unlock cage."

When she put it that way, it didn't seem good. And the plants were still growing, creaking and rustling, sealing them in.

CHAPTER 60

Danby

D anby stood in the elevator cage, listening to Sylvia and Janie's footsteps receding up the tunnel: Sylvia deliberate in high heels, Janie hurried and light. He considered Magnusson lying on his stomach with his cheek to the bloody ground, wide-eyed and staring. A humiliating position. It was time to reassess. Danby had planned to get rid of Magnusson, but not yet. This wasn't how he'd intended things to go.

He pulled on Sylvia's padlock with his handcuffed hands. It was a good lock, solid and heavy. He inspected the rusted hinges of the cage door.

Shouts came from the direction of the mill, followed a few moments later by a smell. Not a good smell. It wasn't the sulfuric acid used to leach the uranium from the ore, but it was similar in its noxiousness.

Danby had often thought about smell, how the sense communicated information to the human brain on the most primitive level: *this* is good to eat, *this* is rotten, *this* is poison.

In that instinctive way, he knew that the smell that came to him now was not healthy.

Other people knew it, too, and they were running. Danby heard footsteps, and people calling. He reached down with both linked hands and pulled up his khaki trouser leg. He squeezed the release to draw a knife from the scabbard strapped to his calf. The knife was RAF aircrew issue, meant for cutting harnesses in case of a crash, but sometimes you had to improvise. He wedged the base of the blade behind the top hinge on the cage's door and put his weight against it, testing the strength of the tempered steel knife against the brittle, rusting hinge. The hinge began to bend, but it had no flexibility. It snapped off. The top of the door was free.

Two men came running past, and Danby slid his knife awkwardly into his sleeve. "Let me out!" he shouted, to keep up appearances. The men ignored him and were gone.

He brought the knife out again to work on the middle hinge, which was stronger and took more time. But then it, too, snapped. He pushed at the door. It gave a little, but the gap wasn't large enough for him to step through. So he wedged his knife behind the bottom hinge, the last barrier to his freedom. It was awkward, this low one, and he swore with the effort. It snapped.

He pushed open the door in the dim light. With his wrists still linked together, he felt for Magnusson's pulse. The skin was prickly with a day's beard, the muscle thick, the jowls incipient. He searched for the carotid artery, for any sign of life, and felt nothing.

Sylvia had taken his cash, but he would have enough of that soon. When the United States and Britain consider you a spy and a traitor, and the Soviet Union considers you a disappointing failure, your options for career advancement become strikingly limited. It was a self-fulfilling prophecy: When the world considers you to be an international criminal, you must become one. You have little choice.

The smell was getting worse, but he didn't panic and run from the mine with the others. He walked deeper into the earth. The poisonous smoke would rise, so the air would be safe below. This tunnel would connect to other tunnels. He had work to do.

CHAPTER 61

Arrival

Pip peered out the window of the plane at the island. It looked just like it had on the charts: rounded at both ends, with a curved narrow section in the middle. He couldn't believe he was finally *here*.

Getting Angelica to lose patience with Hawaii had been the greatest challenge of his life so far. She was spoiled and quickly bored, that was true, but Hawaii was such an easy place to love. The ocean was so blue, the air so soft. The bartender at the Royal Hawaiian made banana-pineapple-coconut milk shakes.

So he had gone to work. He'd sprinkled sand in her clothes and in her shoes. He'd pulled a surfboard out from under her feet while pretending to help her catch a wave. He'd steered her into a jellyfish, which stung her leg.

"It's so beautiful here," she'd said, after examining the red welts on her shin. "It's paradise."

"Paradise is boring!" Pip said.

"No, it's not."

So Pip had turned his focus to her father. First he disabled his hotel room ceiling fan. Mr. Lowell was a big man, quick to sweat, and he complained at breakfast, hot and groggy. Pip replaced the sunscreen in his bottle with ordinary hand lotion, and watched him fall asleep on the beach. By afternoon he was the color of a cooked lobster.

At dinner that night in a Chinese restaurant, Mr. Lowell ordered his kung pao chicken extra spicy, and Pip slipped the waiter a dollar to triple the chili. Mr. Lowell was too proud to admit that the heat was too much, and turned purple. Pip almost started to feel sorry for the guy.

Back at the hotel, maintenance had fixed Mr. Lowell's ceiling fan, so Pip blew the fuse for his room.

In the morning, Mr. Lowell gave in. "We're going home," he said.

"No!" Angelica wailed.

"In the villa *I* want to go to," Pip offered, "all the rooms are air-conditioned."

Mr. Lowell brightened through his crimson sunburn. "What do you say, sweetheart? A compromise?"

"I want to stay *here*," Angelica said.

"That's not an option," her father said. It was the first time Pip had heard him defy his daughter, and it was a sweet, sweet sound.

As they drew closer to the island, Pip saw a grand white house at the southern end, with a green tower attached to one side of it. Pip had never seen a tower like that. Was it a giant hedge? There was also a sparkling blue swimming pool, a few small white cottages, a lagoon, and a grass landing strip.

At the northern end, there was a cluster of tiny, identical houses, a warehouse, and a pier. A boat was approaching the pier. It looked like a landing craft with a flat-nosed bow. Pip had been enjoying the triumph of arrival, but now he felt apprehensive. His old itching feeling was back.

Angelica's father made an expert landing, rumbled down the grass runway, and cut the engine. As the propellers slowed, the island seemed unsettlingly quiet. Even the insects were startled mute by the plane's arrival.

Pip climbed warily out, looking for signs of life. He walked with Angelica and her father up the road past a beach and the lagoon, and toward the big white house. The gate hung open. If anyone noticed the gaily dressed newcomers in Hawaiian prints, they ignored them. Pip felt like a ghost—like a party of ghosts all killed at a luau, coming back to haunt the living, only to find that the living couldn't spare the time to be haunted.

"I want to go for a swim," Angelica said, her voice ringing out in the stillness.

"Shh!" Pip whispered.

"What?" she said. "I'm hot. I'm going to find the pool."

Her father followed her, and Pip headed for the tower of vines. Its top was higher than the house, and there was a man in a green uniform stuck in the branches, twenty feet in the air.

"Get me down!" the man said.

Pip heard a rustle of branches lower down. "Hullo?" he called. "Anyone in there?"

There was a surprised silence, and then a girl's voice said, "*Pip?*"

"Janie!"

"We heard a plane! Was that you?"

"It was," Pip said. "Are you expecting a boat?"

There was a brief silence behind the green wall, and then he heard Benjamin's voice. "What kind of boat?"

"Some kind of landing craft, you know, where the front folds open."

"You're sure it was coming here?"

"Think so."

Benjamin's voice was urgent. "Pip, listen. We need an ax or—a saw. Anything like that. Quickly!"

Pip ran round the side of the house. Where would he be if he were an ax? He tried a door that opened: an entryway to a big kitchen. He heard a noise and crept closer. Sitting on the floor against the cupboards was a blond woman with her knees drawn up and her shoes kicked off. Beside her on the floor was a pistol with a fat silencer. She had her face in her hands, and her shoulders shook with sobbing. There might be knives in the kitchen, but they weren't worth getting past *that*. Pip let himself silently back outside.

He ran down to the white cottages and found an equipment shed. Hanging on the wall were two pruning saws. He grabbed them both and turned to see a man in a green uniform crouching against the wall.

"You scared me," Pip said.

"Are they still growing?" the man asked.

"What?"

"The plants!"

"I think they've stopped."

"They grabbed my friend!" the man said.

"The one up in the air?"

"Is he dead?"

"No, he's all right," Pip said. "Chin up."

He ran back toward the house and set to work with one of the pruning saws, ignoring the pleas of the man in the air, until he had a hole big enough to pass the other saw through to Benjamin. It was faster when they worked from both sides. Finally the gap was big enough for a smallish person to climb through. Janie squeezed out first, the branches grabbing at her clothes. She hugged Pip. "I can't believe you came all this way!" she said.

"It was nothing," he said, suddenly bashful.

Benjamin squeezed out next, shook Pip's hand gratefully, and said, "Now show us that boat."

CHAPTER 62

Fugitive

Benjamin, Pip, and Janie raced toward the north end of the island in a golf cart. Benjamin drove, not particularly well, and tried not to think the worst thoughts: *A boat arriving—Danby escaping—Danby gone.*

When they got to the pier, Magnusson's motorboat was scuttled and sinking beside the pier, useless, the bow and the radio mast still sticking up out of the water.

"There!" Pip said, and he pointed out to sea. "That's it!"

Benjamin saw the landing craft heading away, already half a mile off. On the deck, something white caught his eye. He shaded his eyes to look.

The flash of white looked like a flag of truce, or a girl's handkerchief waving from an ocean liner. But it wasn't either of those. It was a tall, straight figure, looking back at the island from the stern. The sunlight caught his shock of white hair. Danby. Benjamin felt disappointment hit him hard, like a blow to the ribs. It took a moment before he could breathe again.

"Maybe we could follow in Pip's airplane," Janie said.

"And then what?"

"Watch where Danby goes?"

"It was hard enough to get the plane *here*," Pip said. "No way they're leaving already."

When they got back to the villa, a girl in a lavender bikini appeared from the direction of the pool and put her hands on her hips. "This is *not* a resort hotel," she said. "And there is *no* royalty here."

Benjamin stared at her, confused. She looked very clean, with blue-gray eyes and long brown hair.

"Angelica, can we use your plane?" Pip asked. "It's important."

"No!" she said. "We just got here!"

Pip shrugged at Benjamin and Janie. "May I present Angelica Lowell?"

The girl smiled at Janie's filthy pajamas. "You must be Janie," she said, her tone false and slighting. "I've heard so much about you." Benjamin hadn't heard anyone talk like that since he left school, two years earlier, and it was so ridiculous that it made him want to laugh.

Then Jin Lo emerged from the direction of the overgrown garden. "Benjamin," she said, ignoring the newcomers. Her hair was coming out of her braid, and the breeze whipped it across her face. She pushed it away. Tears had left dirty tracks on her face.

"What is it?" Benjamin asked.

Jin Lo's eyes were desolate. "You should come."

CHAPTER 63

The Apothecary

Marcus Burrows felt a hand take his, and he opened his eyes to see his son beside him. He closed his eyes again. *Like an ostrich,* he thought, with his diminished strength. *With my head in the sand.* Did he think he could hide from his son, at the last moment? Now was the moment he must not hide. The pain in his chest was sharp, and there was a dark cloud in his mind. It chased his thoughts in all directions. He forced himself to look at his son, whose eyes were so like Susan's—like his mother's.

"I'm sorry," he whispered. He had so little breath.

"Don't leave me!" Benjamin said.

"I meant what I said. You've surpassed me. You'll do great things."

"Not without you!" Benjamin said. "There's too much I don't know."

"You'll learn."

"How?" Benjamin asked.

"You'll have the book."

His son shook his head, looking wretched.

"And listen, Benjamin. This is important. The work—" He took a gasping breath that raked his lungs. The dark cloud loomed, but he had things to say first.

"Yes?" Benjamin wiped his eyes.

"We don't originate it. The work is being done by the universe. We are the instrument, the vessel through which it flows. You understand?"

"No," Benjamin said.

He wished for more eloquence. He wished for more strength. "You are the vessel. You can't be collapsed by grief, or anger—by bitterness, or guilt, or revenge. What happened here was not your fault."

"It was!"

"*Please,*" he said. Another rasping breath. "You are my hope. What you've done on your own—sometimes I think that no one has ever needed a mentor less than you."

His son was crying openly now. He wished he could protect Benjamin from this pain, but that was impossible, when it was the pain of losing him. He felt himself chasing the tail of his own thought. He hadn't been a perfect father. He had wanted to protect Benjamin, and let him be a child while he still could. And then he had wanted to prepare him to be a man. But he wasn't sure he had done either of those things. He saw that the American girl was here—Janie—even as white spots seemed to invade his vision. She looked distraught.

"Take care of him, Janie," he said. His son would be an orphan now, but the girl loved him. "Will you? Will you take him home?"

She nodded, tears running down her cheeks.

"That would be good," he said.

But there was still the thing he didn't want to think about, scattering his thoughts. He had to face it. He had been working to save Benjamin, in the mill, but that had not been the right act, for the end of his life. "Benjamin, the uranium," he said. An antic dwarf came into his mind—but why? He was growing confused. "I turned straw into gold. Not much, not even a barrel, but that could be enough. A seed. Don't let it get away."

It was so important to explain, but so difficult. He couldn't even hold on to consciousness. He seemed unable to push enough air out of his lungs to make room for another breath. He had succeeded. He had turned straw into gold, at the wicked king's command. He had let the work flow through him for the wrong purpose. Benjamin's face, with his mother's worried eyes, vanished. The bright spots closed in.

CHAPTER 64

The Envoy

The distant tops of the grape and vanilla vines swayed in the tropical breeze, but inside the garden, the air was still and warm. Janie sat with Benjamin at his father's side. The apothecary looked like a wax figure on the ground, so unnaturally still. His chest no longer rose and fell with his labored breaths. Janie felt a sharp pain in her own chest—but if that was true, then how must it be for Benjamin?

He shouted at Jin Lo, "Can't you do *anything*?"

Jin Lo looked crumpled and streaked with tears. She shook her head.

"How could he say it wasn't my fault?" Benjamin was hoarse with anger. "It's *entirely* my fault."

"I'm the reason you're on the island," Janie said. "It's my fault."

Benjamin whirled on her. "But I wasn't supposed to contact you!" he said. "He told me it wasn't safe! And I ignored him!"

"He said you can't give in to anger and guilt."

"I did what *I* wanted to do," he said. "Magnusson only kidnapped you because you were in contact with *me*!" He pressed his palms against his eyes as if he could push the tears back inside his skull.

Janie put her hand on his shoulder, but he shook it off. "Don't," he said. "Just—don't."

She looked around the green cave for help and caught Pip's eye, in his incongruously cheerful shirt with palm trees on it. Pip pointed in the air.

"Listen," he said.

There were two distinct, distant noises, coming from two different directions. They blended together, but one seemed to be a whine from the sea, and the other a thudding from the sky. Pip disappeared through the hole in the green wall, and Janie followed.

She looked into the slanting afternoon light and saw a helicopter approaching the island. It was painted a yellow gold.

As it banked, Janie saw an elaborate design on the side, a dragon curled in a circle, and she recognized the insignia: Opal had it embossed on creamy white stationery. It was her grandfather the sultan's crest.

The whine from the sea grew louder. A black motorboat cut daggerlike through the water. It eased up as it approached, the engine growling to protest the slowness.

The helicopter settled on the lawn like a noisy dragonfly, and Janie and Pip ducked in the wind from the rotors. The first two men who climbed out were elaborately dressed in dark red uniforms, carrying rifles. Another man in a yellow robe climbed out after them.

Janie was about to step forward, but she guessed they would prefer to talk to a man—or at least a boy. She pushed Pip forward.

"Hiya," Pip said over the noise. He folded his arms in defiance over his Hawaiian shirt.

"You wish to speak English?" the robed man asked.

"Yeah," Pip said. "I do."

Janie winced. She was upset, too, but she wished Pip would be diplomatic and obliging for just a minute or two.

"I am the envoy of His Exalted Highness the Sultan," the robed man said.

"I know who you are," Pip said. "I sent you lot a telegram when the sultan's granddaughter needed help, and you never answered it. His own granddaughter! If you'd answered, we'd never be in this mess!"

The envoy frowned. "I know nothing of this telegram."

"Well, maybe you *should've* known," Pip said.

The envoy drew himself up to his full height. "We are reclaiming this island as property of the sultanate," he said. "The princess demands a divorce from Magnus Magnusson."

"She won't need one," Pip said. "He's dead."

"Dead!" the envoy said. "Then we must—speak with the proper delegate!"

"How 'bout you kiss my proper arse?" Pip said.

The envoy looked outraged, and the guards stepped forward with their rifles, but Janie saw a man in a pale linen suit walking up the road from the beach. Now he was striding up the lawn. He was plump, but moved lightly, and carried a package under his arm, wrapped in oilcloth. His hair had been blown back by the wind, and he wore aviator-style sunglasses.

Janie said, "Excuse me. Your most esteemed royal envoy, sir. Allow me to introduce our proper delegate. This is the man you'll wish to speak to about the situation on the island—His Excellency Count Vilmos Hadik de Galántha." The envoy seemed interested, so she kept going: "Professor of Pharmacology, Doctor of Letters, and—Honorary Consul of the Hapsburgs."

Count Vili took off his sunglasses and bowed deeply. He said how honored he was to make the envoy's acquaintance.

He was eager to discuss the situation on the island, and was convinced they could resolve it to everyone's satisfaction. Then he asked for a moment to speak with his niece, and drew Janie away.

"I had a devil of a time getting Vinoray to let me take the Pharmacopoeia," he said in a low voice. "I promised to deliver it *only* into the hands of Marcus Burrows."

Janie felt her eyes filling with tears. She didn't want to tell Vili. She watched as sorrow came over the count's sunny face.

CHAPTER 65

A Midsummer Night's Dream

There was a feast, of sorts, on the island. It was not a victory celebration. It was a reunion, and it was a diplomatic dinner. But mostly it was *food*. No one had eaten since the day before, and they fell upon the plates Osman brought. They sat outside in the warm air, beside the pool at the villa, with lanterns lit in the equatorial twilight. They ate rice steamed in coconut milk, a spicy stew, and hauntingly sweet mangosteens, the white segments of fruit nestled inside the thick purple rind.

Jin Lo wanted to go after Danby in Count Vili's boat, but Vili said that night was falling. There were islands and reefs, invisible in the darkness. Danby could have gone in any direction, and his landing craft could stop on any island to hide. They would go after him, but they would do it deliberately, with preparation.

"When you are in a hurry, dress slowly," Jin Lo said.

"Exactly," Vili said.

"I do not like this rule."

He put a plate of food in her hands. "Too bad," he said. "Now eat."

The crew of the *Payday* had come ashore, and Harry and Charlotte sat in deck chairs on either side of Janie. "So you're the girl Benjamin came all this way for," Harry said. "I told him not to do it. I said when a girl runs off, she usually has a good reason."

"I didn't want to run off," Janie said.

"I know you're an infant," Charlotte said, "too young to think about these things, but Benjamin's a good one. He's a keeper."

"I'm sixteen," Janie said.

"Good lord," Charlotte said. "What I didn't know at sixteen."

"I know a *lot*," Janie said.

Charlotte looked wistful. "That's what I thought, too."

Angelica Lowell sat next to Pip. Her father, eating happily, asked Osman if he was looking for a new cooking job. Osman glanced at Count Vili, who was talking with the sultan's envoy, and said he thought he already had one.

They had cut Magnusson's guard down out of the vines, and brought his terrified friend out of the gardening shed, and the two guards sat at the edge of the lantern light, eating gratefully. Sylvia had locked two more guards up in a storage closet, and knocked one over the head with the butt of her pistol, but he was recovering. The two miners who had carried the apothecary went back to their families with food. They nodded in consolation to Benjamin as they slipped away.

Some of the miners would leave and go to their home islands, Osman predicted, and some would stay to see what the new ownership of the island would bring.

Tessel and Efa tried to cheer Benjamin up, but they were awed by his desolation. He sat in furious silence, consumed by grief and guilt. It was exactly what his father had told him not to do. Janie ached for him.

After dinner, Vili appeared with a tray of champagne flutes, the liquid golden in the lantern light. The forgetting wine.

"I would like to propose a toast," he said, handing the narrow glasses to Harry and Charlotte, to Angelica and her father, to Sylvia and to Magnusson's guards. Osman followed with a second tray of sparkling cider for the envoy's party, who didn't drink alcohol. Janie didn't get a champagne flute. Neither did Pip or Benjamin.

"Here, take mine," Harry said to Janie.

"I'm happy with lemonade," she said. "I'm an infant, remember?"

Count Vili stood among the group in the flickering light. "To Marcus Burrows," he said. "Who was my friend. And my colleague. And my teacher. He had a devotion to his work that most of us can only envy. And an equal devotion to his son, of whom he was deeply proud, although perhaps he didn't always know how to show it. But everything he did for the world, he did for Benjamin."

Janie looked to Benjamin, whose face was stormy.

"Marcus Burrows was a true master of his craft," the count went on. "And more than that, he was a guardian of peace. I promise you that we will honor his memory and continue his cause. In that way, he will live on." He lifted his glass. "*Fenékig,* as they say in my country. It means, 'To the bottom of the glass.'"

"*Fenékig!*" Charlotte said cheerfully.

"*Pro,*" the sultan's envoy said.

"Cheers," Angelica's father said.

"*Gan bei,*" Jin Lo said quietly, lifting her lemonade.

Janie watched as everyone drained their glasses. She drank to Marcus Burrows, too, and her lemonade was icy cold.

Another dinner was held, after an endless series of flights, at Janie's parents' house in Ann Arbor. She had brought Benjamin home, and Count Vili had come along in the role of rescuer, to smooth the reentry. Janie had made him promise he wouldn't give her parents any champagne.

"It would make everything so much easier," Vili said.

"I don't care," she said. She could face her parents' anger, but it was too horrible to make them forget.

Her parents weren't just angry, they were *furious,* and exhausted from driving around Florida on a wild-goose chase. The road trip had used up all their considerable goodwill. And they had no memory of Janie's trip to Nova Zembla, so they were unprepared for a trip to Malaya. But as dinner went on, they listened and asked questions, and Janie told them a version of what had happened: how Magnusson was after Marcus Burrows's scientific secrets, and she was taken as bait, and Benjamin and Vili had rescued her.

"What kind of scientific secrets?" her father asked.

"I don't really understand it all," she said.

"And why don't we remember Benjamin?"

"You met him in England, Dad. You just forgot. You called him Figment as a joke."

Benjamin nodded confirmation.

Her parents looked sheepish. "I guess we were a little pre-occupied at the time," her father said.

Janie wondered if Vili had slipped them something that made them more pliable and accepting, but she decided not to ask.

Benjamin, who had barely spoken on the flight home, or during the meal, excused himself when they got to the part about his father's death. Janie guessed he was going to sit alone and read the Pharmacopoeia, which he did a lot lately. He was an orphan now, and didn't have anywhere else to go. She told her parents about Mr. Burrows asking, before he died, if Benjamin could live with her, and they looked at each other for a long moment, and then her father sighed.

"Okay," he said. "But it's *our rules* from here on out. No lies, and no major omissions, like not telling us that you've been kicked out of school. And no running off to other countries. I think that should go without saying."

Janie agreed to all their terms.

Count Vili left to help Jin Lo go after Danby, and Janie and Benjamin enrolled at the local high school. She set about being a normal American teen, but it wasn't easy. She chafed at her parents' rules, at the way they chaperoned her all the time and treated her like a child. They didn't seem to understand that she had been on her own at Grayson, and they couldn't keep an eye on her every minute.

Benjamin still wasn't speaking, or wasn't speaking much. Sometimes he would launch into anguished monologues about how he had failed his father. If Janie told him that wasn't true, he would argue with her, with some of his old fire. Then he would sink beneath the waves of his despair and go quiet again.

In February, they went to Grayson to collect her things, and to fulfill a promise. The New Hampshire cold was biting, and Janie wrapped her scarf around her neck and took her parents and Benjamin to the auditorium at East High.

The theater, empty and dark on the morning she had tried to contact Benjamin, was bright and full of the happy clamor of people greeting each other and finding their seats. Janie saw Opal and Mrs. Magnusson in the aisle, and her heart thudded. She still wasn't sure what she was going to say to her roommate. Opal had stopped wearing the heavy glasses and looked beautiful, but Benjamin didn't stop and stare, he just said "How do you do," and went to take his seat. Mrs. Magnusson wore an orange silk dress and held her fur coat in her arms, like an enormous pet. She stood protectively close to Opal.

"I'm so sorry about your dad," Janie said.

Opal's naked eyes looked vulnerable and sad. "Were you there when it happened?" she asked.

"There's an official inquiry," Mrs. Magnusson said briskly. "Everything will be taken care of, and answered by the envoy."

But Opal searched Janie's face. "Did my dad say anything about me?"

Janie considered lying, saying that he'd praised Opal to the moon. "You don't have to prove anything to him," she finally said. "He was wrong about everything."

Opal nodded sadly. "That's what my analyst says."

"It's true," Janie said.

"What happened to Pip?"

"He went back to England." He had a costume fitting for *Robin Hood*, and he'd taken Sylvia with him. He said in a year she'd either be running a studio or she'd be a star.

"I liked him," Opal said wistfully.

"Me too."

Janie felt a tug on her scarf and turned to see Tadpole Porter, radiant in his brown suit. "Are you coming back to Grayson?" he asked.

"No, I go to school in Michigan now."

His face fell. "Oh. Because I was going to ask if you'd be on the dance committee. There's a spring formal coming up."

"I wish I could."

"I'll be on the dance committee," Opal offered.

Tadpole's eyes widened. "You *will?*"

The house lights flashed and then dimmed, and they all hurried to their seats. The crowd quieted, and the red curtain opened to reveal the painted set of a Grecian palace. Behind the stones, Janie could see a forest hung with papier-mâché trees and tumbling painted branches.

Raffaello came onstage as Demetrius, who was arrogant and cruel to the girl who loved him, and determined to force the girl who didn't love him into marriage. He was a good actor. And it wasn't just because he was ridiculously handsome, all lit up with stage lights. Or because he was Janie's friend. It was also the way he talked to the other actors. He drew the audience in, even playing a villain. Janie guessed that the girls of East High were thinking less about the play and more about going backstage to tell Raffaello how wonderful he had been.

Benjamin, sitting on the other side of Janie's father, leaned forward in the dark. "*That's him?*" he whispered.

Janie leaned forward, too, and nodded.

"He's a big jerk," Benjamin whispered.

Janie tried not to laugh. It was the first thing Benjamin had said since his father's death that had any lightness in it. She feared her relief might bubble up and come out as some really embarrassing noise. She whispered, *"He's acting."*

"Shh," her father said.

In the dark, looking across her father's lap, Janie saw something in Benjamin's eyes that wasn't sadness or heartache. She thought it might replace the sadness, given time. They both sat back to watch the play. Demetrius was still being horrible to Helena, a tall, pretty blonde who loved him. Even with her father between them, Janie could feel Benjamin relax. She thought she could see inside his mind—not in the glassine-envelope way, but in the usual way of guessing someone's thoughts. He had been afraid she was in love with Raffaello, but he was reassured now, because how could anyone be in love with a jerk like that?

Benjamin's hand was on the armrest. Janie reached across her father, just for a second, took his hand, and squeezed.

Her father shot her a look.

But Benjamin squeezed back.

EPILOGUE

Cargo

A twin-propeller plane rumbled to a stop at the end of the island. The landing strip wasn't paved, but it was kept clear and smooth by the islanders, in anticipation of the return of John Frum. The people gathered with weapons to receive the visitors from the sky, having suffered two rounds of bird people who'd caused nothing but trouble. The airplane had a design painted on the side, a golden creature like a winged crocodile curled into a circle, which seemed to bode ill.

Then the plane's door opened, and Tessel and Efa bounded out, talking so fast they could barely be understood. They had been in an airplane! They had flown through the air! They had sailed a boat for the most *foolish* white people, who never knew where they were! They had been on an island with a swimming pool like a blue box in the earth and there was an enormous house there, with a tower of vines! There were so many stories, they might never run out.

But first there were the boxes to be unpacked, in the hold

of the airplane. Efa knew what everything was, and was ready to explain it all:

There were bandages and gauze, which must be left in the sterile packaging until there was a wound to wrap. And there were special pills: If a wound became infected, or a child became ill in her throat or her lungs, the pills would drive the infection out.

There were three fat pink pigs in a crate, with curly tails, who squealed furiously at their captivity and tumbled out into a pen.

There were two sealed ice chests full of ice and cold bottles of Coca-Cola, an especial gift for Toby Prophet and meant to be opened *only* for the feast to welcome Efa and Tessel home. Efa was very clear about the necessity of the welcoming feast.

There were fishhooks and fishing line and beautiful fishing poles. The hooks were fine and slender and sparkled silver in the light, except you couldn't wear them as necklaces, because they had very sharp barbs at the end.

Efa already had a necklace: a gold elephant on a chain from the woman on the boat. She hoped one day to see a real elephant. Charlotte had said she thought she would. She said Efa might sail a boat someday to the places where elephants lived.

There was a gramophone and records, and Efa went through the stack: Fats Domino, and Big Mama Thornton, and Bill Haley and the Comets. These were for dancing, Efa said. Harry and Charlotte had picked them out.

There were also slates and chalk for drawing, and notebooks full of clean white paper, and Efa's favorite gift:

beautiful soft pencils in all different colors, for making pictures on the white paper.

All tabu was cast off Efa in her role as the deliverer of cargo and the explainer of its uses. There was respectful silence as she took the colored pencils and drew a picture of the enormous white house covered in vines, and the lagoon with a tunnel that went to the sea, and the sparkling blue swimming pool. Not everyone believed it was a true drawing, although Tessel backed her up. Because why would anyone need a house so large? And why dig a pool so close to a lagoon? There was some discussion about whether the lagoon might have crocodiles.

Tessel was forgiven, too, although he could no longer be a kava-maker, polluted as he was by the outside world. A new boy had already taken over making the kava, and the new boy had shown both skill and obedience, so there was no great loss.